"THE LADIES!"

"THE LADIES!"

A SHINING CONSTELLATION OF
WIT AND BEAUTY

BY

E. BARRINGTON

Illustrated with Portraits

THE ATLANTIC MONTHLY PRESS
BOSTON

PREFACE

THE aim of these stories is not historical exactitude nor unbending accuracy in dates or juxtaposition. They are rather an attempt to re-create the personalities of a succession of charming women, ranging from Elizabeth Pepys, wife of the Diarist, to Fanny Burney and her experiences at the Court of Queen Charlotte. As I have imagined them, so I have set them forth, and if what is written can at all revive their perished grace and the unfading delight of days that now belong to the ages, and to men no more, I shall not have failed. Much is imagination, more is truth, but which is which I scarcely can tell myself. I have wished to set them in other circumstances than those we know.

What would Elizabeth Pepys have felt if she had read the secrets of the Diary? If Stella and Vanessa had met — Ah, that is a tenderness and terror almost beyond all thinking! How would my Lady Mary's smarting pride have blistered herself and others if the Fleet marriage of her eccentric son—whose wife she never saw — had actually come between the wind and her nobility? Was there no finer, more ethereal touch in Elizabeth Gunning's stolen marriage with her Duke than is recorded in Horace Walpole's malicious gossip? Could such beauty have been utterly sordid? What were the fears and hopes of the lovely Maria Walpole as, after long concealment of her marriage, she trembled on the

steps of a throne? How did those about her judge of
Fanny Burney in the Digby affair? Did she wholly
conceal her heart? From her Diary we know what
she wished to feel — very certainly not entirely what
she felt.

Perhaps of all these women we know best that Elizabeth who never lived — Elizabeth Bennet. She is
the most real because her inner being is laid open to
us by her great creator. I have not dared to touch
her save as a shadow picture in the background of the
quiet English country-life which now is gone for ever.
But her fragrance — stimulating rather than sweet,
like lavender and rosemary — could not be forgotten in
any picture of the late eighteenth or early nineteenth
centuries and among the women whom all the world
remembers. They, one and all, can only move in
dreamland now. Their lives are but stories in a
printed book, and a heroine of Jane Austen's is as real
as Stella or the fair Walpole. So I apologise for nothing. I have dreamed. I may hope that others will
dream with me.

E. Barrington

TABLE OF CONTENTS

ILLUSTRATIONS

THE DIURNAL OF
ELIZABETH PEPYS

ELIZABETH PEPYS
1640 – 1669

"So home to dinner with my wife, very pleasant and pleased with one another's company, and in our general enjoyment one of another, better we think than most other couples do."

Elizabeth St. Michel, daughter of a French Huguenot, was fifteen when Pepys married her. She was only twenty-nine when she died. Pepys himself at their marriage was twenty-two. It is the skirmishing of young folk that he describes when he reports such animated scenes as the occasion when his wife threatened him with the red-hot tongs. They had their brisk encounters and their affectionate interludes as well, when "very merry we were with our pasty, well-baked, and a good dish of roasted chickens; pease, lobsters, strawberries."

In odd moments, Pepys applied himself to his wife's education. Dismissing her dancing-master by reason of jealousy, he began instead a course in Arithmetic. He himself taught her Addition, Subtraction, and the Multiplication Tables; but, says he, "I purpose not to trouble her yet with Division, but to begin with the Globes to her now."

At her early death he mourned sincerely, and erected a memorial celebrating the accomplished charms of Elizabeth, his wife, —

"FORMA, ARTIBUS, LINGUIS CULTISSIMA."

Hayls, Pinx   Hollyer, Sculpsit

Mrs. Pepys as St. Katharine

I

THE DIURNAL OF MRS ELIZ[TH] PEPYS

2d *May*. — Sam[1] now in great honour at the Navy Office, whereat my heart do rejoice, and the less for the havings, which do daily increase, than that I would willingly see him worshipfully received, the which indeede his hard work do plentifully deserve, he sparing himselfe in nothing for the advancing of his busyness.

And I do reason with myselfe that though he have faults many and great (which God knowes is true) yet he do come up in the world and our gettings are very good and do daily increase. How they go I know not, for that little and grudging is spent on my clothes, and though Sam[1] goes very noble still it is not possible but much is saved, though he do lament himself in very high wordes of our spendthrift way of life and small saving.

But of this more anon.

Up and dressed a pease pudding with boyled rabbets and bacon to dinner for want of a cook-mayde, Sarah leaving us at dawn, and he loving it mightily. The which he should not have this day but that I have a month's mind to a slashte wastcote which hitherto he hath soured upon. This done, a brave dish of cream in the which he takes great delight ; and so seeing him in Tune I to lament the ill wear of my velvet wastcote as desiring a Better, whereon he soured. We jangling mightily on this I did object his new Jackanapes coat with silver buttons, but to no purpose. He reading in the Passionate Pillgrim which he do of all things love. But angry to prayers and to Bed.

But it is observable that this day I discover Sam[1] in the keeping of a Journal and very secret in this, and come at it I will, he being much abroad on his occasions the while I sit at home.

3d. — This day awakes Sam[1] in a musty humour as much over-served with meat and Drink, and in great discontent calling me, do bid me rise and fetch his Pills that olde Mother Wigsworth did give him at Brampton. I merry and named him the Passionate Pillgrim from his love to these, whereupon he flings the Pills in my face and all scattered, Deb grudging to gather them it being Lord's Day. So I to churche, leaving him singing and playing "Beauty, Retire" to his Viall, a song not worthy to be sung on a holy Day however he do conceit his skill therein. His brown beauty Mrs Lethulier in the pew against us and I do perceive her turn her Eye to see if Sam[1] do come after. She very brave in hanging sleeves, yet an ill-lookt jade · if one do but consider, but with the seeking Eye that men look to, and Sam[1] in especial. Fried Loyne of mutton to dinner, and Sam[1] his head akeing I did sit beside him discoursing of the new hangings for the small closet, wherein great pleasure for it will be most neat and fine. And great content have we in such discourse and in our house and the good we are come to.

4th. — This day do Sam[1] speak handsomely enough of his humour yesterday, charging it upon the

Catherine Read, pinx.

Elizabeth
Duchess of Hamilton and Argyll
née Gunning

Rabbets, and so I left it. And strange it is how when he do so repent my heart do take part with him though I would better renounce him awhile to learn him manners. So he to the Exchange and buys me a piece of Paragon to a pettycote, and though it be not what I would have of my own choosing yet I do receive it with many goode words as hoping all will yet be as I desire. So to sup on a good dish of beef *à la mode*, and he well content, it appearing he have this day bestowed upon himself at the Exchange a good Theorbo, four Bookes, and a payre of Globes, talking very high how these be for my instruction rather than his own liking. The which I receive smyling, but do think — Lord! what fools men be that will have a woman so lightly deceived, fine wordes buttering no parsnips. Sure they be but Children when all said and done, and their Innocency in this a pleasant thing to see.

Comes Mr Collins with his new Wife, a pretty well-shaped Woman with black hayre and Eyes, and she, much cried up for her skill on the Theorbo, do after play a Lesson upon it, but very ill, and pretty to see Sam[1] that was hoping great things (loving musique) in pain and grief to hear her mean false playing and yet making fine wordes of it to please her, and they gone, do call her slut and baggage and I know not what all. So to prayers and bed.

5th. — Sam[1] this day reading over his vows not to drink strong waters or wines nor yet go to the play for two weekes. But I do ask myself (though not Sam[1]) whether these vows be convenient. For I do surely think he do it only because it is the greater pleasure to drink and see the play, it being thus forbid. And in Sam[1] it is to be noted and methinks in other Men also that they do suck more pleasure from a thing forbidden and hard to come at than from the same thing when comely and convenient to be done in the sight of all. This day, he being with his Lordship, I to gain a sight of his Journal, he carelessly leaving it about, but took nothing by my pains, it being writ in secret writing, which do plainly show it to be what he would be shamed if known. Whereas mine owne is voide of all offence, and I do lay it under the smocks in the great armoire only because it is not seemly that Sam[1] should know my thoughts, I having to deal with him as best I may.

Mem. To ask of Mrs Jemimah Crosby if her father, being a scrivener, knoweth and can instruct in secret writings.

Sam[1] home late this day, and the supper, a calve's head, very good, with a noble Barell of oysters, he bringing with him Mr S. Lucy, and so supt very merry, and after in the garden, Sam[1] to play on his flageolette, it being full moon. So to bed, omitting prayers. A pleasant day and content together.

6th. — This day, seeing Mrs Jemimah Crosby, I to ask her earnestly if her father the scrivener do teach the secret writing, and she replying that so it was, I after the mayde's cleaning the house, do forth and to his lodging behind Paternoster Row, he being a worthy olde Gentleman with a long white bearde, very reverend. I enjoining him to be secret, which

he the more willingly promised that I have obliged
him and Mrs Jem with codiniac and quince marma-
lett of my own making, do tell him how my father
(which is unknown to him) have documents and
papers which he would willingly decipher but for his
bad Eyes. Wherein God forgive me, for his eyes are
the best Part of him. Olde Mr Crosby thereon
urgent that my father entrust him with the worke,
but I sticking at the expense, no more said. So I to
show him a line of Dots and hooks which I did copy
from Sam[1] his Journal, and he reading it with ease,
what should it prove to be but this : —

"Took occasion to fall out with my wife very highly
about her ribbands being ill matcht and of two
colours, and to very high words, so that I did call her
Beaste."

So finding all as I thought and it being very needful that I should know Sam[1] his thoughts (and indeed
he is very simple to write them unless he think he have
a fool to his wife) I do covenant with the olde Gentleman for Lessons which are dear enough, but to be
paid from the housekeeping, and indeed the better
that Sam[1] should live plaine awhile in consideration
of his ailing. So home in good time, and do find Sam[1]
and our she-cousin Scott very merry with capping of
Epitaphs and sayings, wherein I also delighte. A
very merry witty woman and harmlesse. Suppt on a
Westfalia Ham and so with prayers content to bed.

7th. — This day Sam[1] returning from the Office
takes me to a fine collacion at Hamling's house,

wherein the fine silver set forth upon the table do give us great pleasure, but I a little shamed because the ladies so brave, Mrs Hamling very Rich in an embroidered suit, and Mrs Pegg Penn in flowered sattin, which God knows she do not become, and heads set out with the new French frizzle. I very plain in my olde black silk new-laced all over with black silk gimp, Sam[1] declaring I am very pretty in this, but I trust him not herein, he willing to save his Purse. One passage of Sam[1] kissing the little black beauty, Mrs Deakin, that he do call his Morena, displeased me, she being known for a frolicsome jade. He later singing, "Gaze not on Swans," and "Goe and be Hanged — that 's Good-bye," all did applaud, and great mirth. It was observable that Captain Wade, kissing me on parting, did a little detain my Hand, and for this Sam[1] did so betwit and becall me, returning in the Coach, that I pretended sleep, which did put him in a great discontent and so angry and without Prayers to bed. Yet sure this shows his good liking to me, and I think his heart sound, though he do Friske as I would he did not.

8th. — This day hear that my Lady Sandwich is Delivered of a young Lady and all well. Sam[1] thinking (on some jest of my Lord's) to stand Godfather and give the name — though how to call the Babe for him I see not — do at once provide silver Spoons and a Porringer. Which, seeing he is not yet bidden, doth I confesse, appear exceeding foolish and like a man that hath more silly pride than sense, the rather that I lack a French mantle that he hath promist but not

performed.   But I say nothing, according to the olde
wise saw of Goody Gorum, —

Nothing say,
But take your way.

He this day in his new Cote of the fashion and half
cloth stockings going to give my Lord joy, do indeed
seem very brave and noble, and hath a neat legg, and
it pleases me to see him go as he should, for he is a
personable man when well set out.   And if he did but
consider how it is to his honour that his Wife should go
as fine as he I could the more rejoice therein, but it is
not so, and great dishonour it is to him to consider how
this quarter he hath spent fifty pounds on his clothes
and but twelve on me, a thing not fit to be said of him.
But I wait my time.

10th. — This day Sam[1] refuses me the French
mantle as beyond his Purse, but offers a payre of
gloves — I refusing this.   Slipt out for Lesson, olde
Mr Crosby being a worthy and patient teacher, but
it is a science very hard to be come at, and I weary
enough in the learning of it, though indeed it be so
needful.   Still, some progress, and he saying merrily I
would be at some mischief in this, with love Letters or
such Toys, do make me to blush, so as I never did but
when Sam[1] was courting me.   Yet no guilty deed, but
what is very fitting for a woman.   Was instant with
the olde Gentleman that he should speake of my Lessons to none, the more so (I did say) that my father
would not have these papers known to any, great matters hanging on it.   Which indeed is true though not
as he takes it.

So I home and with Sam[1] to the Play, where my
Lady Castlemaine, which indeed is a great Beauty,
nor can I deny it, but sure it is not hard to be a beauty
in Clothes and jewels that do dazzle the Eyes of all
that Gaze upon her.   But, Lord! to see how bold and
unmannerly in staring upon strangers and the men on
the stage, and in fine do not please me with her Freedoms.   This Sam[1] disputing very hotly after we had
supt upon a Jowl of Salmon, I to speake my mind,
asking if he would have his Wife casting oranges to the
actors and blowing Kisses all about the house, and he
not knowing what to answer, I do say, "Then prayse
it not in others, for, if you will have me a bold Slut,
no doubt but I will do my endeavours to please you,"
and so whiskte off, he sitting astonied.   And strange
how men will like in otheres what in their own Wives
they love not but fear.

14th. — This day I by my Lady's desire to see the
young Lady which is a fine Babe and like to do well.
But no word of Sam[1] to stand Godfather, and Sir J.
Minnes and Lrd Brouncker spoke of, which is no
more than I thought, but will make Sam[1] madd with
his spoones.   But no loss herein if it do make him
more biddable in women's matters.   Her La[ship] observing that my Lutestring suit is well worn and do
me no credit, I did adventure to beseech her that she
would break a word with Sam[1] on his next waiting
upon her that he would give me a Gown of Moyre
which is now all the fashion, and this, with many good
words she promist very lovingly, desiring that I would
come in a weeks time to learn how she hath sped.   So

I home in good Tune as knowing he oweth his duty to
my Lord and Lady and will be said by her.   In comes
fayre Mrs Margaret Wight to sup on a dish of Eggs
and butter of Sparagus that Sam[1] hath ate with my
Lord Carlingford and do highly commend.   And indeed it is rare meat.   After, we dancing and very
merry with Mrs Margaret, and she gone, I take occasion to tell Sam[1] of the Godfathers like to stand for
the young Lady.   Whereat he in a great Tosse, but I
willing to smoothe all betwixt him and my Lady do
tell him the honourable words she have spoke of him
to myself and others, the more especially of his Velvet
suit with scarlet ribands.   The which pleasing him,
we fall to discourse of what to do with the Spoons and
Porringer, resolving the spoons do go to Betty Michell
where certayne it is I do stand Godmother, and the
Porringer to Mrs Lane, whose name I know not but
will come at shortly, and he do cry her up for a sober
and God-fearing woman.   So pleasantly to bed and
good frends.

16th. — This day comes my new cook-Mayd, Jane
Gentleman, and heaven send she prove worthy of her
name, for I am drove almost madd with mayds that
are not mayds but Sluts and know not diligence nor
cleanliness, to their own undoing and mine.   And
strange it is to consider how in the olden days before
my mother and Grandmother (who suffered great
horroures from the like) the mayds were a peaceable
and diligent folk, going about their busyness to the
great content of all housewives.   But now it is not so.
And it is only two days sennight that I coming sud-

denly in did find Sarah with my new silk Hood upon
her Frowsy head and Will discoursing with her and
thrumming upon Sam[1] his viallin. Whereat I did
catch her a sound souse of the Ear, but she never a
whit the better of it and answering me so sawcily that
we parted on it, Sam[1] upholding me in this, though it
be hard enough to fill her place the wench being a good
Cooke-mayde, though sluttish.

20th. — Sam[1] to visit my Lady, who receives him
with great content and satisfaction, though she railed
bitterly at my Lord that is so taken up with his pleasures and amusements that he goeth not to Court as he
should, and she fears will be passed over and forgot
for others that keep more stir. Requiring Sam[1] that
he would deal plainly with my Lord on this, making
known to him that his Reputacion do hereby decay.
But this methinks is a difficult matter, and I do
counsel Sam[1] that he put not his finger between the
Bark and the Tree, lest it come by a shrewd squeeze,
but let rather my Lady deal with her Lord as a Wife
should do. But he would not harken, whereby I foresee trouble.

He then, pulling out of his pocket a little Packett,
do say pleasantly, "What, my Deare, shall you and I
never go a-fairing again? What think you I have
here? And how many Kisses will you bid me for a
sight?"

Much merriment and pleasure from this, he holding it high, and I leaping for it like a Dogg. At the
last he opens it, and lo a fine Lace of the new fashion
for my bosom, and I do well perceive that my Lady

hath been at him, and am well content I did break the matter to her, though an honest gown had been more to my Purpose. Yet well begun is half done. Though but half, as Sam[1] shall find.

Our she-cousin Scott did visit me this day with sore complaints of her husband's humours and constant drizzling, which is more than a woman can or ought to bear. Therefore I should remember that with Sam[1] it is not so, but a spurt or flame of anger when he will be very high with me, yet quickly snuft out and friends again. And generally, it is noticeable, with some little gift for peacemaking, so that I have more than once of set purpose Baited him to this end. Yet not often. Considering therefore the husbands I do know, I think Sam[1] no worse a bargain than any and better than some, but shall be better assured in this when I shall come at his Journal. My seventh lesson today in the secret writing, and progress made, but it do make my head ake extremely and were it not needful would not continue on therein.

Comes this day my old Mayd Gosnell that Sam[1] and I do call our Marmotte, she telling me that Jane my mayde is naught and she hath herself seen her abroade in light company. Yet cooking as she cooks Sam[1] sticks on this and bids me wink my eyes and observe nothing, and such like are men!

21st. — This day Sam[1] his feast for the recovery of his ailment which he do always solemnly keep with great store of meat and Drink and company. And this is a great day with him and a troublous one with me, and to the Mayds also such as would madd a

Saint.   Yet all said and done a noble Dinner, enough
and to spare, being a dish of Marrowbones, a legg of
Mutton, a loin of Veal, a dish of fowl, being three Pul-
lets and 24 Larks all in a great dish, a Tart, a neat's
tongue, a dish of anchovies, a dish of Prawns and
cheese.   His company seven men (Captain Fenner
and both Sir Williams among them) and seven women
and all reasonable merry.   But I beseeching Sam[1]
privately to eat and Drink sparingly for the pain in
his Toe, he do so becall me that it was ten to an Ace
that I did hurle the Spit and the birds withal into the
fire.   Yet knowing he would pay dear next day, I
said the less and so continued on, bidding him take
his own way and pay for his liking.   But indeed great
company and the Dinner well cooked and served and
they did drink my health on it.   Also the house very
handsome with Plate displayed and fires where the
Company did sit.   And the greatness of living we are
come to did make Mrs Pierce's Mouth to water
though she in her flowered Lutestring and liking well
of it.   So she green and yellow with spite as I did well
perceive.   Great Musique after, with "Great, good
and just," and Sam[1] at the top of his Tune, and so to
cards and wine.   Weary to bed, Sam[1] starting up in
the night with Nightmare not knowing what he did,
and did so shreeke and cry that the Mayds in affright
did run in, and the Watchmen passing called to know
was any poor Soul murthered within.   But this no
more than my Expectation, and so quietly to sleep.

22d. — This day a noble gift of Plate being two
Candelsticks and a dish from Capt Salmon, he look-

ing for favour from Sam[1] concerning the Henrietta
shippe that he would have on next going to Sea.
Which do plainly prove to what honour and advancement we are come to be so courted, and do gladde his
heart and mine. Sat long discoursing of this, and,
turning the case, what should fall out but a ring set
with an Orient perle for me, which as not expecting I
received with great good will. Sam[1] to the office and
I to my lesson wherein very diligent and commended
of olde Mr Crosby, and indeed I am come already to
the reading of many wordes, yet not glibbly. So
home, but Sam[1] coming home and I combing his hayre
he did say, "Who do I meet this day in Broade Street
but olde Crosby, Mrs Jem's father, that I did think
long dead and buried, not having seen him this year
and more, and so to talk with him."

And, Lord! to see how I did redden, my heart so
beating in my bosom as I could have thought it would
choak me, and do even sweat in the writing of it. For
sure it might well be the olde Gentleman would think
Sam[1] did know all my father's business and speak
thereon. But I could not speak and my hand shaked
so in the Combing that I did drop the comb. And he
continuing, "So I asked him how he did and he answered, 'Bravely'; and more I would have said for it
is a worthy man, but little Mrs Deakin passing, that
I do call my Morena, I would not be seen talking to
one so scurvily clad, and so incontinently left him
standing and hasted away."

So it passed, nor did I ask him if he hasted after his
Morena, for heaven be thankt that she did pass by,

though I thought not to live to say it. But I will
take order with olde Mr Crosby, for olde men be
tattlers more than any woman or is convenient. And
so a great escape.

So Sam[1] carries me to the Paynter where he sits for
his face and very like it is, yet do not please, he thinking it do make his Eyes too small and ill-favoured,
but I not so, and Lord! to see him sit Smirking upon
Mr Savile since Mrs Knipp hath commended his
Smyle! But Mr Savile the Paynter seeing me did
speak in very handsome language, telling Sam[1] he
hath a Beauty to his wife worthy that her picture
should be with the Court Ladies' pictures, and much
more fine things, harping on the same string, whereto
Sam[1] made answer that he would consider of it. But
to see the Vanity of men, when all the world knows
that the sight of a pretty Woman's face is worth all
the men that ever were or will be! So I sat devising
how to set myself off if this should be, and did like
well of my Cardinal sattin suit with a chapeau de poil
tied beneath my chin. Or it may be, perles in my
hayre, and to borrow my Lady's if so she will. Fritters
for supper, the best I ever did eat, Sam[1] confirming
me in this, and he discoursing very high of the cor-
ruption of the times, and no regard to clean living in
court or city, and glad I am that thus he thinks, and
do hope he acts answerably, as he should.

27th. — This day, by long promise, Sam[1] do carry
me to White Hall to see the Queen in her presence
Chamber playing at Cards with her ladies, and the
people looking and crowding upon them. He com-

mending Mrs Stewart for a great Beauty and so indeede she is, and one I do not weary in looking on,
and do far outshine my Lady Castlemaine as I well
perceive His Maj^{tie} do also thinke. Her Maj^{tie} appearing very comely in a Gown of silver lace, but
Lord! how no one takes heed of her when my Lady
Castlemaine is by, which is a great dishonour to a
sweete Lady in her owne Court, and I am much mistook if Her Maj^{tie} be not the best Lady of them all,
and that not saying much! But strange to see how
beauty sways all and how Sam[1] do uphold my Lady
Castlemaine in all things.

Captain Holmes accosted us and very fine in his
gold laced suit, and it is noticeable that Sam[1] troubled
in mind because he well knows that Captain H——
hath called me for a Toast and the greatest Beauty in
Town. And this Sam[1] likes well of for his own Pride,
yet not for me to know. So saying we must return
in Haste, he would bid adieu to the Captain, but he
followed and escorted me very gallant to the Coche,
hat under his arm, and so kissed my hand at parting
not once but twice. Now I know well to make Captain Holmes or any other Captain keepe his Distance,
but Sam[1], thinking all one as himself, in a sadd musty
humour, and yet would not come forth with what ailed
him. So I do Debate with myself if it be not well he
should see that Men of court and Fashion do judge me
worth a thought. And I think it be, and so I do learn
my Part.

In comes Mrs. Knipp to play and sing. Very witty
and pleasant doubtlesse, and they very merry. I

with Jane, contriving my olde pettycote with a broade
blacke lace at the foot to hide the wear.   But indeede
I begin to be full of thoughts considering if I do well
in going to Brampton, when Sam[1] alone in Towne do
friske and please himself as he will, Jane confirming
me in this.   He home with Knipp, returning in a
great Tosse because I did not bid her to sup with us,
and do pull his supper all about the floor, a good hasht
hen as ever a man did eat, when he should the rather
soberly thank heaven for meat and appettite.   But
sorry later, there being nought else but sops and wine.
And so, good friends and to bed, the Storms coming
and going, but I think he do love me at heart. and
indeede I do love him well.

28th. — Lord's Day.   To church at St. Olave's
where a poor dull sermon from a bawling Scotman,
and Sam[1] to sleep, a thing unseemly in the Church,
but I awake and did fix in my mind the pattern of my
Lady Batten's Hood, the which I would not ask of
her for that we do of late a little make ourselves
strange to her and her family, but the less matter because I now have it in my Eye.   Mrs Lethulier
masqued, which methought a strange thing to be seen
at Worshipp, though the great Ladies do now carry
their masques to the Play that none may see them
Blush, or rather, as Sam[1] do say, that none may see
they cannot blush if they would.   And indeed all the
Men do now complain that the Beauties hide their
faces.

Mem. To Buy a masque in Paternoster Row when
I do go to Mr Crosby.   This night to bed in the little

green chamber — the Chymney swepers in our own.

1st *June*. — To my Lady this day and do give her my thankfull gratitude for that she hath spoke with Sam[1] concerning my poore clothes, telling her of the Lace he did give, she pishing and pshawing it for a meane gift, remembering the money that do pass through his hands whereof my Lord hath informed her. Comes Sam[1] later to carry me home, and my Lady speaking with him of my Lady Jem's marriage with young Mr Carteret do say he is so abasht and so little coming forward with his courtship that it do much discomfort poor Lady Jem as not knowing what he would be at. So my Lady beseecht Sam[1] that he would instruct him how to court a lady, he otherwise doing very well, and a worthy Gentleman, and one my Lady Jem could like of if not so shamefaced. Sam[1] simpring upon this, as who should say, "None better," do make us merry, seeing him already conning over what manner of Speeches and approaches will grace the Gentleman, but I do know him well able in such matters. And indeed in all.

2d *July*. — Lesson, and do now begin well to read. Bought masque of the Toy woman, in the Row, she saying, "Lord! is this the fayre Mrs Pepys, wife to Mr Sam[1] Pepys, that is known for a great man to be? Sure Madam was well pleased with the French mantle that he did buy for her a sennight come Saturday?"

So seeing she was a little ugly talking woman, I did sound her on this, for it vexed me cruelly since he hath sent it to another. And for all, I do and will believe it is but sporting and jesting, which if I did not, God help us all! So sadly and soberly home, but yet said nothing. Pray God all be well.

24th *July*. — For many days have I not writ, for at the last I did come to read what I would, and though not all, for some is in Greeke or I know not what, yet what I did read hath broke my heart. His Mrs Lane that he did prayse for a God-fearing woman, his Deb — but what do I say? — sure he hath not a heart but a stone. So I telling him certayne things of my knowledge (and yet not how I did know them), he in great fear and terrour and as I thought unlike a man of Courage. Which did shame me for him that I could scarce bring myself to look in his face and see him thus, remembering his high carriage that I did use to see in him. And times there were when I would the rather he did Brazen it out, it seeming so poor a thing to see him so low, and times again when in Madness I would have taken a knife to him, but he did pull it away with weeping Teares and promise of amendment. But how to trust him or any I cannot tell. And I have bid Will Hewer (Sam[1] humbly agreeing thereto) that he continue with his master and oversee him in all his walks abroad, doing me to wit where he goeth. Yet, how to trust Will — for sure all men are alike and will give the other countenance in Deceit. So what way to surety, for if a man regard not his wife where shall she look for good? And truly I do believe that in such Trafficking men do chip and whittle away their heart till none be left and they cannot love if they would, and no anchorage in so rotten a Holding ground. And thus have I learned that a woman may be young and yet aweary of her life, which I did not think to be true.

Sometimes I would I had not read, and again I would know more and run the knife yet deeper in my heart, and in that curst book never will I read again, and even in the writing of this well do I know I cannot forbear to read, and so Teares my drink and all my content gone. But let me remember there was here and there a word where he hath writ tenderly of his poor Wife, and when I did see him weep my heart did pity him. But what hope or help, for a Jar mended may hold water, but yet the Cracks remain, and the worth gone for ever and a Day.

Well, God mend all, and yet I think He cannot. But in this Booke of mine will I never write more, for the mirth and the little Frets that I did think so great alike do pierce my heart to read. So farewell, my Booke, that was a good friend in sunshine but an ill friend in storm, for I am done with thee and with many things more this day.

And so to the work that must be done and the day that must be lived though Brows ake and heart break.

(Elizabeth Pepys died at the age of twenty-nine.)

THE MYSTERY OF STELLA

ESTHER JOHNSON
"STELLA"
1681–1728

JONATHAN SWIFT's cousin and biographer sums up his views of the mystery of Stella in definite fashion: "For that she was married to Dr Swift about the year 1716, I am thoroughly persuaded, although it is certain they continued to live in separate Houses in the same manner they had usually done before." Other contemporaries of Swift are equally persuaded that no marriage took place at all. Under the circumstances, it is no great marvel if, as one gossip suggests, " her spirits might have become dejected, by her frequent revolving in her mind the Odness of her Situation."

When Esther Johnson's mother was companion to Lady Giffard, sister of Sir William Temple, the "Platonick" friendship between the young girl and Temple's secretary began. There are reports of Stella's charm, not only in the Journal, but in a general tradition that she was "surrounded by every Grace and blessed with every Virtue that could allure the Affections and captivate the Soul of the most stubborn Philosopher." Says John Hawkesworth: " There was a natural musick in her Voice, and a pleasing complacency in her aspect when she spoke. As to her wit, it was confessed by all her acquaintance and particularly by the Dean, that she never failed to say the best thing that was said whenever she was in company."

She died at forty-seven, and was buried in St. Patrick's Cathedral, where Swift, seventeen years later, by his own instructions, was buried at her side.

Sir G. Kneller, pinx

Esther Johnson
"Stella"

II

THE MYSTERY OF STELLA

This paper have I wrote for certain grave considerations which make me suppose it well it were one day placed in the hands of the Dean. 'T is, however, possible I may destroy it, but this time shall determine ere my death. Writ an: 1727 by me, ESTHER JOHNSON.

WHEN the Dean paid his last visit to London, an: 1726, he writ thus in a letter directed to Mrs Dingley, but for her and me: —

"Farewell, my dearest lives and delights I love you better than ever, as hope saved, and ever will. I can count on nothing but MD's love and kindness, and so, farewell, dearest MD. PRESTO."

So he signs himself, and so it seems the old screen will still be kept up and the letters to me wrote to her also, and in the child's talk that pleaseth him, lest any in the world suspect the famous divine hath a man's heart. But hath he? This I have not known, nor shall. Let me tell my own heart yet again how deep my debt to him, remembering the sickly child of Moor Park, to whom he brought not alone learning but companionship, and all the joy known to her childhood. For it pleased Dr Swift, then a young man, to condescend to a child's humours, to solace her solitary hours, forsook as she was of her mother's company, and not alone to teach her to write, but all her store of knowledge. And Dr Swift hath since been pleased to acknowledge that, having instilled in this poor child the principles of honour and virtue, she hath not swerved from them in any passage of her life.

Yet have I not?   Again I question my heart. 'T is the most I can hope that the woman hath repaid the child's debt.   On this I will be judged.

A keen remembrance begins not much before the age of eight, nor can I recall a time when I did not love him.   My mother's time was took up in making her court to my Lady Giffard, sister to our benefactor, Sir William Temple; and Rebecca Dingley's (a kinswoman of the Temples) in making her court to all; and the child Esther might run as she pleased, chid only when she was remembered.

And this young man took pity on her.   I remember very well Dr Swift's face in youth.   'T was extraordinary handsome and commanding, the eyes blue and piercing, the features strong, and a something that very early distinguisht him from others, so that great persons coming of errands to Sir William Temple were not seldom drawn into intercourse with his secretary.

Mr Swift was not then so prudent as he became later.   What need with a child?   He permitted his fancy to range in all he said; and seated by the lake at Moor Park, with this child at his knee looking up into his face, he would discourse of things in heaven and earth, forgetting his hearer.   For he who could charm all charmed himself no less, and often hath said to me laughing: —

"There 's no company so good as Jonathan Swift's — and he himself would choose it before all others!" Of this I am not certain, for the Dean hath been and is very partial to the company of the great and famous of either sex.

'T was thus, sitting by the lake and gazing down the great perspective cut in the trees, he saw the peasants going homeward up the hill, no greater than ants, and looking into my eyes (from which and my name he called me Star, and later, Stella), he said:—

"What say you, Mrs Star, if these folk were really no bigger than now they seem? What if this country were peopled by a race of little creeping Hop-o'-my-Thumbs?"

"O rare, rare!" I cried, and clapt my hands. "Tell me the history of them, Mr Swift, and their little homely ways and houses like bees' cells for size."

And as I looked up and the words came from him, truly all was visible before me. 'T is a gift Mr Swift hath had from the beginning, that men should see what he would. And women, — O Father Almighty, — women!

So that was the beginning of Gulliver his travels, that being told for a child's pleasure hath since become a world's wonder. It had not then the meanings he gave it later, nor were there any Yahoos.

If I ask myself when this harmless love did change to a woman's, I cannot tell, because with my growth it grew. But the first pain it brought (and sure pain is love's shadow) was an: 1697, when I was sixteen years of age. For I sat by the housekeeper's window, and Sir William and Mr Swift were pacing the path, their voices coming and going. Mr Swift was now dressed as the young Levite he sometimes called himself since he returned from Ireland a clergyman; and he walked with his eyes fixed moodily on the ground, listening to Sir William.

"Why, as to that, Jonathan," said he familiarly, "I ever thought it behoves a parson to marry when he hath got preferment. There is room for Mrs Parson's help with the women and children of the parish and 't is meet she should set an example with her neat parsonage, and be a notable woman with her possets and cordials for the sick. Now what like is this pretty Varina that Dr Holmes hath brought news of from Belfast?"

"Miss Waring," says Mr Swift, very grave, "is a commendable young lady, but I design not for marriage as yet, Sir, nor for a long time to come."

They past out of hearing and, returning, I heard but the last part of Sir William's words: —

"'T is a cruel thing for a man to raise hopes he means not to be answerable for, and I am told the young lady grows very melancholy upon it. True it is, a man must sow his wild oats even though he honour his cloth; but 't is not well to sow them in a harmless girl's acre, Jonathan. Sow them by the wayside, and then they come not up to her confusion and your own."

"A sound precept, Sir; but better still to sow none. This shall be my care. As to the connection you speak of, 't is long broke off, and was at all times impossible, the lady having no portion, and myself — as you know!"

His brow was like a thunder-cloud ere it bursts; but, looking up, he catcht sight of me, and continued with no pause : —

"As for that matter of the publishers, Sir — they have writ to say that they wait your commands anent the Letters of Phalaris. Asking your pardon, time goes, and we should be speaking of this and not of child's toys."

I knew by the black blink of his eyes that I had heard what he would not; and as they turned, my heart beat so that I laid my hand on it, as if that poor fence might hide its throbbing. And for the first time in my life I knew I had in this world an enemy, and that was this Varina; and from that hour mine eyes waited on him.

More often mine eyes than my company, for, especially since this conversation with Sir William, Mr Swift was now grown very cautious. In public he addressed me as "Mrs Johnson," or, when Sir William rallied him, as "Mrs Esther," affecting an awful distance, which was not in his heart, for therein was still the tenderness for his child and pupil, as he had used to call me. And he was good enough to signify to Mrs Dingley, who carried it to me, that he found me grown to his liking; "beautiful, graceful, and agreeable," says he, and condescended to praise even my black hair and pale face, after which I would not have exchanged it against the golden hair of Helen. But still held aloof except when I was in company with others. And I took note that, of all the ladies that came and went at Moor Park, there was not one but hung upon his talk, and held up her head when he came near, spreading out all her graces. Mr Swift had always that power with our sex and, if he used it, 't is but what all men do. Providence made us fair game, to our undoing and theirs. 'T is not all men who have this gift, and never have I seen one who, having it, spared to use it, whether from liking or policy.

Yet he used it strangely. I remember, when the fair Lady Mary Fane came to Moor Park, — a widowed beauty and toast, — the look of scorn she cast from her fine eyes on the young secretary.

"I marvel, Sir William," says she, "that you will have your servant ever at your elbow, so that a body hath never a word with you alone. I would not presume to censure, but certainly my father's chaplain does not so intrude himself into company; and 't is difficult for persons of quality to speak their mind in such underbred society."

"Why, your Ladyship," says he, laughing, "be gracious to my young Levite. He is not of the common sort of creeping parson, but I dare venture will yet be heard of. Simple as your Ladyship thinks him, he is at home in all company, be it great or little; and I had not known him three year when I sent him to London on a secret errand — and I was not mistook."

"Such persons," says the lady, very haughty, "are paid to exert themselves in our service. We may expect no less."

So it passed; but a busybody carried this, with other tattle, to Mr Swift, who questioned me also. I looked to see him mighty angry; and first his brows frowned, and then he laughed, as if a thought pleased him.

"Said she so, the painted jade! What, Madam Stella, shall not a stinking pride be taught its place by the Church? I 'll give the hussy her lesson."

That very day, my Lady Mary sitting to embroidery on the great terrace in the shade, and I holding her threads, she threw Mr Swift a word as he past, to ask the name of the nymph that was turned to a bush to escape the pursuit of Apollo; for that was the subject of her needle.

"Daphne, Madam," says he. "Have I your permission to look upon your work? Oh, fie! — this bush — 't is a rosebush, and Daphne became a laurel. Sure, a lady with your Ladyship's reputation for wit will not be in error."

She stopped with the needle in her hand and lookt at him angrily.

"Sir, if you know better than Mrs Weyland who drew my pattern, instruct me. I am not too proud to learn from my — betters."

She made the word an insult, and went on: —

"Have I done amiss to give Apollo wings to his feet?"

"Why, indeed, Madam, 't is Mercury carries the wings. In another lady's presence I had said 't is Cupid, but from some ladies love cannot fly."

So it began. In a moment more she had bid him

be seated, and tell her stories that a lady might paint with her needle. And presently her hands dropt in her lap, and her eyes fixed on his face, and 't was not long ere I was dismist.

That evening he came into Dingley's room, where I sat with her to repair the household linen, and rattled on, full of wit and good humour; and when Dingley went out to fetch a cordial for him, he says: —

"Well, Mistress Stella, did we give the lying slut her lesson today — did we? Sure, 't was a pure bite!"

And says I : —

"I have seldom heard your Reverence more entertaining."

And he, laughing hugely : —

"A cat may be choked with cream as well as fishbones, Mrs Stella. Keep your pretty little eyes open, child, and thou shalt see."

In a week she was his humble servant. 'T is scarce credible, but I saw her once lay her hand, sparkling with jewels, upon his, and he shake it off as if 't were dirt. I saw the water brim her eyes as she lookt at him and he laught and turned away. Indeed, her Ladyship had her lesson ere she left Moor Park, and I knew not then enough to pity her. Pity — 't is a flower that grows in the furrows of a heart ploughed over by sorrow, and my day was not yet come. He laught with me over the disconsolate beauty, when she importuned him to be her son's tutor, and he replied he had far other views.

Yet for all his caution we met sometimes, when I

would be gathering flowers and lavender, or fruit for Mrs Groson the cook. And I knew he loved to talk with me. He loves it still. Many was the jest we had — jests with their root in childhood and folly to all but him and me.

So came the day that changed all.

'T was a fair sunset, with one star shining, and I stood in the copse far from the house, to hear the nightingale; and, though I thought of him, did not see that he leaned against the King's Beech, until he stirred and made my heart to flutter.

"I watch your namesake, Stella," says he, "and wonder if in that sweet star are plots and envyings — a Marlborough intriguing against his King, a Burnet plotting for an archbishopric, an ugly Dutch monster-kin on the throne — and a naughty rogue called Stella, that hath forgot her old tutor and loves him no more. Yet if that love should miscarry, I know not —"

"If it miscarry," says I, trembling, "there will be many to succeed it. But I think, Mr Swift, it cannot."

"Many?" he answered, and up went his brows. "Such as my Lady Mary and such-like? But that is no love, Stellakin. 'T is only thy innocence could mistake it. The true name is none so pretty, and not for thy lips. Get thee to a nunnery, child — the world is not for such as thee."

So I faltered out: "What is love?"

"A thing that hath no existence between man and woman in this world, so mixed is it with lust and hatred and jealousy. True, there is love, but it is not that one. 'T is the loves filial and paternal, and friendship, better than all the loves the rhymesters hang with their namby-pamby. The love between the sexes—'t is a game wherein the weaker loses, and then — *vœ victis!* Hast forgot thy Latin, child?"

And then I broke out into a great sobbing, as if my bursting heart would break; for, I know not why, but this cut me like a knife. And he took my hand with anxious kindness to soothe me; and at the bird's rustle in the tree, dropt it and stood apart. He lived in the eye of the world even in such affections as he owned. But I sobbed on.

"Pray, pray, don't sob, Stella," he says. "This is mighty, mighty ill and like a child. Dry those pretty eyes, — prettier, gadso! than any Lady Mary's of them all! — and tell me wherein I have offended. 'T was not willingly."

So, drowned in tears, I lookt up, and having lookt, turned away weeping, and could say no more. For what skill had I to argufy with a man of such infinite parts? And yet well I knew that in this matter of love I was the wiser, though but a simpleton. But he caught my hands.

"Have I hurt thee, Stella? I were a devil if I did. What ails my girl at love? What is it to thee? Keep away from that raging fire. Souse it with every stream of reason and honour. Heap the ice of the Pole on it, for it is not only hell itself but feeds the flame of hell eternal."

He so wrung my hand that it pained; and I saw his

face work like a man most desperately sick and ill. It dried the tears in my eyes, and I stood trembling and staring upon him, and the twilight was sweet about us with a smell of grass and growing things and flowers; a night for lovers — and I most miserable.

"I doubt —" he began and stopt; and then, with a cry that choked in his throat, he put his arms about me and I laid my head on his breast.

Should I blame myself for that half-hour? Should I blame my Dear, the Desire of mine eyes? 'T was but a step to take across the line that parts innocence from — No, no, never will I say guilt! 'T was not guilt, if all the tongues of men and angels should so preach. 'T is in the later denial of love that guilt lay hid. But these things I did not then know, and I thought in my simplicity the world changed and the foolish girl become a woman and beloved, and our lives together in a fair prospect before us.

And suddenly — "Go — go!" he cried, rejecting me and thrusting me from him. "Go, and never again let me see your face. I sicken — I sicken at what is done. No — no! Speak not, utter not, lest I strike you and myself dead. Leave me, for God's pity's sake! Go!"

So did the Angel with the flaming sword drive our first parents out of Paradise. I drew apart shuddering, and he cried after me in a loud whisper: —

"Let none see your face. Go in by the covered door, and so to your room, and plead headache if Dingley see you. Go."

I left him in the dark. I drew my palatine about

my face and none saw; and so to my room, and outed
the light, and sat by the window till the dawn came.

Now, if I am condemned herein, I take the blame,
but cannot change my thought. What woman in
giving all met ever so sorry a return — and why?
I broke my brain with thinking, and at that time
found no answer. Later, I knew. But to escape
the hue and cry of question, I washed the tears from
my eyes in the morning, and so to the housekeeper's
room. And he was there, reading in a great book,
and my heart leapt like the last leap of a hare with
the dogs on it.

"Why, Stellakin — saucy-nose!" says he, laughing, but his face was pale. He could cheat with his
words, but I saw his face bleacht like a linen clout
behind his laugh, and I swear at that time he loved
me, though he loved advancement better. "You are
bright and early, young woman! Are you for the
garden, to get you a stomach for breakfast? Well,
so-so! and pray for poor Presto as you go; for in honour and conscience, his Ppt is the child of his heart."

How could I endure this? I closed the door, and
left him laughing with white lips.

So went the day, and now I saw his drift. He
would hold the little language of childhood for a shield
betwixt us. I should be nothing more for ever than
Ppt, — poor pretty thing, — Stellakin, the pretty
rogue. He would not fail in this, but only in all my
hopes. He would give me all but that I longed for.
He would glut me with sugar-comfits but never a
taste of the living bread.

And next day a new thing. Dingley and I sitting together, he came upon us, and in all he said included her. She was his second MD. He was her poor Presto, also. I saw his will and knew he built a fence about himself.

Sometimes I thought I had but a mean spirit so to live, and thought to ask his meaning; but dared not, for he struck an awe into my very soul. So gradually the days covered that sunset, and 't was impossible I should speak; and life went by, and still I studied with him, but Dingley always present.

Hath he a heart? I know not. That sunset was a grave between us; and had the corpse risen and stared him in the face, I think he had run mad. In my solitary hours, I would imagine I spoke. Sometimes I would kneel before him entreating, and he would raise me up, as a certain king did another Esther. Sometimes he would fall at my knees, and I would bow my head upon him, weeping for joy.

But yet always I knew that, if we glanced near that secret, he would rise and stare upon me with a ghastly face, and I would see him no more. Yet at that time he loved me. To himself he will not lie in reading this.

'T was in 1699 Sir William Temple died, and the household at Moor Park was broke up. Mr Swift took the kindest part in my settlement and the laying out of my little fortune. "And be easy about money, you nauti-nauti, dear girls," says he to old Dingley and me; "for what is mine is yours; and were it my blood, 't is all one."

And so laid his plans that we should come to Ireland, where he had preferment at Laracor near Dublin, and the prebend of Dunlavin in St. Patrick's Cathedral. And, God forgive me, I asked myself if the thought to keep me under his guidance mingled not itself with all his kindness.

So I, being twenty years old, and Dingley a kind bustling woman, we went; and Ireland was a kindly home, for 't was near him, and I might see him. Not as I would — oh, never that! but as a friend, provided 't was with caution. For as he now mounted in the Church, and his ambition strengthened on him (and sure Wolsey himself did not more suffer from that failing of noble minds), caution grew to be his main thought; for he said the adventure of our coming looked so like a frolic that censure might hold as if there were a secret history in such a removal; but this would soon blow over by circumspect conduct, and this too was used to put a distance between us. But 't was the condition of our intercourse, and thus I accepted it. For aught I could discern, all else was clean forgot, and we lodged near him and met as friends — no more.

Nor could I think otherwise when Mr Tisdall, his friend, made suit to me. I was cold, — what else, — for I thought myself a wife, if a forsaken one, and Mr Tisdall imagined that Dr Swift opposed his suit, objecting that his means did not come up to the expectation he formed for me, who was, he said, in a manner, his ward.

Poor Mr Tisdall writ in haste on this, and brought

me Dr Swift's reply (who had not broke the matter to
me) and thus it ran : —

My conjecture is that you think I obstruct your inclina-
tions to please my own. In answer to all which I will,
upon my conscience and honour, tell you the naked truth.
[The naked truth ! O God, if it were told !] If my fortunes
and humour served me to think of that state, I should certainly make your choice, because I never saw that person
whose conversation I entirely valued but hers. This was
the utmost I ever gave way to. [But once — but once !]
And this regard of mine never once entered my head as an
impediment to you, since it is held so necessary and convenient a thing for ladies to marry, and that time takes off
the lustre of virgins in all other eyes but mine.

This Mr Tisdall offered on his knees, declaring it
must remove my last objections, since the worthy
friend of my childhood supported his suit. I received it sedately, and dismist him with the compunc-
tion so worthy a gentleman merited. Was this letter
honest to his friend? I say not.

Henceforth he disliked Mr Tisdall. Could I im-
pute this to jealousy? Why not? A man will be
jealous if his dog but lick the hand of another; and,
though he reserve himself perfect freedom, no man
must so much as sigh for the woman he hath once
honoured with his regard. Truly there is a something Oriental in the passions of men; and if a woman
break through this, 't is at her peril.

So stood matters when the Doctor went to London,
an: 1710, on his errand of obtaining the First Fruits
for the Irish Church from the Crown — and he chosen
from all others to this, for his commanding talent and

presence, though then but forty-two years of age, and
many dignitaries older, yet not wiser. It created
much envy.

I missed him, and yet took a sad ease in his going.
'Twas the easier to talk with Dingley, to play at
ombre with the Dean and Mrs Walls; for when he
was in presence, my heart waited upon his speech, and
he wounded with many a word and look he thought
not on. And he writ often in the form of a Journal
to Dingley and me, saying: —

"I will write something every day to MD, and
when it is full, will send it; and that will be pretty,
and I will always be in conversation with MD, and
MD with Presto."

'T was near a year since his going when Mrs Coleburn came to Dublin, full of London talk, and her
friendship with the great Dr Swift, the hope of the
Tories. Indeed, it made her a great woman with the
clergy in Dublin, that she knew so much of his sayings
and doings, and in what high company he was got,
and the clutter he made in London. Much was true,
as I knew under his own hand. Much was idle
twattle and the giddiness of a woman that will be
talking. Now, one day, she visited me, dressed out
in the last London mode, and talked as I knotted, and
presently says she: —

"And, Mrs Johnson, what will be said, the Doctor
being made a Bishop as he now looks for, if he bring
home a fine young bride from London? Sure he lives
at Mrs Vanhomrigh's, so often is he there; and Miss

Hessy is as pretty a girl as eye can see, in her young twenties and a bit of a fortune to boot. I have ever said the Doctor was not on the market for nothing. He is not the man for a portionless beauty. Hath he wrote of this? for all the tongues are wagging, and the lady in such a blaze with the tender passion that she can't by any means smother it."

"Doctor Swift hath often writ of Mrs Vanhomrigh and her hospitalities," says I, smiling. "Also of the charming Miss V. Her name is no stranger here."

So I baffled the woman, and could see her petty malice dumbed. I held the smile on my face like a mask.

"Well, 'tis a charming creature, and the Doctor commends her wit in all quarters; and 'tis certain he should be a judge, for he tutors her in Latin. There's many a man would gladly tutor the seductive Miss Hessy."

When she took leave, I writ to the kind Patty Rolt in London. When her reply returned, 'twas but to confirm Mrs Coleburn. Then I turned over all his letters — yet did not need — for mention of this woman, and found but three, though of the mother and her house he writ in almost every letter, but making somewhat too light of it. 'Twas a raging pain that he should be her tutor — I had thought that was mine only and not to recur — a memory stored where neither rust nor moth might touch it. Well — what could I but hate the girl? And to hate is a bitter thing: it saps the life and breaks the strength, and so

no escape night or day. I must then fancy his letters
cooling, and later says Dingley unprompted : —

"The Doctor is took up with his fine friends and his
business. La! — for sure he writes not as he did, but
is plaguey busy. Two simple women can't expect so
much of his time that duchesses go begging for."

He stayed long away, and Patty Rolt writ often,
discreet and willing to serve me ; and one day comes a
packet from her, and when I cut the seals, out falls a
letter — his. I read it first.

Miss Hessy, I am so weary of this place ['t was Windsor]
that I am resolved to leave it in two days. I will come as
early on Monday as I can find opportunity, and will take
a little Grub Street lodgings pretty near where I did before,
and will dine with you three times a week and tell you a
thousand secrets, provided you will have no quarrels with
me. I long to drink a dish of coffee in the sluttery, and
hear you dun me for secrets, and "Drink your coffee —
why don't you drink your coffee?"

So he writ, and more — much more could I read
unsaid. For him, this was much — I knew it. Then,
another letter — a woman's hand.

It is inexpressible the concern I am in ever since I
heard from Mrs Lewis that your head is so much out of
order. Who is your physician? Satisfy me so much as to
tell me what medicines you have took and do take. O
what would I give to know how you do this instant. My
fortune is too hard. Your absence was enough without
this cruel addition. I have done all that was possible to
hinder myself from writing for fear of breaking my promise ; but it is all in vain ; for had I vowed neither to touch

pen, ink, or paper, I certainly should have had some other
invention, and I am impatient to the last degree to hear
how you are. I hope I shall soon have you here.

The two were wrapt in a sheet from Patty who had
writ thereon : — "Dropt by the Doctor when in a
giddy attack, visiting me."

I think she was shamed. So was not I. As well
ask the hound if he is shamed when tracking the deer.
Had it been to save my life, instead of lose it, I had
less eagerly read. 'T was clear they understood one
another. With me, in his caution, Dingley must be
joined when he writ. With her, not so. Her happiness was a knife turned in a bleeding wound.

So I writ him, in a letter of many matters, somewhat scornfully of the family as marvelling a little
that he whom all solicited could be satisfied with such
inconsiderable people. In time he replied thus : —

Sir A. Fountaine and I dined by invitation with Mrs V.
You say they are of no consequence — why, they keep as
good female company as I do male. I see all the drabs of
quality at this end of the town with them. I saw two
Lady Bettys there this afternoon. Rare walking in the
Park now. Why don't you walk in the Green of St. Ste-
phen's? What beasts the Irish women are, never to walk.

Men hide not matters so well as women. They say
too much or not enough.

Much later he writ : "I found Mrs V. all in com-
bustion with her landlord. Her eldest daughter is of
age, and going to Ireland to look after her fortune and
get it in her own hands."

So I was to think it concerned them not to be apart.
Immediately I set my wits to discover where was her
estate, and 't was not long ere I knew 't was Marlay
Abbey, near Celbridge; but the lady would reside in
Dublin while making her dispositions, being Mrs
Emerson's guest, and was like to be at a rout at her
house. 'T was long since I attended a rout, but I
intrigued to be bidden as courtiers intrigue for an inch
of blue ribbon; and in such a fever and anguish as I
think I had died of it if not successful.

So, when the day was come, I went with Mrs
Stoyte; and the first person I saw was a young lady
on the stair-head as we went up, and Mrs Emerson
presenting her to many. A fine young London
madam, who curtseyed to me, taking no more heed
than of any other.

Shall I admit her beauty? I did not think her
charming, despite fine sparkling eyes and a luxuriance
of brown hair. Her lips were full and her chin round,
but she looked full her age, and between the brows
was a line that I would call the Doctor's sign-manual.
I have it myself — I have seen it in others — 't is the
claw-foot of care, care never-ending and cruel unrest,
and hope that sickens the spirit and fades the bloom;
and in her, though but just of age, the first bloom was
gone that is like morning dew in a young girl's eyes.
He loves to tyrannise over women and show his fam-
iliarity by a certain brutality of address, and the line
comes not slowly.

I caught sight of her person with mine in a long
glass — she in her sea-green sacque flowered with

Hester Vanhomrigh
"Vanessa"

pink, and myself in gray, — "an angel's face a little cracked," — that was the best he could say for Stella! She gave not a thought to the faded Dublin lady that would have given all but her eternal hope to read in that girl's soul. Oh, the mask of the human face behind which none may look!

So she went, and after a year he returned, now Dean of St. Patrick. He was kind, but 't was a kindness that stood apart and viewed itself carefully, lest it diminish my due. 'T was easy seen he was engaged in thought. Well — shall a woman expect more from a man in the world's eye? Let her be humbly grateful for the crumbs he lets fall.

Also for the crumbs from her rival's table; for Miss Hessy following, and now an orphan, was established soon after at Marlay; and whether I would or not, I knew when the Dean's rides took him that way, my Mrs Prue being courted by his man Samuel, and all he did trickling through that channel. 'T was at this time also that copies were handed about of his poem, "Cadenus and Vanessa," and 't was the very top of talk and admiration. Many might guess who was the lady, and 'the Dean was mighty angry, and said 't was but a jest, and no friend to him who took it otherwise.

He asked me with a feigned carelessness if I had read it; and I replying carelessly that I thought it extreme fine and could wish he would write oftener in that vein, he smiled and looked pleased, and so it passed. But again and yet again I conned the lines: —

'T is to the world a secret yet
  Whether the nymph, to please her swain,
  Talks in a high romantic strain,
Or whether he at last descends
To act with less seraphic ends.
  Or, to compound the business, whether
  They temper love and books together,
Must never to mankind be told,
Nor shall the conscious Muse unfold.

I knew the meaning of that passage where others guesst. I read it by the light of a sunset many years gone, and lived in hell.

'T was when Mr Dean was next in London, came a letter to me

Madam, I have great and urgent reason to wish the honour of meeting you and a half hour's conversation. Any place you may condescend to appoint will be perfectly agreeable and the favour prized by
                Your obedient humble servant,
                      ESTHER VANHOMRIGH

(who would not ask it unless it concerned Mrs Johnson as nearly as herself).

I broke my brains thinking, should I or should I not? Nor can I now unravel all the motives at work. But in two days' time I writ : —

Madam, I have a difficulty to come at the reason for your request, but am compelled by courtesy to appoint three o' the clock at the rooms of Mrs Dew, my old servant, at Kidder Street, No. 12. Your obt humble servant,
                      ESTHER JOHNSON.

Strange our names should be alike!

She was the first at the meeting. I ensured this, delaying my chair at the corner of Kidder Street till I saw her enter.

The room was small and poorly decent, and her hoop and mine filled it. She curtseyed low, as did I, and though she aimed at composure, I could see her lips work. The line between her brows was eight years deeper, her face pale, the bloom faded, and her mouth droopt. Had she been any other, I had pitied her. His friendship is fatal to my sex, though I have wore it like an honour. For me, I was composed. It 's not for nothing I have spent my life in that school — she was a newer pupil.

Being seated, I asked her to favour me with her commands, and she came straight at the business with a kind of directness pitiable enough.

"Madam, all the world talks of the goodness of Mrs Johnson. I am not long a resident of these parts, but am no stranger to your merits. 'T is my confidence in them causes this explanation. May I ask pardon for plain speaking?"

"Madam, if the subject is one I can admit of, speech cannot be too plain."

"So I have been told. Accept me therefore as a plain-dealer, Madam, and have the goodness to read what I cannot speak. But first," — she put her hand to her throat as if she might swoon, and so closing her eyes for a moment, opened them clearly on me, — "Madam, between a certain gentleman and myself have been love-passages tending, as I believed — hoped — to marriage. A passion that, with due regard to honour, hath been the ruler of my life hath brought me to Celbridge, as I did think for the happiness of both. Being arrived, I have the happiness to see this gentleman often, and he hath had the goodness to say that no person hath ever been so loved, honoured, esteemed, ADORED by him as your humble servant. Yet I am told that a former attachment doth so constrain his honour that little can be hoped." — (Her voice broke.) "Madam, will you read this paper, and say Yes or No?"

I opened it, and thus read: —

Madam, of your angelic goodness be pleased to answer, are you indeed the wife of one I name not? If it be true, I will utterly withdraw my intrusive presence. In pity, answer me.

It seemed many minutes I sat with this in my hand, and she dropt on her knee at my feet, looking up in agony. Time passed and I heard my voice as if it were another's, and strange to me.

"Madam, am I expected to disclose my secrets to one of whom I know not if she tells truth? What are you to the Dean, and what proof do you give of what you are, that I should answer?"

She said very low: —

"I had not thought of that. But 't is very true." And, trembling and looking fearfully about her, she put her hand inside the whalebone of her bodice and drew out letters.

"I thought not these would be seen by any, but buried with me when I die; but 't is impossible you should know me for honest, and because honour speaks in your face — read these."

I took them, trembling inwardly. She, poor wretch, was newer to her trade, and was like to faint. I knew the writing.

I will see you tomorrow, if possible. You know it is not above five days since I saw you, and that I would ten times more, if it were at all convenient. — Cad bids me tell you that, if you complain of difficult writing, he will give you enough to complain of.

"Cad"? Then I remembered — "Cadenus and Vanessa." So — *she* might call him by a little familiar name, but I, never. I stopt there.

"Madam, have you thus writ to him?"

"Always of late, Madam. With a dash before it, as here you will see the cause."

She pushed a letter into my hand, eager, as I thought, to convince not only me but herself of his regard. And thus it read : —

I wish your letters were as difficult (cautious) as mine, for then they would be of no consequence if dropped by careless messengers. A stroke thus — signifies all that may be said to Cad at beginning or conclusion.

"So," says I, "a stroke means endearments. Otherwise 't is difficult to conclude these sentimental letters."

"Madam," she broke out, "it means more than tongue can tell. And since you still doubt, have the condescension to read this letter of my own which he returned to me in rebuke. 'T will show you our terms."

— Cad, you are good beyond expression. I thought that last letter I writ was obscure and restrained enough. I took pains to write it after your manner. I am sorry my jealousy should hinder you from writing more love letters. Pray tell me, did you not wish to come where that road to the left would have led you? I am now as happy as I can be without seeing — Cad. I beg you will continue happiness to your own Heskinage.

I read, and was silent — reading this letter by the light of a dead sunset. I never dared so write. There was that between them that he had never shared with me, and yet all his old caution, as with me. I thought not, however, so much of his feelings as of hers, for I think his care for women is but skin-deep at best. He was ever willing to take the tribute of their hearts — nay, of their lives; but should they incommode him, or trespass across the line he hath marked — this careless liking is changed to hatred, and he will avenge himself brutally on the weak creatures that love him.

Who should know this but I — I who have lived beside him and retained his friendship only because I have in all things submitted to his will — silent to death? Had I anything to lose to this unfortunate woman? No, I had lost all many a long year ago. She still had hopes; I, none. Why torture a wretch so miserable?

She kneeled before me, pale as a corpse. 'T was the strangest meeting. I could scarce hear her voice.

"Madam," says she, "I have put my life in your hand; for if Mr Dean knew that I had come here — that I had dared — O Madam, he can be cruel to women!"

I strove to collect my thoughts; then heard my own voice as a stranger's: —

"Madam, to your question, the answer is No. There is no marriage between Mr Dean and me. I have no claim on him that obstructs your own."

She looked up like one in a stupor of amazement — so dazed and white that I repeated my words. Then, suddenly, she gathered herself into composure like my own, but her poor lips trembled. I saw in her my girlhood long dead.

"If I say I thank you, Madam, with all my heart and soul for thus opening your mind to a most miserable woman, I say little. What is left of my life shall be a study to deserve your compassion. What would you have me do?"

I replied: "I think you will not fail in what honour and conscience dictate. 'T is not for me to say. 'T is between you and Mr Dean. And now, Madam, will you give me leave to withdraw, for this hath been a painful meeting for us both."

"Not before I bless you with all my broken heart," she cried, and took my hand. "For I will now tell you that, for all these letters, I know he loves not me, nor any. I may please him better than another in moments, but there's no security. He hath a contempt for women that scorches, and to hurt them — but 't is not this I would say. I feared to find an ex-

ulting rival when I came to you, Madam, and instead
I find an angel of compassion. Sure I read it in your
eyes. In this life we shall meet no more; but in my
prayers you will be present, and I beseech you, as the
last favour, to give me an interest in yours, that I may
know myself not utterly forsook. My one sister is
not long dead — I am utterly alone in the world."

She could not continue, but kissed my hand, and
her tears fell on it. I told her that this meeting
should remain secret, but she needed not assurance.
We embraced, and so, curtseying, separated, she departing first. A good woman, if I have known one.
'T is of good women men make their victims. The
ill women cannot and do not suffer; they but repay
our score. When I reached home I found her paper
still in my hand.

I must now be brief. Mr Dean returned, and all
was as before; but I wearied yet more of the child's
play and prattle he still continued for my amusement.
He was much engaged with writing. I thought him
ill at ease.

I was seated by the window on a day he will recall,
when he entered pale and furious.

"What hath gone amiss?" I cried, starting up.

"This," says he, in a voice I scarce knew, so awful
was it; and laid before me the poor Vanessa's paper
that I believed I had destroyed weeks agone. O,
what had I done? 'T was another paper I had burned, and this had lain in my pocket. 'T was most
certainly Mrs Prue — But what matter? He had
what for her sake and mine I had died to hide.

"Hath that vixen dared to come anigh you?" he cried. "Hath she ventured to disquiet my friends, the wanton jade, the scheming —" and so on, pouring horrid words upon her that chilled my blood. 'T was terrible in him, that he could so swiftly change to these furies with one he had favoured, and to a rage frightful to see.

I tried to moderate him, to speak for her; but nothing availed. Finally I rose to withdraw, for he would hear nothing.

"But I 'll break her spirit," he said, with clenched hands. "I 'll ride to Celbridge and face her with her crime —"

I held him back. "For God's sake, no. Have patience. She hath done no harm, and no eye but mine saw the paper. I pitied her — we parted friends."

"Then you saw her? She came?"

But I can write no more. He tore his coat from me, and so down the stair like a madman; and I heard his horse clatter down the street, while I prayed for a soul in agony, and that she might not think I betrayed her.

Hours went by. He returned, still riding furiously, and told me how he had dashed the paper on the table before her, and how she had sunk down speechless when he so spoke as satisfied even his vengeance. And so continued: —

"But I am resolved. Such sluts, such tongue-snakes shall not cross my path. You have been obedient, Stella, through good and ill report, and merit reward. I will speak with the Bishop of Clogher and he shall marry us forthwith, though privately. And we will live apart, for I cannot bend my will and habits to live with any woman; but Stella shall know she is my wife, and the knowledge pierce that ——'s heart."

So, at last, the words I had once died to hear came and found me cold. Indeed, I despised them, though still I honour my friend. I mused, while he leaned against the window, breathing heavily and waiting my reply.

"It comes too late," I said. "There was a time when it had been welcome, but not now. Also, my sympathies are engaged in a quarter where I think a little mercy had become you. With your permission, Mr Dean, this is a subject that shall detain us no more."

I pickt up my knotting as Dingley entered. He stared upon me and went out, nor was it ever again mentioned.

After, she writ me a word: "Madam and my friend, I know 't was not your doing. That needs no words. I am very ill, and were it possible we should meet, 't would be my solace, but 't is impossible. May the happiness the good should enjoy attend you, as do my prayers. Your grateful humble servant, E. V."

I answered thus: "Madam and my friend, God be with you in life and death. The question you put to me I shall for ever answer as then. Comfort yourself, for sure there is a world that sets this right, else were we of all men most miserable."

She was dead in three weeks, of a broken heart. For me, my own hour draws on. I have writ this paper, yet think to destroy it, and know not what is best. No happiness lies before him in old age, for 't is a plant he pulled up by the roots for himself and others — alas! how many. Should I then cause him to suffer more? He hath had the mercy of my silence for a lifetime. 'T is not so hard to be silent in the grave.

(Stella died in the year 1727. The letters in this story to or from Dean Swift are authentic.)

MY LADY MARY

LADY MARY WORTLEY MONTAGU

1689–1792

"I THANK God witches are out of fashion," observes Lady Mary, in a letter to her daughter, when spicy gossip about her doings abroad had been circulated in London, "or I should expect to have it deponed, by several credible witnesses, that I had been seen flying through the air on a broomstick."

Conspicuous always, she was nominated a "toast" in the Kit-Kat Club when she was eight, occupied herself with Latin at ten, was married when she was twenty-three, began her campaign for smallpox inoculation when she was twenty-nine, held salons in London, Constantinople, Brescia, Rome, and Venice, and died when she was seventy-three, bequeathing a fortune and twenty large manuscript volumes of prose and verse to her daughter, one guinea to her son, and two volumes of correspondence to a gentleman in Holland, with the request that the letters be published at once.

"Her family," writes Horace Walpole, "are in terror lest they should be, and have tried to get them. Though I do not doubt but they are an olio of lies and scandal, I should like to see them. She had parts, and had seen much."

Admirers and foes alike will be pleased to note that Edward Wortley Montagu, in the days of courtship, used to direct his love letters to her, simply, —

The Lady Mary Pierrpont
With Care and Speed.

Sir G. Kneller, pinx.   Dawson, ph. sc.

Lady Mary Wortley Montagu

III

MY LADY MARY

[Letters from my Lady Mary Wortley Montagu, cele-
brated for her Beauty and Talents no less than for the
introduction of the Practice of Inoculation for the Small-
pox into England, to her Friend the Lady D——n in
Paris. These Letters will dispel the Mystery to the
Publick of the Lady M.W.M.'s quitting England in
the year 1739.]
Writ in the year 1737, Their Majesties George II &
Queen Caroline reigning.

I RESUME my pen, my dear Madam, to acquaint
you with the news of the day, though 't is what you
scarce deserve from your silence, unless indeed a letter
have miscarried, and 't will not surprise me if my last
hath not come to your hands, which if so, is provoking, it being writ in my best manner. I willingly
would hear from you, was it but to say you still exist,
for I begin to find myself in the mind of the worshipper
of Minerva, who, receiving no answer to prayers and
vows, discharged a pitcher of foul water in her God-
dess-ship's face, declaring he would not longer be at
the trouble to address a lady who would not be at
the trouble to listen, and she might go to the devil
for him. 'T is not however quite come to this with
me, so I continue.

The world riots on at its common pace, and is now
come to the pass that vice is scarce worth the pain of

concealing. Yet when it becomes the general rule, sure there is nothing so stale! Its facility damns it, and it then must simulate some of the airs of virtue to be alluring. Indeed, I conclude it not wholly imaginary that, if it was made easier to be virtuous than vicious, the whole moral balance of the universe would shift and our present monarch and Madame Walmoden be the saints of a new calendar. 'T is here we need the clergy, and, for the life of me, I see not how else. They lend a *haut goût* to vice by condemning it; and if they should disappear, vice must cease to interest and go with them. I gave this for my opinion to the Queen and Lady Sundon, when they were fond to discuss metaphysics, adding that the Seven Deadly Sins required the flames of the infernal regions for their heating and the Ten Commandments for their encouragement if they could be hoped to flourish in the future as at present — and they had the condescension to agree.

All this being so, it will give you neither surprise nor concern to hear my Lord H——d hath run off with his ward, Miss Nanny Graves, leaving his lady with four children. We shall have them back in a few months with reputations so little worse crackt than those of the decentest among us as will not be worth the trouble of censuring, and give neither themselves nor others the smallest uneasiness.

His Majesty is happy at present in the loss of "that old deaf woman," as he lately called my Lady Suffolk, who was once his greatest blessing. There is much I could tell you, but think best not to commit to paper, save that I hear from my Lord Hervey (who is as much as ever in the Queen's confidence) of the farewell of Lady Suffolk to Her Majesty. She lamented to the Queen that she no longer met with the same attention from His Majesty. "I told her," said the Queen, "that she and I were no longer of an age to think of these sort of things in such a romantic way, and as wishing not to encourage it, bade her take a week to consider of the business and give me her word to read no romances meanwhile, and I was sure she would think better of her present concern."

She cares little who rules the King, so she and Sir Robert Walpole rule the kingdom; and indeed does both with the skill of a juggler tossing balls at Bartholomew Fair. Suffice it to say that she is as complaisant as ever, and treats the favourites, be they who they will, with a condescending and smiling geniality that enables her to give many an unexpected stab — the dagger hid in flowers. 'T is thus, in my opinion, every sensible woman in the like case should carry herself. 'T is not tears and agonies that move that sex, but good humour and composure, and thus are they left to their follies while common sense pursues its own objects. Yet, will a future age credit (what my Lord Hervey tells me) that our sovereign Lord, wishing to meet the daughter of the French Regent, — a Princess whose reputation is known to all the world, — writ thus to his Queen, "C'est un plaisir que je suis sûr, ma chère Caroline, vous serez bien aise de me procurer, quand je vous dis combien je le souhaite"?

Never was woman mistress of so much tact, nor with more need of it. He struts like a little despot while the beggars sing in the street : —

You may strut, dapper George, but 't will all be in vain,
We know 't is Queen Caroline, not you, that reign.

He thinks her his slave, and all his sultanas tremble at her nod! Lord, what a world do we live in! I wonder in how many private homes 't is the same.

She is, indeed, an extraordinary woman ; and for my part, despising men and women alike for their motives, I could at this instant form a ministry of women, with the Queen at their head, no more silly and impudent than they who now suppose themselves to guide the fortunes of the country. If the Gods have any relish of humour, — and 't is to be thought they have, else had they not created such a miserable little crawling species, — they must often be witty at our expense. *Quelle vie!*

I comprehend her well. When I give my friendship and confidence and meet with a scurvy return, 't is not anger nor aversion it produces in me, but a complete indifference. Was I to hear tomorrow that Mr Wortley had a train of charmers as long as Captain Macheath's in the "Beggars' Opera," 't would not inflict a pang, so long as he kept within the bounds of prudence and family decency ; and indeed, 't is as my poor sister Gower said to me more than once : "'T is you, sister, for a merciless good sense that makes you accommodate yourself without complaint to what had drove another woman distracted." We

were not married two years before I had to complain
of his indifference and negligence (though no worse),
and writ him plainly to that effect, concluding in the
words that, as this was my first complaint, so it
should be my last. I kept my word, and he his
course, and we now correspond with good temper on
family interests, and no more.

But since I have spoke of the "Beggars' Opera,"
know that I have myself become possessed of a Polly
lovelier than any Lavinia Fenton that ever played
the part. 'T is a romance — heaven send it go no
further! Here is the first chapter.

Being some weeks since at Twicknam, I did not see
company awhile, owing to my cousin's death; for
though, as I writ at the time of my father's, I don't
know why filial piety should exceed fatherly fondness,
and still less cousinly, still there is a decency to be
exprest in black bombazine and retirement. Be-
sides, a thousand nothings kept me engaged. I
passed a part of the time writing satires upon the
little crooked viper of Twicknam, Pope — that may
appear one day with a decoration from my Lord
Hervey's pen; for Pope's last lampoon on me is
a disgrace to any nature above that of a baboon. So
all was pastoral and tranquil.

But, as the Fates would have it, walking one day
by the river and (I suppose) pulling off my glove, I
lost the diamond ring that was my mother's, — the
plainest thing and such as may be found anywhere, —
a ring about the finger, of small brilliant sparks.
'T was not the value, which is nothing, but I returned

home in a scold with my woman Pratt, that was
walking behind me and thinking of nothing but her
face, which some commending have turned her head
or she must have seen it fall.   She is a fool, even for
her nauseous class.   Seeing nothing better to be
done, I caused notices to be writ and stuck about the
village that a Lady of Quality having dropt her ring,
etc., would give a reward.   And having wrote of my
loss to Mr Wortley, my son, and a few friends, fixed
my mind with my usual good sense that I would see
it no more.

For upwards of a week nothing took place.   I was
seated in the garden with my tent-stitch, when out
comes Pratt to say a young woman requested an
audience of me.   I was vexed to be disturbed, having
on my mind a letter that morning received to say
that young rake, my son, was run off from Hinchinbrook and none knew where — but you are no
stranger to his behaviour.   I therefore sent word by
Pratt that I could not see her, well knowing she would
add any force to the information that my words lackt.
But I was vexed to the blood by my young rogue,
knowing not where to find him, and suspecting some
low haunt in the Fleet.

To my astonishment returns Pratt presently,
flouncing and bridling, and with her a young woman
— Heavens! No, but one of the nymphs of the
Thames, or rather, for they are somewhat oozy here-
abouts, a dryad of the Richmond woods, indeed as
beautiful a person as ever I saw in my life. There's
not one of our reigning girls to be compared with her

for a moment, and even my Lord Hervey's Molly
Lepel would vanish beside her, nor could Paris have
any doubt where to bestow the apple. I am an amateur of beauty and can't forget your Ladyship's
praise of my commendation of the fair Fatima, saying
you never before knew one fine woman do such justice
to another. So here I repeat myself.

This fair creature was drest in a plain suit of *minunet*
that had seen better days, and a straw hat tied with
ribbons over a cap of thread lace. But her eyes!
large, black, and languishing, they would have recalled
to me those verses addrest to the daughter of Sultan
Achmet, —

> Your eyes are black and lovely,
> But wild and disdainful as those of a stag,

but for the fall of lashes that hid their soft fire; her
hair raven-black, a bloom I never saw equalled in this
country, and her lips a veritable scarlet and shaped
for every sweetness.

Thinks I — 't is well the Duke of Wharton and his
club for gallantry can't see this paragon, else — but
I leave the rest to your discretion, for your Ladyship
knows "Sophia" as I call him, as well as I. However,
the agreeablest girl in the world came forward and
dropt a curtsey, with her eyes on the ground, and
offered my ring, excusing herself on the scruple that
she must needs give it into my own hand — and all
this in a voice like music.

I leave you to guess if I was pleased, for the ring
was on my mother's hand when she died, and 't was
so prettily tendered, too.

"Well, child, I thank you for your pains," says I, "and will, of course, be answerable for the reward; but give me leave to add that, if I can serve you in any other manner, 't is not my custom to leave a service forgot; if I am not mistook, your mind is not as free from care as a well-wisher could like to see it."

Indeed, there was an air of melancholy about her which moved me prodigiously, and seeing Pratt flouncing and bustling in such a manner as denoted her curiosity and jealousy, I dismist her to the house. She can't endure a face that eclipses her own curds-and-whey skin, and lookt upon my little thread-satin beauty with a true court malice. I was, however, really desirous myself to know what had brought so much beauty to misfortune.

"Madam," says she, "my story is so common that it needs not detain your ear. My father was a rich Turkey merchant, and I wanted for nothing that money could buy. But he was bit by some scheme for making more, three years since; a scheme he compared — alas, too late! — to the South Sea Bubble itself. And in this he lost all, and I had the pious duty to support him by my needleworks. However, he sunk under his miseries into a melancholy that deprived him of life two years since. I nursed him to his last sigh and then, desiring to lead a life of virtue, I entered the family of Mrs Lamb, the Levant merchant's lady and a cousin of my father, to care her children. She carried them down here for an airing, and walking with the little misses yesterday, I found this ring and have the happiness to restore it."

She spoke with a propriety I can't describe, and curtseyed to retire. Indeed, my dear Lady D——n, you had yourself been seduced into the step I next took, though how far 't was prudent, I leave you to judge, allowing the uneasiness beauty causes, go where it will.

"Child," says I, "I thank you, and as for the reward—"

She stopt me with a simplicity and integrity that could not but confirm my first opinion.

"'T is not possible, Madam, I should accept it for an act of honesty common to all decent persons. Refuse me not that privilege, and permit me to retire, with thanks to your Ladyship for so encouraging a reception."

Again she curtseyed, but I detained her. 'T was truly a pleasure to see so charming a creature.

"Child, if not possible I should serve you in one way, it may in another. If the question be not disagreeable, are you happily placed with this city lady?"

Her fine eyes moistened.

"No, Madam. Not but what Madam means well, but she possesses not an easy humour, and Miss Nanny, Susan, Betty, and the rest are hard to be controlled. I receive but my clothes and food and 't is very true —"

She stopt what she would have said, with all the easiness of a girl of quality, but a modesty they have exchanged for the paint-pot and whitewash in which they now blaze out. What she did not say left much to be guessed. 'T is certainly these rich city folk for an illiberality of mind and petty spitefullness that inflicts countless stings on their dependants. 'T was a weakness, I own, but it then came into my mind on a high point of generosity (with which I am sometimes took like a colic) to do what I could for the poor creature. 'T was to be seen she was educated, and she presently confirmed my belief that she could read, write, and cast accompts to perfection, and was skilled in needleworks and household management. Her expectations of payment did not run high, and 't is but reasonable I should consider of this. So was I tempted into what you may censure as an indiscretion, and said I was in need of one to overlook my family of servants, and be about myself and my girl, who hath picked up some little grossnesses from Pratt that I like not. Not that I would dismiss Pratt, but put this one somewhat above her as her training deserves. 'T was charity and carefulness combined.

Sure never was gratitude more lively exprest than when she fell on her knee and kist my hand, protesting and vowing her life should be the monument to my goodness. And indeed, think what you will, Madam, 't is a girl more suited to the company of persons of quality than to city dames that drive behind a pair of Suffolk Dumplings with coachman to match, their own hair and portliness dressed out in the last mode but three. For this girl fashion mattered not. I dare to swear the more she put off, the fairer she must appear, even as our general mother Eve gained no lustre from her fig leaves nor furs,

'T was not till the matter was settled and she retired, that my good sense asserted itself, and thus it said : —

"Come, Madam, what do you know of this nymph that you should be in such haste to make yourself her guardian? Did you ever know gratitude, or even decency, in return for a favour? And here have you took a girl into your family that will certainly draw every rake within thirty miles to hunt down the prey?" — "No matter," says my conscience (did you credit its existence, my dear Lady D——n? for so did not I), "if you take not pity on the wench, she will in three years' time be chargeable to the parish, with a brat in either hand, cast off for a newer face." 'T is the way of the men, and those that trust them embark their little capital into worse than the South Sea Bubble. I resolved to keep her very secluded and say nothing of my Polly Peachum (whose name, by the way, is Anne Wentworth) outside the house, but indeed might as well endeavour to stifle a promising scandal as such beauty! However, she arrived a week later with her meagre outfit. 'T was an odd whim, I own.

Don't I see you now, saying as you read, "Well do I know the sequel. Mr Wortley comes up from Hinchinbrook and loses the acorn he is pleased to call his heart to Mrs Anne." You are much mistook, Madam, and was it to be she, I had as soon that as another, for I might thus acquire the merit with my husband which the Queen gains with hers by choosing his inamoratas. It fell out far otherwise to your

expectations; and, but for Pratt's gruntings and
grumblings about cuckoos picked up in the street,
which Mrs Anne bore with smiling patience, I had
vaunted every day my good fortune in lighting on
such beauty and merit.

My first alarm took place when Molly Skerret
comes down one day and sees her engaged over the
lace ruffles of my *negligée*. Says she: —

"Are you mad, Lady Mary, that you will needs
have a beauty about you like yonder? All the men
will be running after her. She is a close resemblance
to Sally Salisbury, that hath been the rage — she
that some time back stabbed young Finch and fled
to France."

I set it down to spite, for dear Molly is no beauty
herself. But the very next day my troubles begun,
for the viper of Twicknam, happening to spy her in
the garden in attendance on my girl, went home swelling with poison and writ the following, which was
handed about all over the place and in the town.

> Narcissa wisely from the world retired
> So soon 's she saw her slighted charms expired.
> But since she still must hope another spring,
> (As snakes collect their poison ere they sting,)
> She chose a lovely nymph to keep her sweet,
> And, willing to be cheated as to cheat,
> When in her glass the glowing charmer shone,
> She fondly dreamed the image was her own.

This made a great talk, which was against my wish
to keep the girl retired. But you will credit, my
dear Lady D., that the malice of this little crooked
monster, who should from affinity be conversant with

the habits of snakes, would not set me against the poor innocent wench that caused it, and I contented myself with the caution to her that she should keep in the garden and speak with no men but what I judged proper. I fear none the less that there may be a difficulty in keeping her, impossible to be overcome, but will tell you further in replying to your obliging favour just received.

Before concluding this epistle, which indeed is more truly to be called a novel, I would have you know that Lady Polden was inoculated, together with all her family, for the smallpox two months since, excepting only Miss Jenny, that none could persuade from fear of the lancet. All recovered after a day or two's disagreeables, but poor Miss Jenny catching the distemper, supposedly at a masquerade, fell a victim at the age of eighteen, and was buried a week last Monday in all the forms. 'T is certain there are those would sooner die with the approval of the doctors than live to dance on their graves without it.

My daughter presents her duty to you. I have designs myself to cross to France ere long, but will not be particular as to plans until I am more resolved.

I am affectionately yours.

(*Two months later*)

My dear Madam, —

I know not whether I do well or ill in acquainting you with a matter so delicate, as there is none other but my Lord Hervey to whom I dare confide it, and

't is but to you and to him I would be obliged for
assistance. But friendship, if an illusion, is the last
left me, and I won't dismiss it until I am compelled.
'T is certainly absurd that one human being should
depend upon any other for anything, for alone we
are born and die, and it may be thought the Great
Author of our being intended us to walk the way alone
that conducts from the one to the other, else had he
made our minds more accessible. For my part, if
truth be a merit, I can say I never had an affection,
but what I regretted it sooner or later, or made a
confidence, but what I wished it recalled. Excepting
in one case, which I leave to your discernment. And
such is my vexation at this minute that, was I to be
born in another incarnation as Pythagoras pretends,
I would be a foundling, indebted to none who could
exact repayment of the gift of life forced upon an
unwilling victim to please the humour of others.

If I write a little bitter I know your kind concern
will excuse me in view of what I relate. I am extreme
annoyed and fluttered, yet would not be a vain lamenter neither. Life is still endurable when met
with an easy common sense, and this I call to my aid
on this occasion.

I had a mind to return to London about a month
since, when word came that my young rake of a son
would come hither for a few days, with his friend
Carew. I knew not the young man, but remember
his father in the Thoresby days, and the old man now
being dead, the youth is well to pass in the world in
a small way and hath inherited the old Devon grange.

However, I took this as a sign of grace in my prodigal, and desired Anne to see the rooms prepared and that she should not attend me with my tent-stitch after dinner, as wishing to keep flint and steel apart, which your Ladyship will admit was a prudence to be desired. And so went down to receive the young men.

You are not now to learn that Edward, with all his follies, hath a very pleasant humour when he chooses, and a tongue not unworthy of his family; and young Carew being very conversable and well-featured and full of odd stories of the authorities at Oxford and the liberties they allow themselves under the mask of gravity, the evening past extreme agreeably, and it was late when I left them to their bottle.

Pratt and Anne Wentworth attended me to bed, and I desired the last to put my pearl necklace into my dressing-box with the dressing-plate, with which she complied in her obliging manner and took the key as customary. This done, I dismist them and writ a few lines to my Lord Hervey, and so to sleep.

The next day we past on the river in a water party and sillabubs at Richmond and what not; and evening come I asked for my necklace and — Lord bless me! — 't was not to be found. Anne, pale as her smock, was looking in all corners, — and Pratt, also, but with purst lips as who should say, "Your Ladyship now sees what comes of whimsies and foundlings," — till I was vexed to the blood with them both, and knew not what to say next; the more so, since I had seen Mrs Anne gathering flowers for the bowpots

after sunrise, and young Carew staring after her like
a zany. I don't doubt but what there had been a
thousand sweet nothings before I opened my window.
The house was hunted in vain, and all the comfort
Edward could give me was the assurance of his
father's anger at my folly in taking a stranger into
the house; which is most abominably true, Mr
Wortley loving to find fault and invent it where not
found.

By this time Pratt was weeping like a crocodile,
and the Bow Street runners sent for to come and take
particulars lest the pearls be sold in Drury Lane.
Indeed, my dear Madam, I could not close an eye
for vexation, and to complete it could not but remark
that young Carew kept casting sheep's eyes at Mrs
Anne that looked as lovely as a weeping angel, could
such be supposed. How different are tears in one
woman and another! Pratt, her nose inflamed, her
eyes scarce visible in swelled lids, might have been
exposed to the Duke of Wharton and his "Schemers"
without an ounce of virtue lost on either side; whereas
Anne, with the liquid pearls hung on her lashes as if to
replace the lost ones, was a dish for the Gods. 'T is
no manner of use to scold the Fates for what they
give or withhold; but I swear 't is easy known they
are women, such favourites do they make without
reason.

We returned to London without loss of time, and
the young men remained on in my family for awhile,
a course I took because the investigators are such
filthy drunken beasts as I would not bring myself

to endure their presence, and thought it more fitting that Edward should direct them. 'T was more than a week ere they returned, with the news that pearls answerable to the description were sold at a receiving "ken" about Drury Lane. My blessed offspring, who (by the way) is grown extreme handsome, endeavoured to learn more certainly, but was told with surprising impudence that they were likely out of the kingdom by this time. The wretch that kept the place was took in custody and closely questioned; but naught could be got from him but that a young madam whom he supposed a nymph of Drury Lane had sold it, saying she had it from her young cully of a lover, and she would not have the sale known for worlds, but had occasion for the money. Asked to describe her, he said so many were his dealings as he took no particular heed beyond that she was handsome, and a way with her, says he, that would whistle a bird off a bough.

God forgive me — 't was not wonderful I looked at Mrs Anne, and the thought came in my mind how little I knew but her own story, and my own folly that took up with a stranger on what I might call a mere spasm of liking. She saw it, for she hath a gift of reading faces, and says she : —

"Your Ladyship, I am sensible that suspicion is like to rest on me, for Mrs Pratt is some time in your family and I but new come. This is a hanging matter, Madam, and I beseech you have so much pity for a poor girl as permit me a few days more before I am handed over to these cruel men. 'T is the bare truth that, so far from stealing, I would give my life to repay the debt I owe your goodness. And sure I that restored a jewel unasked am scarce to be now held guilty. Have pity upon your poor girl, Madam! and delay but till Mrs Lamb and her family return from the Wells to speak for me."

'T was so well exprest and carried so much truth that, though I called myself a thousand weak fools, I could not refuse her, and so set a week and la-mented my own weakness in regard of beauty, that might be a man for the sensibility I have for it but that I detect their little cunning tricks. I know not how I am so oddly made up, unless it be the merciless good sense of which my poor sister Gower com-plained; but I am no more like to believe a woman ill-behaved because she is handsome (as women do), than to think her innocent (as a man would do) for the same excellent reason.

Some more days past, and I had other cause to regret my course; for passing a door ajar, I looked through the crack, hearing voices, and found Mrs Pratt conversing very much at her ease with my prodigal — a thing which, though well enough in Congreve's comedies, is what I will not have in my family. I am so ill-bred as to be quite insensible to the romantic flights that are now the vogue and, walking into the room, spoke my mind, desiring Mrs Pratt to be so good as pack her boxes and depart within the hour, which was accordingly done, I hav-ing her boxes looked through ere she went, so much assurance awaking my suspicion that perhaps she could tell more of the pearls than anyone, if so disposed. However, nothing found, and so off she went in a sulky silence, my son and heir talking very high and railing upon me for injustice. He took himself off next morning with young Carew (who however behaved very genteelly throughout), saying as he flung away, that God only knew but they might next be suspected, and they had better depart while their characters were safe. You know the silly cant he is apt to talk as well as any.

I was fluttered and wearied when they departed, and had, what is rare with me, a touch of the vapours; but there was Anne, hearing me come up, and did all to support me that a feeling heart and good sense could dictate. Will your Ladyship credit me when I tell you the poor girl had had good reason all along to suspect Mrs Pratt might have a hand in the thievery, but would not speak as knowing nothing for certain, and sparing to trouble me with the understanding she surprised between Pratt and my young gentleman. Her good sense and heart were a cordial, and I drew a little consolation in considering that I would now retain her about my person and enjoy a little peace in a worthy attendant. For, though I have known no instances of honour and integrity but among those of high birth, still there are exceptions, no doubt, to be found to any rule. So resolving, I sat down to write to my rake that I had sufficient reason to think his Dulcinea might know more of the pearls, and to request he would oblige me by using his best endeavours to trace them.

What a bubble is hope! Two days later comes a letter from young Carew, expressing himself with decency and respect, to tell me that with my permission he had made up his mind to marry Mrs Anne Wentworth, who was not unwilling to hear his suit, since he knew not where else he could find so much beauty coupled with good sense and modesty. He doubted not but I would approve his resolution.

'T was somewhat of a blow. I had come to like the girl about me as a lap dog or any other little fondling. Her every look was a caress, and her voice as soft as violets. Also she hath mended my girl's manners of a hundred little indelicacies gathered from Pratt's pertness. I had willingly kept her, but 't was not to be. What! shall a young beauty refuse a comfortable home and other matrimonial delights for a lonely woman! Not she!

I gave them what, by courtesy, may be called my blessing, and my suit of blue lutestring to Mrs Bride, and she threw herself at my feet, and I actually came near shedding a tear to see her overflowing gratitude. 'T was worthy such a set of verses as Pope writ when the rural lovers were killed in each other's arms by a stroke of lightning.

No doubt Carew is a fool — yet I think a wise one. She will play him no tricks and stratagems, and will be a fair Lady Bountiful in his moated grange, and will care her children and the poor, and con possets and caudles with the parson's wife — Pshaw! what sickly stuff do I write that should know better. 'T is liker she will play him false in a year, with some booby

squire that rides to hounds and swaggers in with his
boots a mass of mud to drink himself silly after a
dinner of roast pig. And for me, I have replaced
her next day with a Mrs Susan — the Duchess of
Montagu's late woman, that hath all the pertnesses
and the tricks of her trade.

Well — 't is the way of the world. Set not your
heart on anything. A hard heart that values nothing
is the only wear, and 't is evident Scripture so enjoins
it. My glass tells me I am still a personable woman,
and 't is open to me to find amusement in making a
lover — and myself — happy if so I choose — and if
't were not so dull a pastime. And there is crimp and
quadrille for the asking, and the new game that is just
come up.

Horace Walpole is crossing the Channel and will
give this to your Ladyship's hand. And the favour
I would have of you (in all secrecy) is this — that you
would cause enquiry to be made with caution at
Breguet's in the Rue des Moineaux, whether he hath
had lately any sale of pearls from England. 'T was
a thing spoke of as not impossible, that they should
find their way there, for I hear from H. W. and others
that the man is a well-practised receiver of such goods
from England. But with caution, I entreat, and
with no mention to H. W., for I begin to have an
anxiety that I have not as yet mentioned to any.

Pray be so good as send your reply by special hand.
I await it uneasily. It may be that I have the spleen,
but though I have done with knight-errantry for dis-
trest beauty, I wonder sometimes whether my little

Anne Carew have not a happier fate than any woman of fashion. 'T is but a modest grange in Devon; but those two simple souls will taste of happiness there and in each other, and the world will not trouble them. The seasons will come and go, and when they lie in the churchyard 't will not be with tons of marble and scutcheons of lies above 'em, but with nature's covering of snow in winter and leaves and flowers in summer. They 'll sleep the sweeter. I would willingly have her with me still. Present my compliments to our Embassador. I may yet have to ask his good offices, but am still in hopes to avoid this.

Your Ladyship's most affectionate, as ever.

(A month later)

MY DEAR MADAM, —

Herewith the end of the romance I have inflicted on your obliging attention, and I am now to tell you your comments were fully justified and I have writ myself down an ass and invoked as fine a lampoon as Pope could write in gall and vinegar. "Sappho" will be as nothing to it, and indeed that I, that know the world or should know it, should behave so like a country bumpkin new come to town is gall and wormwood to myself. I cannot hide from a friend what all the world will soon ridicule, and had sooner you heard it from me than another. Was you to reproach my folly as I deserve, you will write volumes and I promise to read with seasonable humility. Sure I must be falling into premature dotage.

I was at Twicknam again, somewhat ailing with

my common swelled face, when I was told Mr Carew would see me. I refused, but he would take no denial and indeed forced his way in — so pale that I could expect nothing but the worst news of my son and implored him to speak. 'T was some time and took a dram to restore him before he could answer, what with his haste and fluttered spirits. But when he did — 't was to tell me Madam had flown the day they married. The ceremony was scarce over and they returned to the house, when, making some excuse, she slipt from the room. He waited as long as a bridegroom's patience would hold out and followed her; but found she was nowhere to be seen. Your kindness, Madam, will conceive the horror with which he searched everywhere, but could get no news. The least he could suppose was that she was murdered for the diamond ring he gave her on the occasion.

At the last he had recourse to the law, and what a discovery was there. Who think you was my paragon — the compendium in little of all the female virtues? Why, Sally Salisbury's niece! and the equal of Sally herself for worthless good looks and behaviour. She is not yet well known to the town or I could not have been so took in. But you will recall that Molly Skerret observed the likeness to that drab Sally on seeing her. Good Heaven, that I had heeded, and not harboured the slut!

Yet there is worse to follow, and I know not how to tell such folly, but must do so. She is the wife of my son, whom indeed I knew capable of any wick-

edness short of robbing his mother. He picked the
hussy up in the Fleet and wed her, and then, being
in debt, the thought struck the promising pair that
my jewels might meet their needs. He took advantage of the loss of my ring to have it copied, and the
rest followed easy with a fool like me.

"But I beseech you, Madam," says poor Carew,
shaking in every limb, "that you would have the
goodness to review your jewels, since the only way
I can reason upon her continuing with you and pretending to accept my addresses was to take time
while Mrs Pratt was under suspicion to make off
with more and keep you easy about them. The pretended love-affair with Mrs Pratt was plainly to be
a false scent."

I sent for my cases, and find my chain of diamonds,
my gold etui set with diamonds, my Turkish clasp
with emeralds, and other things disappeared with
my Venus. I enclose the list and description, for I
learn Miss Sally Salisbury is now in Paris, and it is
probable that her niece and nephew (my son) have
joined her or committed the jewels to her good offices.
I am ashamed to give your Ladyship such trouble
about this trifle, yet beg your obliging enquiries in the
Rue des Moineaux or where else your Lord may sug-
gest. But by all means keep it from Horace Walpole.
I want not his bitter tongue to lick my sores. 'T is
of course certain we cannot use the law, considering
who is involved — a point Madam no doubt laid her
account with when she carried through the plot.

Lord, when I think of my sentiment wasted on the

arrant hussy! My green churchyards and Lady
Bountifuls and all the praise of simplicity and parade
of folly that took me because of a pretty face and arts
from the gutter. Well, 't is the miserable truth that
this young fool (who sure must get it from his mother)
did wed this slut at the Fleet two years since, and
hath damned himself for life. He is now as weary of
her as is to be expected, and besought me to deliver
him from the consequence of his folly. Beside that
fact the affair of the diamonds seems shrunk, for
nothing can be done, nor does he deserve it. He
whines like a whipt dog in his letters.

I would my father had lived to see the soundness of
Mr Wortley's reasoning, when he refused to entail
his estates upon a future child of whose vices and
disposition he could know nothing. 'T would certainly be the young gentleman's utter ruin had he
money to handle in reversion. I will not trouble you
with the number of falsehoods he has stuft into his
letters.

I have trained myself to fortitude, and go about
with as many knives stuck in my heart as our Lady
of the Seven Dolours that I saw in Vienna, but make
much less display of them. The best news I could
have at this moment would be the young villain's
death, for the misery he will yet bring upon himself
and others is too certain. For Madam, she will
doubtless be heard of yet in a manner that the decency of my sex obliges me to soften. I doubt they
will both end on the gallows, though indeed her face
will probably save her that or any penalty.

Well, I have done with such fragments of a heart as I had, and wish it may never trouble me more. I am sick of the cant of sentiment and duties and suchlike, which is the mask men use to cover what will not bear considering. Let me write of it no more. The open wickedness of the world we live in is preferable to hypocrisy and cringing. I will rather laugh with others than be a laughing-stock. I sicken at this complication of folly and falsity. I go to the Bath shortly, and look for change and pleasure there, though Mr Wortley speaks of passing through on his way to Bristol, I know not for what. Lord Hervey is resolved to come there, though I fear it will not please his lady, who seems resolved to keep so general a blessing to herself, which is more than she or any can hope. She takes it, however, with easy good sense, and wisely, for there's nothing on earth, I protest, worth a tear.

The rage for cards runs higher than ever, and let me conclude my romance and this long paper with a pretty parable of them that is making the round of the town. Will your Ladyship guess the author? 'T is called "The Goddesses of Chance."

"There was long since in the Moon four Goddesses. One was the Queen of Riches, the second the Queen of Love, the third the Queen of Power, and of the fourth you 'll hear anon. 'T is to be supposed the fourth received the most homage; for a thing known loses its value, as when a man despises his own wife and thinks Lord M.'s a descended Venus, when, was the case reversed, his own would be his object.

"On a certain day these ladies, being, after all, women, disputed between themselves on a point of precedence.

"Says the Goddess of Riches, jingling her diamonds: —

"'I come first with all. I am worshipt in every polite country, and even the blacks fight over the shells that are their coinage. I give not only gold but all it can buy, inclusive of such bagatelles as love and honour, and all the other little nothings men cry up when they have a mind to be droll. I need give no examples though I might cite the late marriage of my Lady M. E. at the age of fifteen to a wealthy lord of seventy-five that shall be nameless. Undoubtedly I am Queen of all.'

"'Not by any means,' says the Goddess of Hearts, adjusting her crown with a simper. ''T is I am supreme. 'T is known a young rake will sell his last estate to win a smile from Miss Sally Salisbury and other worthy ladies. And hath not the Countess of H——t lately run off with her footman? I lead statesmen and kings by the nose. Many such moral examples could I give if needful.'

"The Goddess of Power, brandishing her club with a brawny arm, then replied: —

"'I beg your Ladyships would cease twattling when 't is in my power with a crack of my club to silence you all. I leave you to judge whether anything in life is so powerful as what can end it. What 's love when a crack on the sconce can kill it, or riches when a blow can turn it over to the grimacing heir-at-law? No, no, ladies. Strength comes first, and this was seen when the Strong Man was at Bartholomew Fair and half the beauties ran after him and poured their gold in a perfect Pactolus at his feet. Show your good sense, therefore, by a discreet silence.'

"But still they disputed, and at last the fourth said : —

"'Sisters, let us descend to earth, that we may settle the question which I see not how else to conclude.'

"'But how shall we go?' says the three at once.

"'We will go as the Queens of Chance, and men may sport with us, play with us, revile us, men and women alike. And they shall sell us their honour, love, and whatever else they have marketable, and on the day of Judgment we four will see whose bag is fullest of their commodities. 'T is the only way to settle the dispute. And in the end all shall come to me.'

"And the three said : 'And who are you, Madam?'

"And says she : 'With my black spade I dig the earth where all shall lie. 'T is I will be the Black Hag of the Pack, and you shall strip them and I will dig their graves. Be it known to you that I am Destiny herself.'

"So they came to earth, and are the Queens of Diamonds, Hearts, and Clubs. But if the Queen of Spades be in your hand, say the gambler's prayer backward, for she is the chance you can't reckon in the game, or in life or death."

I think it neatly turned, whoever did it, and I

declare this little writing hath so affrighted the fine
ladies, that Mrs Murray swooned away at the
Duchess of Manchester's, finding the Queen of Spades
in her hand at commerce, and was forced to be re-
vived with strong waters. His Grace of Wharton,
known to you and me as "Sophia," hath given up
cards altogether, though whether it be the parable,
I know not. And the viper of Twicknam is so jealous
that he did not himself write this piece, that he spews
his venom in all directions, in hope some will settle
on the author. His pleasure to scourge alike the
follies and virtues of mankind is, for aught I know,
the liveliest this world affords. The follies are, at
least, inexhaustible, and none need be at a loss for
amusement that can taste them, whether in themselves or others.

The Queen, who I can't undertake to commiserate
for bad health, so hard a life as she leads, hath had
the unspeakable blessing to see her lord return from
Hanover, after a storm which induced his faithful
subjects to believe they had lost him. Will your
Ladyship credit that the wits affixed a paper to the
walls of St. James's Palace with, writ on it, this
following : —

"Lost or strayed out of this house, a man who has
left a wife and six children on the parish. Whoever
will give tidings of him to the churchwardens of St.
James's Palace, so as he may be got again, shall
receive four shillings and sixpence reward. — N.B.
This reward will not be increased, nobody judging
him to be worth a crown."

Impudence indeed! But I hear from Lord Hervey that she is counselled by Sir Robert Walpole to invite Madame Walmoden hither from Hanover, to amuse his leisure. 'T is done as you might throw a bone to a dog, while Her Majesty and the Walpole pursue the business of governing. I have no sort of liking for either, but own, had that woman been a man, she had been a great one, so entirely does she subdue her heart and all the femininities in her to what her reason demands. When she dies, and it can't be long first, from what I hear, the fool she leaves will drift like a stick in a stream.

Well, I sicken of England and of the town and the wits and all else. My mind is made up to quit this country ere long, and seek peace abroad, where I found it when I was younger than I am now. Folly! I tell myself so, and yet I will do it, when one or two businesses I must attend on are finished. 'T is not that I am a lamenter over that I have told you. I care not what happens to my prodigal, and had sooner be out of hearing of his doings. When a cup is broke, throw it from you and think of it no more. But whether 't is the spleen or the vapours, I have a mind to cross the water and seek a new earth, if not a new heaven. Here I am in neither, but in purgatory. *Quelle vie!* — 'T is what I say daily.

Adieu, my dearest Madam — may it not be long before we meet.

Inviolably yours,

M. W. M.

(The son of Lady Mary Wortley Montagu was the misery of her life, and it is the historic truth that he made much such a marriage as I have described. It is said he turned Mohammedan after the death of his parents. A portrait of him in a most aggressive turban is in existence. The reason for Lady Mary's leaving England in 1739, and returning only to die in 1762, has never been known.)

THE GOLDEN VANITY

MARIA GUNNING
Countess of Coventry
1733–1760

ELIZABETH GUNNING
Duchess of Hamilton and of Argyll
1734–1790

" 'T is a warm day," remarks George Selwyn in a
letter to Lord Carlisle, "and someone proposes a
stroll to Betty's front shop; suddenly the cry is
raised, 'The Gunnings are coming,' and we all
tumble out to gaze and to criticize."

The two lovely sisters from Roscommon in Ireland, introduced by their beauty, were the sensa-
tion of fashionable England in 1751. Maria, a
year the elder, was the more dashing and at first
the more conspicuous of the two. She became
Countess of Coventry, and died at twenty-seven.
Elizabeth married the Duke of Hamilton, after his
death, refused the Duke of Bridgewater, but later
married the Duke of Argyll. Four of her children
were Dukes, two of Hamilton and two of Argyll.

So much Irish luck and beauty kept the Gunnings constantly in the centre of court affairs. A
poem celebrating their conquests was entitled,
"The Grand Contest between the Fair Hibernians
and the English Toasts."

The Queen of the Bluestockings said of them,
when she saw them together, "Indeed very handsome ; *nonpareille*, for the sisters are just alike take
them together, and there is nothing like them."

Cotes, pinx

Maria Gunning

IV

THE GOLDEN VANITY

A Story of the First Irish Beauties
The Gunnings

It was the year of grace 1750, and old Mother Corrigan sat outside her door in Slattern Alley, smoking her short black pipe with a relish; and 't was a good day with her, for she had told his fortune that morning for Squire Tyrconnel, on his way to fight a duel in the Phœnix Park with Lawyer Daly; and when it was finished, says she to him: —

"Let you count the buttons on his body-coat, your Honour, and fix the third from the top in your eye. And when you stand up to him, say a prayer and pink him with your swordeen in that very spot, and the Lord grant him a bed in heaven, the old villain, for he 'll never be asking one on earth again."

And as she said, so it was, and old Daly turned up his toes and never spoke more, when the Squire got him in the third button. And an hour after, Squire Tyrconnel sent his purse with five golden guineas in it, and a pound of the best rappee to be found in the Four Courts, and all for Mother Corrigan, and she was a proud woman that day. Her house was stuffed as full of money as an egg of meat; but no one would think it to look at her; for she had it all hid away like an old fairy, so that no one would give a thought to it.

She was sitting at her door at the top of Slattern Alley where it turns into Britain Street, and she in the best of good tempers, when a lady came by with two young daughters beside her — a tall woman, with a fine blossoming colour in her face and an air like a peacock spreading his tail and her eyes as clear as spring water. It would be hard to see a finer woman of her age in a day's walk, and all the gentlemen going to and from the Castle must turn to have another look at the three of them. Her dress might be handsome at first sight; but, closer, you could see she had it held up with pins and stitches, and a bit of good lace fell over it to hide the wear in the front. Also, she drew her feet under her hoop, that they might not be noticed, though they were as small as a young child's. And so she minced along with steps like mice, for fear of showing the burst in her shoe.

But for all that she held up her head like the deer in the Lord Lieutenant's park, and her pride was enough for a queen, and too much for a poor lady walking the Dublin streets and holding her skirt up out of the mud.

But it was the two she had with her that any lady might be proud of. There were never two such out of heaven; and sure it may be believed, for the world has said it often enough since that day, and will say it to the end of time. For the elder was a sweet rogue, with hair like red gold clean out of the fire, and eyes like a blue June morning, and cheeks like May flowers that a rose has kissed, and lips that better than a rose would kneel to kiss one day; and her smile lit up the street, and she tripped along as light as a spring breeze.

But the younger — sure the Lord was well pleased the day he made her face, for 't was perfection's self. Her hair was a dark brown veined with gold, and her eyes like purple violets with the rain on them; and when she closed her long lashes 't was like a cloud over the stars; and her mouth, and the soft smile, and the dimple that dipped when she laughed — a man would stand all day to watch her and not think long.   'T is a strange thing that one girl will be like that, all beauty and shining sweetness, and another, perhaps as good, — for better she could not be in her heart, — will be a poor sorrowful little victim that a cat would not look at in the dark!

And old Mother Corrigan saw them coming, and she took her pipe out from between her teeth, and says she: —

"Halt here, my ladies, the three of you, and hear the fortune that 's waiting you — the way you 'll be ready when it comes."

"Fortune!" says the lady, stopping, a girl in each hand; "'T is the black fortune and the sad fortune that befell me since the day the gold ring was on my finger. And I don't want to hear any more, so I don't; for if I had more to bear than I have this minute I would n't face the morn's morrow."

But Mother Corrigan rose up as nimbly as a woman to a dance, and she looked the lady in the eyes as if she was as tall as herself, and, "Come in," says she, "for though 't is a poor place, the beauty of the three of you will light it like candles, and 't is here your luck begins."

So they went in, and the lady said she had not so much as a silver bit to cross her hand with, and indeed would have pulled her daughters back; but the old woman would not have it.

"Leave it so," says Mother Corrigan, "what matters an empty hand today when you 'll fill the two hands of me with gold when the luck comes that 's coming? Give me your word, my lady, and I 'll take it for as good as five guineas."

So she gave her word to fill Mother Corrigan's hand with golden guineas; and the two young girls were standing by, their cheeks like burning roses for fear and hope, as the old witch caught the lady's hand, and gabbled something that was not a prayer, and the words came from her like a person talking in their sleep.

"High blood and poverty. Sure, your father had a crown on his head and no gold to gild it with."

But the lady pulled her hand away angrily.

"Then you know who I am. What 's the good of play-acting? I guessed this would be the way of it!"

"I don't know and I don't care," says the old woman with a grin. "I 'm telling you what I see, and till this minute I never laid eye on you or yours. Don't you be speaking again, for there 's no sense in that; but harken!"

So she told her her father was poor and proud, an Irish lord with a castle in a bog and an old coach with the cloth hanging off it in flitters and the plough-horses to draw it; and that he never gave her a penny since she married, for he had it not to give. And she told her her husband was no better, but running after the cards and dice all day, so that all the world cried folly on her for taking up with him.

"But no matter!" says Mother Corrigan, "for you did a good deed for yourself that day you stood up with him in the church."

"A good deed!" says the lady, very angry. "Don't you be a foolish old woman, and you so near your end. For I got nothing out of it but care and crying and pinching poverty and five children that I don't know how to put the bread in their mouths; and this minute I 'm as lonesome as a widow, for my husband is off and away in the country, and here am I in Dublin; and if I know how to get bit or sup for them it 's as much as I do know."

But the old woman shook her head till her teeth rattled.

"Let you be easy and take what 's coming. I see you sitting in a king's house, and the walls all gilded gold, and the carpets like moss that your foot would sink into, and riches and grandeur, and everyone bowing down to the mother of the beauties."

"Well, if the half of it 's true," says the lady, "the first news should come to me is that I 'm a widow; for 't is impossible it should happen as you say with a husband that has n't one penny-piece to rattle on a tombstone."

"You 'll not be a widow for many a day, and 't is your husband's name brings the luck."

"You don't know what his name is. You could n't! If you 'll tell me his name, I 'll engage to believe any mortal thing you tell me."

So the three looked at the old woman; but she took another look at the hand as she might be reading a book, and: —

"Good-day to you, Mrs Gunning, and good-day to his Lordship's daughter, — my Lord Mayo, — and good-day to the mother of the two beauties that 'll sweep the world."

And she clucked and chuckled to herself, highly diverted with their astonishment. How did she know it? What that old woman did not know would make but a short story. 'T was said she had informants over the whole countryside, like a Minister of the Crown.

They stared, for they were new come to Dublin, running from their debts in Roscommon and taking the chance to pick up husbands in the city, and there was not one there who knew them.

So she took the youngest girl's hand in hers and says she: —

"You 'll marry the highest man, bar one or two, in England. And you 'll not be content with that; for when you bury him, you 'll marry the highest man in Scotland; and if I sat here till tomorrow, I could n't tell you the half of the riches and glory that 's waiting for you. You 'll have to crawl through the black mud to get the first; but after that 't is a clear course, and the mud won't stick to a duchess's gown, young Miss Elizabeth Gunning!"

A duchess! Elizabeth's eyes were like winter stars, they so sparkled — they would put out the light of diamonds. She held herself like a young poplar and says she: —

"And if you 're right, old woman, or anything like it, I 'll come and see you when I get promotion, and my Lord Duke shall fill your pockets with gold."

But Mother Corrigan grinned like a dog.

"I have n't a pocket, my Lady's Honour. My hand 's good enough; but I 'll not be here when you come riding back to poor old Dublin in yer coach and six — and now for the fairy of the world!" — And she took the hand of the eldest, who was shaking like a leaf and expecting to hear of a prince and his blue ribbon at the least, and her eyes fixed on the old witch like two blue lakes with the stars dipping in them.

But she shook her head.

"A great man, but not so big a man as your sister's." (The girl looked jealous daggers at Elizabeth.) "A fine man, and the gold lace on him, and velvet and silk stockings, and gold buckles shining in the shoes of him, and a big house to live in, and fine clothes for your back, and —"

She stopped dead, like a horse pulled up on his haunches; but the young Maria twitched her by the raggedy sleeve.

"Go on. What is it? I want to hear."

"Don't ask me, and you so beautiful!"

"I do ask, and I 'll have it out of you. I suppose you mean I 'll get old and ugly like yourself."

"You 'll never be old and ugly. Them that remembers you will remember the loveliest thing God
ever made when he took clay in his two hands."

"I don 't know what she means," says Maria fret-
fully. "But sure some women are handsome till they
die. Tell us when will the luck come, and how ?"

"With the Golden Vanity and a woman with a
man's name. And now leave me, my three queens,
and I 'll have a drop to warm me old bones and a
whiff of the pipe to put the life in me. But don't forget the old woman when the great lords is kneeling
before you and pouring the diamonds out of baskets
before ye — and send the golden guineas, and —"

So she went on mumbling and muttering, and that
was the first and last time the old hag told a fortune
for love and not for money. She had not long to tell
any, for she died next May, and not a soul to cry for
her.

They stepped out into the sunshine, their heads
high, and scarce a word to say to each other; for all
three were thinking of the promises as light and glittering as soap bubbles. And Maria would not spare
a word to Elizabeth, for not a woman but must walk
after the heels of a duchess, and she was all for leading.

"The Golden Vanity !" says Elizabeth. "Mama,
what should that be ? When I 'm a duchess —"

"I don't know, and most likely 't is not worth
knowing." Mrs. Gunning was angry. Her fine
brows were drawn together. "Leave talking of duch-

esses, you silly fools, and go get the herrings for tea.
I have left the children too long as it is."

So she marched down Britain Street like a queen,
for all her burst shoe, — a shabby street it was for
such ladies, — and the two walked off to Fish-
monger's Alley, and not a head but turned to look at
them.

"Faith, they 're goddesses and no mistake!" says
gay Mr Councillor Egan, on the way from the Law
Courts, with his mulberry face and his mulberry velvet coat.   'T was to Lawyer Curran he said it, and in
a small city like Dublin the name held, and the two
were called the Goddesses from that time.

Old Corrigan's words gave them courage for a
while; but what can hold up against a diet of herrings
day in and day out?   And that was all the poor lady
could give her family.   What was she to do?   Mr
Gunning had took himself off to Castle Coote, his beg-
garly place in the country, where he could dice and
drink in peace with the neighboring squireens, and
live off claret and the skinny fowls that pecked about
the avenue; and she had the weight of the children on
her spare shoulders.

'T was about this time that young Harry Lepel, the
first man they met, in a way of speaking, fell in love
with Elizabeth, the younger.   The way it happened
was this.   She was walking down Mount Street with
Maria, and she let fall her purse, and nothing in it
but a pocket-piece to save her gentility.   Harry was
strolling off to my Lord Cappoquin's, from mounting
guard at the Castle (for at that time his Lordship

lived in Merrion Square); and indeed Mr Lepel was as fine a figure of a young man as a girl could wish to see, in his regimentals all laced with gold and his handsome head above them — a brown man with dark eyes. And seeing a young madam drop her purse, he stooped for it and, coming up behind them, saluted very stiff and offered it, and the two turned and looked him in the face.

'T is certain a man might come up a thousand times behind a woman's back and not be startled as Harry Lepel was when he saw them; for there never was, nor will be, two such sisters. 'T was like a battery suddenly unmasked; and what chance had the poor devil that was marching up to it like an innocent? The only thing he could do was to surrender at discretion — but to which lady? That was the trouble. Elizabeth Gunning settled it for him.

"I thank you, Sir," says she, with a smile that had ruined St. Anthony, for she was one that smiled with her eyes as well as her mouth — a golden sunshine that the heart opened to naturally.

He was stuttering and stammering. "Madam, I thank you for the happiness of touching anything your hand hath blessed."

'T was sudden, I allow; but then, so too was her beauty. At all events, he dared no more, not having the courage, though all the will, to linger, and was turning off when a queer thing happened. But 't was to be.

A drunken poltroon of a bargeman was coming up from Liffey-side, lurching and yawing like a Dutch hooker in a gale; and seeing them in a little bunch on the cobblestones, he took an anger at them in his wooden head, and, whether purposely or not I know not, but he elbowed up against Miss Maria and drove her into the dirty kennel; and she gave a faint scream, for her shoes were destroyed with the mud, and it was the only pair she had to her name. So what does Mr Lepel do but let drive straight from the shoulder at the offender, and in a minute the shoes and the lady were out of the kennel and the bargeman lying there as snug as snug, and the oaths he let out of him blackening the air like a flight of crows. So Mr Lepel, smiling with set lips like a picture, says to the girls: —

"Ladies, permit me to escort you to your home. 'T is much to be regretted the streets are not safe for beauty unattended, though to be sure I have the happiness to profit by the circumstance. I trust it hath been no shock to your sensibility?"

And, indeed, tears had gathered in Elizabeth's eyes; but Maria was laughing like a Hebe, and looking up in his face — the blue-eyed lovely rogue!

"We thank you, Sir. 'T is what our own brother had done had he been more than five. But while he is in the nursery, we must be obliged to kind strangers for protection."

"Madam, I would not willingly remain a stranger," says Mr Harry, very eager, and touching his cocked hat. "Permit me to present myself for want of a better introducer. My name is Harry Lepel."

"I thank you, Sir. 'T will be remembered with gratitude. May we now bid you farewell?"

Miss Maria sank down, in a curtsey so well devised that it showed the littlest foot in the world, save only Elizabeth's. A fortunate bootmaker later was to make five guineas an afternoon by showing their shoes at a penny a head to the mob that gathered to stare at them; but that time was not yet come. Mr Lepel spoke earnestly: —

"Madam, you can't suppose—'t is not possible I can permit you to return alone after such an adventure. The sun sinks and the streets are mighty ill lit. If my company is disagreeable, I can walk ten paces behind; but otherwise —"

Here Elizabeth interposed, with a fine colour in her cheek: —

"The company of our protector can't be disagreeable — 't is a favour. But, Sir, I will be frank with you: we are in Dublin *incognita;* our lodging is not equal to our pretensions to birth; and in short —"

She hesitated, with her eyes dropped and the lashes like night upon her cheek. The crimson bow of her upper lip trembled — a seductive picture of troubled beauty. Anyhow it did Mr Harry's business for him. He could no more have tore himself away at that moment than he could have embraced the bargeman swearing blue murder at his feet.

"Madam, these are misfortunes that may happen to the greatest, and 't is easy seen that in your case breeding and birth combine with — beauty. Is it indiscreet to ask the name of the ladies I have the honour to address?"

"'T is very indiscreet," says Miss Maria, with one

of her bright side-glances; "but yet — should we withhold it, sister?"

"Surely not from so kind a friend." Elizabeth spoke eagerly. "Our name, Sir, is Gunning, and we are granddaughters to the late Viscount Mayo and nieces to his present Lordship. And when I add that our parents have fallen into poverty, you will comprehend —"

Her voice paused on a silver note, which had the beginning of a sob; and when Elizabeth saddened, the world must sadden with her, so lovely were her long eyes and the drooping head. Pity poor Mr Harry! Talk of Scylla and Charybdis — he stood between the Sirens, and could he have halved his heart (and many men have that power), one half had gone to either charmer.

"Madam," says he tenderly, "I feel for your sorrows more than I can express. Might I but have the happiness to be presented to your mama; for 't is the most prodigious circumstance — I am the son of Sir Francis Lepel of Tarrington in Yorkshire, and I have heard him speak of my Lord Mayo many a time. His Lordship stood second to my grandfather in his famous duel with Lord Ayrshire thirty year since. My name will not be unknown. Permit me —"

And again he saluted, very gallant, and the three proceeded down the street, the girls on thorns for thinking of the dingy rooms, and their mother down-at-heel, and the everlasting herrings sizzling on the grate, and Lucy and Kitty screaming for their supper. 'T was thinking thus that Maria touched Elizabeth's arm, as much as to say : "Shall we let him go?" For indeed these girls had a perfect language of signs between them, elaborated in the shifts and devices of their life; and Miss Maria, at least, was an accomplished little schemer. But Elizabeth responded not to the pinch.

"Why, Sir," says she sweetly," the name is indeed familiar. Sitting on his Lordship's knee, often have I heard him discourse of Sir Francis. You are no stranger. Yet truth is best. We are poor, Mr Lepel. My sister and I are debarred from all the pleasures of our rank, and our only concern is how to lighten our mama's burden if we could. 'T is this makes us hesitate, for we can't offer you the hospitality we would."

"Name it not, Madam, I entreat," says Mr Harry, trying to look into those too seductive eyes. "God forbid I should add to your anxieties. But had I the happiness to know your mama, whose beauty half Ireland knows by repute, sure I might be permitted to open the way to some pleasures. There is, for instance, a Birthnight ball to be celebrated at the Castle —"

"Sir, you are all goodness, but gentlemen understand little of the difficulties of poor young ladies of quality. How should they? We have no dresses fit for the eyes of his Excellency. Even shoes —"

She permitted a foot to appear beneath the edge of her petticoat and ambushed it again. But it had done its work.

"You tear my heart, Madam. But since that little

marvel of a foot recalls Cinderella's, permit me to say that a fairy godmother smoothed the way for that young lady to a certain ball, and there she met the prince whose throne she afterwards shared."

"There are no fairies in Dublin, Sir." Her voice was like flowing honey, while the little foot so commended was bestowing a sharp kick upon the fair Maria, and thus it said : —

"Run ahead. Turn the corner and run like a lamplighter, and let mama know what is toward. Hide the herrings. Bundle the children to bed. Fling mama's Irish lace over her head. I can hold him fifteen minutes. Speed!"

'T is much to be said in one kick, and it takes a woman to say and a woman to hear; but Miss Maria was a woman, though but eighteen. She smiled like Truth's self.

"Sister, if 't is not disagreeable to you to spare me, I have the message to leave at Mrs Flaherty's, and will go forward and meet with you at our door. Excuse me, Mr Lepel. My sister is a slow walker and I a swift. I knew not 't was so late."

Off went Miss Maria. Turning the corner, she picked up her petticoats and legged it along like a hare at dawn.

It may be thought that the acquaintance ripened in those fifteen minutes, which doubled into thirty. Elizabeth's step was slower, her voice more musical, even as a nightingale sings her sweetest to the moon. The shade of my Lord Mayo might hover about them to safeguard propriety, but Mr Harry drew as near as the rampart of the lady's hoop would permit, bending his head to catch her murmurs, and his nostrils inhaling the faint perfume of silken hair rolled back from the whitest brow in the world.   They made a pair that many would have remarked, but for the ill-lit streets.

Maria awaited them at the shabby door in Britain Street.

"I would not go in, sister, lest mama should scold me for leaving you; and indeed I am but just arrived," says she demurely.   And since she had not entered, 't was singular how neat was the appearance of that dingy room; for 't was dingy, do what you would.

The fire burned brightly, and if there was a delicate odour of herrings and onions, 't was the worst could be said, for none were to be seen.   Indeed, a rich perfume fought with it, as if a hasty hand had dashed the odours of Araby here and there to discourage the herrings.   A large velvet cloak, the worse for wear, disguised the rents of the sofa, whereon sat Mrs Gunning, majestic in another of faded purple satin, beneath which her dress remained conjectural. A noble square of Limerick point was flung over her head and hung veil-like by each ear; and, indeed, with the little cherub Lucy at her feet, she might have sat for an aging Madonna.

Kitty was bundled off to the camp-bed in the back room; and sure the picture was homelike, if you studied the handsome lady rather than the ragged chairs.   'T was the best they could do, poor souls, in fifteen minutes, and wonderful in the time.   'T is

women for quick thinking and quick acting where men
are concerned; and, indeed, the look of astonishment
Mrs Gunning gave as the three entered was inimi-
table, though already she had every particular set
down in her mind. She swept the stateliest curtsey,
and cast a rebuking maternal eye on her daughters,
ere she addressed Mr Lepel.

But, when explanations were made, how did her
brow clear and a fair-weather smile efface the frost!
She welcomed him with cordial kindness, with such
reminiscences of his family as warmed his heart; and
though no hospitality was offered save one, — a
bottle of generous claret in a silver cup enriched with
the Mayo arms, — 't was given with such good-will,
and served by so lovely a cup-bearer, the fair Maria,
that the man does not breathe but must feel it worthy
of the three ladies who tendered it. He toasted them
one and all in turn, and if his bow to Elizabeth was a
little lower, that circumstance did not displease Mrs
Gunning.

"I leave you to judge, Mr Lepel," says she, "what
it costs a mother to see her dear ones exiled from all
the little gay scenes where it would become them to
appear. But what can I do? My father's grand-
children, Mr Gunning's daughters, can't appear except with propriety; and why should I hesitate to tell
so kind a friend that 't is beyond my power?"

'T was discussed between them all for an hour as to
the Birthnight ball; but Mrs Gunning was resolute,
nor could Mr Harry dare to make the offers that
trembled on his lips. He could have groaned aloud

to think on the sums he wasted nightly on gaming —
one half of which would have adorned these beauties
and set them free to flutter their wings in the sunshine
of fashion.   Later Maria, half-smiling, half-sad, told
how they were promised luck by the old witch of
Dublin, though she gave not all the particulars.   She
built not on it, she declared, nor yet did Elizabeth;
and she, a soft sigh parting her lips, confirmed her
sister: "the more so," says she, "that none of us can
imagine what is the Golden Vanity.   Is there such
a ship, to be the ship of our fortunes?   'T is that it
sounds most like."

He shook his head.   Mrs Gunning softly remon-
strated: —

"My dears, be not giddy, nor let your heads run
on such follies.   There is no such name and no such
thing and 't is impossible —"

More she would have said, but a man came crying
somewhat down the street, and beside him went
another with a flambeau, that he might read a paper
in his hand, and what the man cried was this: —

"Let the fashion of Dublin, both ladies and gentlemen, take notice that there comes presently to the
theatre in Aungier Street the dramatic company
which Mr Sheridan presents to his patrons in a new
and luscious play, by name —"

But here was the speaker's voice drowned by a
wagon passing on the cobblestones.

"What is it?" cries Mrs Gunning, running to the
window; for indeed she loved the play as well as did
her girls.   And, as if the question had reached him,

the man turned towards her and bellowed like the bull of Bashan: "The Golden Vanity!"

The little company within stared transfixed upon one another.

For the next fortnight did the three live in a kind of rapture; and 't is not to be wondered at, the name coming so pat on the prophecy. And sure, Mr Lepel was no less moved; for he took a deeper than brotherly interest in all that touched them, his heart being caught that day in Dublin streets; and if he then thought Elizabeth a beauty, it took not a week to rank her an angel. Before the week was out, he laid his heart and the reversion of the baronetcy at her foot, not regarding the worn little shoe that cased it. For, indeed, the sisters wore the same size, and Elizabeth being the better mistress of her wardrobe, 't is to be feared she sought often for her own, to find them gadding abroad on Miss Maria's feet and herself left to luck. 'T was mortifying, and her heavenly blush was as much owing to this circumstance as to the gentleman's ardour.

However, taken by Mr Harry's fine person and clothes (and which was the most potent is not known), she accepted the heart, and he set about to inform his father of his good fortune, for mother he had none. 'T was with inward quakings, for beauty, were it Helen's own, is but a blunted arrow against a seasoned heart of seventy: and Sir Francis Lepel had reached that discreet age. 'T was vain to tell him of celestial eyes and roseate bloom. God help us! 't is little he cared for the like. The baronetcy was poor and Mr Harry expensive, and what Sir Francis looked to was a fat balance at Child's the banker's. Was the lady a fortune? And when Mr Harry, trembling, avowed that a single doit could not be hoped in that quarter, the old gentleman, his temper as well as his foot highly inflamed with gout, swore to disinherit him if the matter went further.

Poor Harry was in a sad quandary. He slept and ate ill, and 't was provoking that Elizabeth bloomed like a rose and troubled not her fair head about Sir Francis. Her mind seemed possessed with but the one thought — to attend the Birthnight ball and, like the planet Venus, shine in her rightful heaven. And indeed Mr Harry could not fancy her heart so deeply engaged as he might wish; for he could scarce get a word in while the two peered into the mercers' shops, gloating on satin and muslin. Mrs Gunning, as improvident, was almost drawn in by them, when word came of a card debt that their papa owed to Sir Horatius Blake, and the unfortunate lady received not even the pittance that provided herrings for six hungry mouths; so that they were like to come down to dry bread, which event fairly ended all talk of the ball.

'T is not to be supposed that Mr Harry did not offer to set all the mantua-makers in Dublin to work, though in his heart he knew his own credit did not stand immaculate. He stormed up and down the room, protesting, vowing, exclaiming; but Mrs Gunning would have none of it. Says she: —

"I do all justice to your kind heart, Mr Lepel, but 't is not, because we are unfortunate, that we have no pride, and 't is impossible Miss Gunning should accept garments from the gentleman she honours with her hand."

And Elizabeth, lovelier than ever in grief, confirmed her mother, Maria stamping her foot like an angry goddess. 'T will be admitted 't was a hard case. And since misfortunes don't come alone, arrived a furious letter from Sir Francis, demanding instantly to see Mr Harry, and acquainting him that his appointment in the Guards was cancelled, and he must join his new regiment in London at a day's notice. Sir Francis had good interest with the lady whose interest with His Majesty was unquestioned, and 't is to be thought this event did not come by chance.

Oh, then were wailings and passionate embraces on the part of Mr Lepel, Miss Elizabeth receiving them with wondering eyes. "For London is not so far but we shall meet again, Harry," says she, with her angelical smile.

He had preferred tears, no doubt; but a man must take what comes his way, and be thankful. He, who had never before been guilty of the like, now composed a set of verses of atrocious demerit. Indeed, the first two lines will suffice : —

> If from my Chloe's snowy breast I part,
> Grant me to know I bear with me her tears.

"'T is very pretty!" says Chloe. "O Harry, I

would you did not love me so ! A girl's affections are cool and temperate, I think — at least 't is so with me. Forget me a little, — though not too much, child, — and be happy."

It might have been her mother who spoke. 'T is certain no person ever had the appearance of sweet simplicity more than Elizabeth Gunning; but whether 't was wholly devoid of art — Ah, well, shall we dissect the rose? Best to enjoy and ask no questions.

The day of parting he came to Britain Street, and solemnly renewed his vows in the presence of Mrs Gunning and Maria.

"And, O my Elizabeth," cries he, "pledge me once more that hand which is all my joy. Swear that neither raging seas" ('t was a day calm as milk and the Irish sea like a mirror) "nor the brutish tyranny of man shall divide us, and that our constant hearts shall never change!"

Miss Elizabeth raises heavenly eyes, a glittering moisture enhancing their brilliance.

"Have I not pledged my word, Harry ; and if you believe not that, what will serve? Sure 't is you that rove and will see fairer faces" (frantic protestations from Mr Lepel) "yet I don't doubt *you*. Farewell, dear Harry, and remember us when you are in the glitter of London."

She covered her face with a handkerchief, and he took the last embrace, kissed Mrs Gunning's hand and Maria's, and hurried madly from the room. Elizabeth unveiled her face and folded the handkerchief for future use.

"He 's gone," says poor Mrs Gunning, seeking her own; "and if I know where tomorrow's dinner is to come from, for you all, I 'm — a Dutchman!"

They mingled their tears, and Elizabeth's were real enough now. 'T is possible, could the matter be sifted, that many more tears have been shed for absent dinners than absent lovers; and certainly, though beauty may survive without the last, it cannot without the first. There was so much of gloomy and terrible in their mama's aspect, that Maria wept also; and Kitty and Lucy, with the little John, who had all been secreted in the bedroom during the adieux, dashed in screaming at the tops of their voices, as if the heavens were falling; and so sat the poor unfortunate family drowned in tears. 'T was not balls they thought of then, nor departing lovers, but simply bread and herrings.

A lady came down the street, picking her way through the garbage that adorned it. Her dress was hooped in the mode, and of a showy brocade, with much tinsel interwoven and very glittering, so that the ragged children in the gutter stood, finger in mouth, to see. She had a muslin cross-over upon an expansive bosom, and 't was finely laced with Mechlin, not too clean, and set off with a black velvet ribbon about the throat, graced with a clasp of paste. A large tilted hat tied beneath her chin shaded an arch and sparkling pair of eyes, which, though not in their first youth, lighted up a face with striking features and an air of easy good-humour. If her critics had accused this lady of being somewhat too good-humoured with the other sex, why 't was perhaps natural to her circumstances and needs no further excuse. Her worst detractors never denied her a good heart, and an ear open to the lament of misery. In her hand she carried a cane of fine ebony, and altogether appeared a radiant vision of a fine woman in the purlieus of Britain Street. She paused and looked about her, bewildered.

"I declare I know not where I am got to !" says she, half aloud. "And these barbarians — 't is hard to be understood or to understand their gibberish. If now —"

And even as the words left her lips, arose a piercing wail from across the street, in which three lusty young throats united — Lucy, Kitty, and John, each out-screaming the other.

"Crimini !" says Madam, "what 's this ? Is Herod abroad in Dublin ?" The screams redoubled. She added : "'T is almost to be wished he was !" And stood half-laughing, half-unwilling to pass on.

"I will !" says she ; and more doubtfully, "I won't ! 'T is not my business. Sure I have enough stage tears and sobs to make me distrust all I hear."

She turned resolutely away, and halted again.

"Poor lady ! 'T is a lady soothing them, and weeping herself. I will ! She can but bid me exit."

And so marched to the open door, and into the narrow passage, and rapped smartly with her cane on the door of the parlour, bringing all her natural assurance to bear.

Dead silence. The screams halted, as if a tap was turned off: whoever was inside was all ears. She rapped again. And now a scuffling; and Maria opened the door, and six pairs of astonished eyes gloated on the stranger. And no less did hers on the party within; for there sat Mrs Gunning, beautiful and maternal, with the little John's curly pate on her bosom; Elizabeth, lovely as the day, leaning on one shoulder of her mother; Kitty and Lucy, golden-curled cherubs, clinging to her gown; and Maria, like a sorrowful wood-nymph, holding the door. Sure, never was such a family, and these children seemed made of some more exquisite clay than ordinary.

"Lord, am I got into heaven, for I see the angels about me!" says Madam, advancing with a reverence lower than the paltry room demanded. "Forgive an intruder, Madam, and confer a benefit. For being newly come to Dublin, I 've lost my way returning from Smock Alley, and while I called up courage to enter and ask it from any other than these savages, I heard a cry that hastened my steps. Be pleased to pardon me, and say if I can be of service to yourself and your sweet family; for 't is the plain truth — I 'm dazzled as I stand, by the beauty of your olive branches."

'T is not possible to mistake the voice of sympathy, and Mrs Gunning rising from her chair, curtseyed in her turn, and begged the visitor to be seated. "Lord, Madam," says she, "you catch us very unfit for company; but so kind a heart needs no excuse, and I will be candid with you. We are of birth and breeding like yourself." ('T was a skilful compliment, and the lady simpered.) "And therefore, as a gentlewoman of quality, you shall understand my grief when I present myself as my Lord Viscount Mayo's daughter, and add that I have not the wherewithal to clothe or feed these innocents! You are yourself too young to be a mother, Madam" (again the lady simpered), "yet will comprehend a mother's anguish. I am Mrs Gunning of Castle Coote, and such is my condition!"

She wept again. The lady applied a laced kerchief to either eye. A touching scene.

"Madam, a heart of marble must feel for you, and mine is not marble — far from it. But sure such beauty must open all doors. Marriage —" She broke off.

"Alas, Madam, in these days of money-grubbing avarice, what is beauty? My second" — she indicated Elizabeth — "is cruelly rejected by the father of a gentleman of birth not near so high as our own, because she has no estates pinned to her petticoat."

"Monster!" cries the lady with spirit.

Mrs Gunning proceeded : —

"And, O, Madam, were you in want, as a lady of quality sometimes is, of a young lady to write letters, to keep accounts, and all those little useful arts such as mending lace and the like, I can truly say that in my Elizabeth you would find solid worth. She is graver than my Maria.

"Sure we cannot have had the happiness to meet you for nothing. 'T was ordained you should walk in

upon us.   Permit me to ask the name of our benefac-
tress."   The lady hummed and hawed a little; but
not being easily daunted, she tossed up her head
bravely enough ere she replied : —

"Gemini, Madam !   We can't all be ladies of quality; and if we could, I see not who could provide the
wants and amusements of the fashionable.   To be
plain with you, I am an actress — and —"

"An actress !" screams Maria, all rapture.   "Sister,
do you hear ?   Was it not this very day I said, would
I could go on the stage like the famous Mrs Woffington, and other beauties such as this lady.   And
then should I be happy and pour all the gold I made
into my mama's lap."

The lady shook her head, a little melancholy.

"Gold ?   Not much of that on the stage, young
miss.   'T is found there — true; but — but — in-
directly.   However, this concerns you not.   Madam,
I am in no need of such an attendant as you describe,
having my dresser and —"

"I might have guessed it !   When did luck ever
come our way ?   Farewell, Madam.   Return to your
own happiness and abandon us to our misery."

Heart-rending !   The lady drew nearer.

"Gemini, Madam !   You misjudge me.   A woman
can but offer what 's in her power.   A good word
from me to our manager, Mr Sheridan, and with such
faces I doubt not small parts can be found for your
daughters in one of the plays to be produced here.
We even now rehearse it, and the parts of Susan and
Peggy Careless go begging, for the girls that took

them are called away by their mama's illness. But
dare I mention such a proposal?"

"Madam, you are all goodness and beauty!" cries
Elizabeth. And Maria fell on her knees like one dis-
traught and kissed the pretty hand in its black mit-
ten. 'T was known to them that Mr Sheridan's
company was from London and would return there;
and indeed this came like a sunburst through the
cloud, for 't was food, clothes, admiration, money,
hope — and many other charming things that set
them dreaming on worlds to conquer.

They swept their mama away on the wave of their
delight; and indeed that poor lady was always prone
to take gilding for gold so long as it glittered sufficiently.

"And what, Madam, is this play in which Susan
and Peggy appear?"

"Child, 't is 'The Golden Vanity' — a play of a
poor girl that weds a rich lord and —"

Heavens and earth! She could not continue, for
how describe the joy and wonder of the family! Reserve fled away. Prudence borrowed the wings of
Hope, and dressed her face with rainbows. Crowding around the stranger, they entreated her name,
that it might grace their prayers; and she, radiant
with the sunshine she dispensed, calls out: —

"Why, girls, sure you have heard it. 'T is I am
the leading lady in all Mr Sheridan produces at present. I am George Anne Bellamy."

"George!" screams Mrs G. "'A woman with a
man's name,' said old Mother Corrigan. Girls, your

luck's come!" And with that falls into strong hysterics and frights them all to death.

But joy is a strong cordial, and 't was not long ere she sat up, panting and dishevelled, with George Anne's hand in hers, telling her the story of Mother Corrigan. 'T is to be supposed Mrs G. had heard that Mrs Bellamy's heart was not marble in any sense; but what was the lady to do? For my Lord Mayo spent his rents five years ahead, and though his good nature would give the coat off his back, that would neither clothe nor feed her family; while, as for Mr Gunning, that gentleman regarded his wife and children no more than the cuckoo that leaves her offspring to chance.

Mrs Bellamy was all ears. 'T was prodigious, 't was vastly astonishing, she vowed. Maria was sent out with half a guinea, and they had a comfortable dish of tea, with currant bread and what not; and she told them tales of the stage and the fine matches made by Mrs This and Signorina That, displaying little of its threadbare and much of its tinsel; and by the time the candles were lit, they were all sworn friends. They parted with embraces; for Mrs G. was as easy as George Anne, and the girls must needs follow the example set.

She had her way with Mr Sheridan, who knew 't was as much as his play was worth to offend Mrs Bellamy; and she returned next day to announce her success, triumphing and rattling on like a girl herself, so pleased was she with their pleasure. All was joy and gladness, and she named the hour of the first

rehearsal and their introduction to Mr Sheridan, who
knew as well as another how pretty faces fill the play-
house; and was proceeding, when Maria, turning
archly upon her, says : —

"Look you here, dearest Mrs Bellamy! Think
what it will cost us to refuse this." And so holds up
a splendid card, thick as boards and embellished with
a gilt edge and the Royal Arms and the Irish Harp,
and Heaven knows what braveries, inviting the Honourable Mrs Gunning, Miss Gunning, and Miss
Elizabeth Gunning to the Birthnight ball at the
Castle, on the part of his Excellency, the Earl of Harrington. Diamonds were never so bright as the eyes
that sparkled above it; for the charming new prospect of the stage had quite effaced the ball, and poor
Mr Harry's trouble in securing the invitation was
like to go for nothing.

"I care nothing now for it!" cries Maria, and Elizabeth echoed her; while George Anne looked thoughtfully at the Lion and Unicorn guarding a Paradise
she could not hope to enter. Maria made to tear the
card across; but Mrs Bellamy caught it from her
hand and did not smile.

"Children," says she at last, "you know not what
you talk of. I would have a word alone with your
mama. Take the little ones in your hand, and go
out a while in the sunshine." She thrust some cream-
cakes upon them, and they did so, looking doubtfully
at her cloudy eyes; and when the door shut, she
turned to Mrs Gunning.

"Madam, you know well 't is my wish to serve you

and yours. But seeing this invitation, there's thoughts comes into my head that I must needs speak out. This" (she flicked the card) " is the life for the Miss Gunnings, and not the stage. 'T would scarce become me to tell a lady like yourself what must be faced there, but — but — 't is much! Ask Peg Woffington — ask Kitty Clive — ask George Anne Bellamy!" She hung her head.

There was silence. Mrs G. stared at her, all aghast.

"Why, yesterday, all your talk was of pleasure and success. Sure, dear Mrs Bellamy, 't was not like your kindness to draw on the poor things till they can think of naught else, and now so far otherwise."

"Why, Madam, I thought there was no other way; and if so, needs must. But seeing this, my mind misgives me and I falter. I'm a plain-dealer, Madam, with all my faults, and 't is easy to be seen your daughters are a world's wonder. I never saw the like, and that being so, 't is certain the dangers are tenfold for them. They'll see the glories and grandeurs, sure enough, but not through a wedding ring."

"If you mean, Madam, that my daughters —" Mrs Gunning flamed out, furious; but George Anne was not to be turned from her purpose. She raised her hand in a fine stage attitude.

"Madam, I wish vastly to serve you. Hear my proposal. Accept this invitation."

"Impossible. We have no dresses, no shoes, no equipage, and no means to get them. 'T is absurd!"

"'T is not absurd. Hear me. In the theatre properties is a fine dress for Lady Modish and two more for Peggy and Susan Careless. Not perhaps what such ladies might expect, but passable. And — I know men. There 's not a man will look at their gowns for looking at their faces, though the suits are well enough when all 's said. I vow, Madam, you have so long lived beside the two that you forget what beauties they are. I wager my next benefit to a China orange that you 'll have no more care once they are seen, but all the women mad with jealousy and the men with love. Indeed, your young madams are what one reads of in romances, but don't see. Give them this chance, and if it fails, I 'm good for my offer; but I 'm much mistook if you hold me to it. Gemini, Madam; use your wits! Would you have them what I won't name, when they may be what your old witch foretold?"

She smiled her charming smile, and pressed Mrs G.'s hand. The lady pondered. 'T was disagreeable to owe such a thing to a mere actress, and one, too, whose reputation was a trifle flyblown. The stage she might have swallowed — being the lady's province and she a queen on the boards. But an entry to the world where she and her daughters had a birthright — Fie! 't was a very different pair of shoes. But George Anne had that in her eye that would be obeyed; and seeing it, Mrs G. dropped her high tone and returned the pressure with an air of sensibility.

"'T was said by old Corrigan that 't was you to

bring us luck, dearest Madam, and 't is certain you are prudence itself. Sure a mother can risk nothing for her darlings. If you will ensure us the dresses, I accept; and, indeed, my Lord Harrington's father was a friend of my own revered father in happier days. 'T is possible —"

" 'T is certain," cries George Anne gaily. "Not a word will I drop to Mr Sheridan, who is a perfect Israelite where theatre matters are in hand. Count on me."

She was gone ere the girls returned, and 't is needless to tell their wonder. They preferred the stage, yet condescended to say they would favour the ball, since Mrs Bellamy counselled it. "But, never, never will it turn my heart from the charming footlights!" says Maria. "What say you, sister?"

"I know not. My taste is quieter than yours. I will tell you my mind the day after the ball. Poor Harry — 't is he has given us this."

She would say no more, but sat thoughtful.

'T was the evening of the Birthnight ball when George Anne arrived, in a hackney coach, attended by her dresser, and scarce visible for mantua boxes. The three children were put away — their usual fate — in the beds within, and though not able to sleep for excitement, were mute as mice, lest they be punished by the closing of the door upon the ravishing glimpses they had of the parlour.

'T is not for a mere scribbler to intrude upon the chaste mysteries of the toilet. Suffice it therefore to

say that, when all was completed, George Anne and
Mrs March the dresser stood back, breathless, to
contemplate the work of their hands.

Mrs Gunning, her fine brown hair piled on her head
into an edifice twisted with gauze and feathers that
granted her five inches more of height, looked a
Roman empress — her fine bust displayed to advantage and sustaining a necklace of stage emeralds set in
pinchbeck, which could not be told from the veritable jewels, so closely were they copied for George
Anne from her Grace the Duchess of Bridgewater's.
Her hoop was very wide, and over it a green satin
brocade flowered with gold, wherein George Anne had
played Lady Modish but twenty times, and so rich
that 't would serve her great-granddaughter. 'T was
ruffled at neck and elbow with Mechlin, and the girls
gazed in awe at their splendid mama. 'T was a
changed woman. She expanded, she glided, she
moved, as a swan floating through her native element differs from the same lurching along the bank.

But Elizabeth — O beautiful! Sure 't was joy to
see her! Her hair, agleam with gold, was rolled
back and carried in massive braids that crowned and
bound her head in the Grecian taste, confined by a
bandeau of pearls that crossed her brow. Her Grecian
robe (indeed the fair Miss Lebeau had played Calista
in it) was a white satin with a fall of lace, and round
her slender throat a chain of seed pearl. Mrs Bellamy knew her business. 'T was simple, but simplicity
becomes a goddess, and frills and flounces can but dis-
tract the eye from loveliness that seems native to

heaven.   Her mother surveyed her in a kind of amaze
and then turned to Maria.

'T was peculiar to these two fair sisters that they
adorned each other and each appeared more beautiful
when both were in company.   Indeed 't was said later
that this contributed much to their triumphs.   Maria
now appeared in a fine India muslin embroidered in
gold wheat-ears — a robe which 't is to be feared Mr
Sidney of the East India Company, the rich nabob of
Jubblepore, had laid at the feet of George Anne in pur-
suance of a suit not wholly disdained.   No matter!
On Maria it shone like the raiment of the youngest of
the angels, draping yet expressing her fair limbs with
a seductive reserve that was art embellishing nature.
She had a row of seed pearl like her sister, and one
rose of faintest pink nestled in her virgin bosom.   Her
hair of burning gold was dressed in curls *à la mouton*,
as Mrs March expressed it, and a string of pearls
wove through the rich tresses.

But 't is useless to describe beauty.   As well dry a
rose in a book and look for bloom and dew.   It de-
pends on bright eye and smiling lip and wordless
sweetness and the fall of exquisite lashes and the tone
of music and — and this poor scribbler lays down his
pen and attempts no more to paint where the great
artists later owned themselves vanquished.

"And all is prepared," cries George Anne, exulting.
"For my mother's job coach is at hand to take my
three beauties; and distress not yourself, my dearest
Madam, for I engage to remain with your little family
and will return in the coach when it deposits you here.

And now, children, peep and whisper no longer, but come see your lovely mama and sisters before they go to conquer the world."

'T was the kindest heart! She clapped her hands, and in rushed the three children like Bedlam let loose, careering round and about the three, shouting, laughing, and begging to be took also. Raisins and oranges from George Anne's reticule alone restored them to their beds in peace.

" 'The Golden Vanity' has sent forth two incomparable beauties," says she at the door as they stepped into the coach. "May it bring them the luck of its heroine and more."

St. Patrick's Hall was all of a blaze with wax candles and flambeaux, and shining mirrors set in with gilt Cupids, and twinkling of fairy lights in the great glass lustres and their glittering chains of drops and pendants. Garlands of green, with roses interspersed, were in swags and loops about the splendid walls, where hung the pictures of bygone viceroys in ribbon and star, in frames to match the mirrors that multiplied the scene a hundredfold.

And, more than all, the handsomest women in Ireland were decked out in silks and satins and all the family jewels, and they sparkling like the lustres above their heads. And all the gentlemen in uniforms and silk stockings showing off their fine calves, and they strutting with their swords and squiring the ladies and bowing. And above it all the Throne, with the velvet canopy and the Royal Arms, and my Lord

Harrington, his Excellency, sitting like a picture of himself, with his stars and orders and his coat of sky-blue velvet laced and embroidered with gold; and as each pretty lady came up to him and swept her curtsey he lifted her by the hand and kissed her cheek; for the Viceroy has that privilege, and many a man envied him a few of the kisses, if they did not envy them all.

And now at the great doors appeared three ladies, quietly, like persons used to assemblies, though to be honest their knees were trembling under them and their little hearts quaking. So they were passed on from one golden image to another, until they arrived before his Excellency, the company politely making way, and a whisper that rose to a buzz running with them. "Lord! who are they?" — "Who can they be?" — "Look at the girls!" — "Exquisite!" — "Beautiful!" — "For my part I see nothing in them. Vilely dressed. Very far from modish." — "Too tall." — "Too short" — in fact, every expression of approval and disfavour. But every lady stood on the tips of her satin shoes to see, and every gentleman took the fullest advantage of his height; and had poor Harry been there, he had died of jealousy. Alas! even his fond letters were not in Elizabeth's gentle bosom, but tossed forgot on the bed in Britain Street, with George Anne casting the eye of sensibility on them.

And now the officer who performed the introduction took Mrs Gunning's gloved hand, very stately, and led her before the Throne.

"The Honourable Mrs Gunning, your Excellency."

Down she flowed in a magnificent curtsey, her hands supporting her brocade on either side, her head bent majestic — Beauty adoring Power. Suddenly my Lord steps nimbly forward on the dais.

"What?" he cries. "Do my eyes deceive me? Impossible! But sure I have the happiness to see the daughter of my old friend, and I am honoured beyond expression to welcome her beneath my roof. Where have you been retired? And what are these two lovely nymphs? Your daughters? No, sure it can't be and you all youth and beauty yourself. Present them."

And while mama blushed and bridled, the magic words were spoke, and the two dropped the gentlest curtseys, and rising, received a salute more than usual warm from his Excellency on either fair blushing cheek. 'T was observed he lingered an instant on Maria's. Viceroys, too, are human.

'T was an instantaneous conquest — how could it be otherwise? A moment later they were the centre of a competing crowd of gentlemen, and glances of coldness and aversion raining on them from ladies only a little less fair and now deserted. That his Excellency was the first victim, none could doubt, for when he was not in company with the beauties, he was discoursing of them to others. True it is that he conducted the Dowager Rathconnel to the supper-table, but equally true that he left the lady seated before such dainties as ensure an old age of gout, disengaging himself with a nimble wit that should

have appeased her, and sought out the mother of the
Graces, devoting himself to memories of old times
with a gusto, while Maria and Elizabeth danced and
smiled on their adorers, blooming and beautiful.

"My dear Madam," says his Lordship, "how is it
possible that you have lived so retired for fifteen
years? 'T was not justice to your admirers — of
whom I was ever one. How came it about?"

"Why, your Excellency," says the lady very serious, "'t was not with my good-will. You know well
that my late father's good heart was his chief possession; and my husband — alas!"

Sure a pause and downcast eyes are more expressive than any words. His Excellency shook his
majestic peruke, and echoed the lady.

"Alas! Cards, horses, the bottle — how many a
wife and mother hath had cause to curse that fatal
trinity! And 't is even so, Madam?"

She applied George Anne's laced handkerchief to
her eye, then smiled faintly and seeing opportunity,
seized it.

"I would not cloud this festive scene, your Excellency, yet why should I reserve from a tried friend
that I and my poor daughters — "

"Yes, yes!" cries his Lordship, very impatient.

"— Are here this night in borrowed dress," con-
tinues Mrs G. solemnly, "and are indebted even for
the shoes upon their feet to the kindness of an actress,
Mrs Bellamy."

"Good Ged!" says Lord Harrington, genuinely
shocked, and the more so that he had himself known

Mrs Bellamy some years since. "Sure it can't be! I won't believe it. Indeed, we must discourse further of this. Come hither!"

Profoundly interested, he led her to a withdrawing-room and there they fell into so deep discussion that never had he been such a negligent host. And when Mrs Gunning left the withdrawing-room, it was with an imperial head held high, and a flush in her cheek which became her so well that the most prying female eye would not give her a day over thirty.

His Excellency led out Maria to a minuet. Twice he took Elizabeth down the country dances. The generous wines had warmed his heart, the glow of beauty kindled it to flame, and it was plain to be seen that his eyes were only for the fair Gunnings. The world followed his example, — when does it otherwise? — and a petal from Maria's rose, a look from the violet dark-lashed eyes of Elizabeth, were the prizes of the night.

A party of noblemen escorted them to the doors on leaving, and 't was with the utmost difficulty Mrs Gunning persuaded them it was unnecessary to ride in cavalcade about the coach to Britain Street. When the ladies were gone, they returned to the Banqueting Hall to toast "The Irish Beauties," and break their glasses in their honour until the floor was strewn with broken crystal, and the celebrants were most of them borne speechless to their beds. Indeed, a challenge passed between my Lords Cappoquin and Tuam upon a dispute as to which lady was the greater Venus.

Never was such a triumph! And Mrs Gunning, falling into George Anne's arms in Britain Street, declared with tears of joy:—

"You were right, entirely right, my dearest Madam. I am promised a handsome pension on the Irish Establishment, and his Excellency counsels me to transport my girls to London, where, he considers, they may pretend to the highest matches, and promises introductions worthy of them. And, O Madam, playing at faro in the cardroom, I won a milleleva — no less! — Fifty guineas! — Lord! was ever anyone so happy!"

Tears of sensibility stood in George Anne's eyes. She was one who shared to the full the griefs or triumphs of her friends. She wrung Mrs G.'s hand and embraced the fair conquerors, scorning to mention the rent in Maria's muslin gown, and the stain of wine on Elizabeth's satin. It was a generous heart, and had earned more gratitude than she afterwards received from two, at least, of the ladies.

'T was amazing to Mrs Gunning and Maria now that ever they had contemplated the stage — so very far below their pretensions; and it took but a week to open the former lady's eyes to the little cracks in George Anne's reputation. She saw plainly that such a friendship could be no aid to their soaring aspirations; and indeed her ambition had now spread its wings to some purpose. The Earl of Harrington having advanced the first installment of her pension, she immediately moved their lodging to the genteeler Mount Street, and Britain Street was forgot, along with George Anne. Sure a mother must be prudent! Elizabeth only forsook not her friend, going to wait upon her and carrying with her many of the posies left in daily homage to her sister and herself. She had little in her power, for money was still none too plenty; but kindness and gratitude smell sweeter even than roses, and these she carried in handfuls straight from a grateful heart to George Anne.

It smoothed not her own path in Mount Street, for Mrs Gunning's pride grew with what fed it, and though admiration was plenty, offers were few. It might be that the enmity of the Dublin ladies stood in their way, for certain it is that Mrs G. was never a favourite. Where she judged well to flatter, she flattered too openly; where she disliked and saw no gain, she insulted; and many gentlemen would have retired from her acquaintance, but for Maria's frolicsome gaiety and the sweetness of Elizabeth. It gained ground about the city that there was much scheming in Mount Street with a view to rich husbands, and it smirched the girls as well as their mama, and put thorns in their way. It made the men bolder than they should be, and the women cold.

Maria was the hardier and took it as a necessity of their situation; but the milder Elizabeth wept often on George Anne's kind bosom over the insults (as she took it) which Mrs Gunning received with rapture, as hopeful signs of love. And, whatever the actress's own case might be, 't is certain she showed more delicacy in dealing with the girl than did her lady mother.

Nor had she much comfort from Mr Harry's letters.   His father remained adamant; and though he
writ, 't was more carelessly, and a rumour reached
Dublin that coupled his name with the great fortune
Miss Hooker, and was generally took for truth.   Mrs
Gunning greeted it with pleasure, regarding Mr
Harry as a gone-by and much below her hopes; but
though Elizabeth's heart was not wounded, her pride
was pierced to the quick.   It seemed that all the
world conspired to humiliate her, and she asked herself what was the use of beauty, if it meant this and
no more.   She sighed and left his last letter un-
answered.

Miss Maria too had her troubles.   My Lord Err-
ington pursued her with ardour, and his handsome
rakish face and gallant impudence drew the pretty
moth towards the heat and flame of a dangerous
candle.   Folly, no more, but his lady took her vengeance in scandals that spread about the town, and a
duel was fought that did Maria no good and kept off
worthier pretenders to her hand; and indeed it was
not a day too soon when the family packed up their
belongings and changed the air to London.   The girls
outshone all others — true! but 't was thought more
in beauty than discretion, for Elizabeth must needs
sink with her family.   The world draws not nice dis-
tinctions.

But to say they were courted in London is to say
little.   They broke triumphant upon the town, supported by letters from his Excellency, and the town
received them with frenzy, as it might the great

Italian singer or the new lions at the Tower, or what
not.   Amongst the greatest, the Duke of Hamilton
put himself at their disposal, urged thereto by a particular letter from my Lord Harrington and his own
love of beauty.   He dangled about them daily, and
it must be owned that from the first moment of meeting Mrs Gunning fixed the eye of cupidity on his
Grace.   For of all the matches of the Kingdom James
Hamilton was the greatest available.   Duke of Brandon in England, of Châtelherault in France, of Hamilton in Scotland, of vast possessions, of suitable age
and gallant presence, a princess need not have disdained his hand.   A great prince, indeed, and knowing it possibly too well, 't was he to dazzle a girl's eye
and carry her heart by storm!   For hearts — it was
never supposed his Grace possessed one; at least, he
wore it not on his sleeve, but was ever cold and
haughty, though it was well known he liked a pretty
woman as well as any — short of the wedding ring.
He hung about the new beauties as a gentleman will,
until wagers began to be laid at White's as to which
had caught his favour, and where would fall the handkerchief of the Grand Bashaw.

Meanwhile, his attentions made them more than
ever the mode, and the town gallants swarmed about
them like bees, at the Assemblies where they figured,
attended by my Lord Duke in ribbon and star.   As
the days went by, however, the anxious mother observed that his preference was for Elizabeth, and that
he had no thought to interfere with my Lord Coventry, who could not keep his eyes off Maria, though he

committed himself no further than the Duke. Indeed, stories were now freely circulated concerning Britain Street and the poverty and shifts of the family, and wagers were laid that neither the one nobleman nor the other looked for more than a few months' amusement with the two loveliest girls in England. Mrs Gunning was openly called the Adventuress, and it was a favourite sport with some ladies to imitate her Irish accent and carnying ways with those she would please; and doubtless Maria angled a little too openly for her lord. They were, in short, easy game for the mockers, and Elizabeth shrunk daily more into the shade. It appeared as if it would be the Dublin story over again.

Mr Harry came at once to their lodging on his return from Yorkshire, and to be sure, had not a word to say of Miss Hooker. He would have saluted Elizabeth, but she drew back with a curtsey, her manner sweet and cold as an autumn dawn with a touch of winter in the air. He found her changed, and no wonder, and said as much with some anger.

"It should not surprise you, Harry," says she serenely. "I am now eighteen, and have seen the world, as you have also. Our betrothal was a child's game. I like you too well to be your ruin. Marry Miss Hooker, of whom I hear. 'T is your best way, and obedience to parents a plain duty."

"You were not so wise in Dublin," replies Mr Lepel, casting a jealous eye on the fair monitress. If her looks had changed it was to a more radiant sweetness, and there was that in the way her long silken

lashes lay on her fair cheek that dwarfed Miss
Hooker's fortune.   He had better have kept his distance from the siren, he thought with bitterness.
But sure a little pleasant dallying could hurt neither
Miss Hooker nor his father — a summer pastime and
no more; and if the tales flying about town were but
the half of them true, he might hope for this, especially with the past pleading for him in Elizabeth's
tender heart.   Sure there was a softening in her
glance.   He pushed his chair somewhat nearer and
took her hand.   She withdrew it, and removed her
seat farther away.

"Is my Elizabeth angry with her Harry," cries he
with a fine dramatic air.   "Does she forget those
happy days when we were all to one another?   What
is Miss Hooker or Miss Any-person to come between
us?   What —"

"Your future wife. as I understand," says Elizabeth, perfectly calm.   "No, Mr Lepel — I know the
world now, better than I could wish" (she sighed),
"and I desire not your attentions.   I —"

But Mr Lepel broke in, pale and furious.

"And is it thus you speak, you heartless jade?
Clothes, jewels, balls, 't is these you value.   Is there
a woman alive that will not sell her soul for the like?
O God, why are fair faces made to madden us?   Now
I have seen you once more, how can I return to that
flat-faced —"

She rose, with a wave of her hand that dismissed
him; but he ranted on in a towering passion of wrath
and grief.   It had all burst up anew in his heart,

in and for a moment. He believed himself hardly used indeed.

"Could I bury my father and inherit his land, you would not use me thus. It is all a cursed thirst for gold, and you are for sale like an Eastern slave. Who is the highest bidder? But I know well. What am I to compare with —"

"His Grace the Duke of Hamilton!" announces Mrs Abigail, very demure in her pinners at the door; and in walks his Grace, magnificent in manners and dress, and Mr Lepel's fury stopped on a breath, though he could not regain countenance as readily as Elizabeth. She rose to meet the visitor — a rose in June; and he might take the blush of anger which was due to Mr Lepel for a welcome to himself.

What could Mr Harry do but draw back, stammering and looking foolish under the cold glance Duke Hamilton bestowed on him. Prudence counselled, "Withdraw. What do you here?" Angry Love retorted "Here I stay. What! Shall I leave the field to a rival?" And so, flung himself in a chair glaring defiance, Elizabeth palpitating between the two. 'T was not surprising that she drew nearer to the Duke, as if for protection; that there was an imploring softness in her face as she looked up to him; that she saw him greater, handsomer, stronger than ever, beside this idle and futile young man who had reviled her. The carelessness of his glance at Mr Lepel seemed to fling his pretensions in the mud — his haughty coolness to degrade the young man; and to such thoughts women are responsive. If her

heart was touched before, the dart went deeper now.
She held her head higher, deerlike, and wasted no
words on the unwelcome guest.

The two gentlemen, seeing neither could outstay
the other, departed presently together, Mr Lepel
saying with assumed lightness as he bowed, hat in
hand, at the door: "We had not the pleasure to see
Madame la mère, your Grace, and no doubt but she
is slipped away on some hunting errand. I wonder
what new fox is broke cover. Half the world bets
on my Lord Coventry still!"

The Duke returned not his salute, and Lepel could
not tell whether or no his arrow had gone home
through the armour of chilly pride and silence. He
himself strode angry and ashamed down the street.

That same evening a Council of Three was held in
the lodging, Mrs. Gunning with her mask of smiles
laid by, Maria fretful, Elizabeth grave and retired
in her own thoughts. The ladies had but the one
bedroom, with a little closet for the youngest adjoin-
ing.

"Girls," says Mrs Gunning, "'T is time I spoke
plain. This six weeks in town hath reduced my purse
till I am frighted to look in it; and what have we to
show? Young women with not half your looks are
married and settled since we came hither. We have
had a vast deal of froth and flutter, but nothing solid.
Were it possible to live on sweetmeats and dress in
posies, we have a fine prospect, but not else. I see
nought before us but Britain Street — or worse."

Maria shrugged her white shoulders.

"What more can we do, mama. Sir James Ramsden has offered marriage, and Captain Golightly; and Mr Lennox has asked Elizabeth, and Mr Lepel —"

"What signifies all that?" cries Mrs Gunning. "Don't let them slip. They 'll serve for the future perhaps, if all fails. Elizabeth, I command you on your duty that you please Mr Lepel, though not more than sufficient to content him. If we can't better him — But, Maria, what said my Lord Coventry to you at Lady Lowther's ball? I saw him very earnest."

"Nothing that might n't be in the news-prints, mama. His breed of black shorthorns filled his thought and tongue. I protest I loathed the man's folly. 'T is an insipid creature when all 's said."

"No man with a coronet is insipid. He is grave and reserved, and I would he had been Elizabeth's admirer rather than yours, for they could have sat silent in a corner together. But what of the Duke, child? My hopes are sadly sunk."

Elizabeth flamed in a blush, less beautiful than painful. A sore heart was behind it. She replied not. Mrs Gunning frowned.

"Well, girls, you 're easy enough, but so am not I. Now therefore listen while I speak my mind."

'T is needless to be particular in recording the lady's speech, which was much to the point in dealing with their needs and stratagems. She spoke for many minutes and at the end tears of shame and

anger were in Maria's lovely eyes. If Elizabeth
wept, 't was behind a sheltering hand.

"What signifies grumbling?" finishes Mrs Gunning. "'T is as plain as the nose on your face. Elizabeth's is the best chance, and if she makes her match,
my Lord Coventry will kiss your slipper, Maria.
The Duchess's sister can marry where she will."

'T was vain to interrupt. Mrs Gunning sailed on,
maternal, imperative, and took no heed. It would
be impertinence to intrude on the talk that followed,
and the plan laid for the entrapping of his Grace, of
whom it may be said that he could protect himself
against even the assaults of beauty better than Mrs
Gunning supposed. But Elizabeth, borne down by
two to her one, fought a losing game.

"I hate the man," she cried with spirit, and knew
't was false as she said it. "I 'd sooner sweep a
crossing —"

Mrs Gunning smiled contemptuous.

"Not you! You came pretty near it in Britain
Street, and 't is known how you relished it. Beggars,
my dear, can't be choosers. The Duchess of Hamilton may have as much delicacy as she pleases. Miss
Elizabeth Gunning can't afford it. There 's no more
to be said."

Yet Elizabeth said it furiously, and in vain.

A subdued light of wax candles — the most flatter-
ing light in the world — made the parlour enchant-
ment when his Grace sauntered in one evening, later.
Posies were in the bowpots, and a delicate scent of

violets in the air.   On a table by the window lay a
magnificent chicken-skin fan sent by my Lord Coventry for Maria's birthday : it was covered with rosy
figures of Cupids swinging garlands in blue air, the
mother-of-pearl sticks latticed with gold.   It lay
beside a lace handkerchief, as if a fair hand had flung
it careless down.   A decanter of purple Burgundy,
with two glasses, was hard by, and a small painting
of the lovely sisters from the hand of Neroni, who had
asked the favour to depict them as wood-nymphs.
They advanced, smiling and bearing a garland between them down a forest glade, while two Cupids
concealed behind a tree aimed a dart at each fair
breast.

The Duke contemplated this work of art, smiling
at his own thoughts, and not pleasantly.   Presently
the door opened and Mrs Gunning and Maria entered, in hats and capes, followed by Elizabeth, dead
pale and in a *negligée* with blue ribbons, her hair falling in long tresses to the knee, confined only with a
fillet of ribbon.   She looked not even her eighteen
years in this dress, and had a most touching beauty.
His Grace kissed Mrs Gunning's hand, yet with the
half-contemptuous air of the great man.   Some
might resent such a kiss as an insult, but the lady's
armour was defensive as well as offensive.   Says she,
curtseying : —

"I beg a thousand pardons, your Grace, but we are
disturbed with an unexpected call.   'T is what we
never imagined, but can't refuse.   Good Mrs Acton,
a friend of our Dublin days, is took ill and hath sent

for us to Harbour Street.   She is unattended in London; I know your Grace's sensibility will excuse us."

"Why, Madam, friendship is so rare a virtue that 't is worth proclaiming at the Exchange.   I will give myself the pleasure to wait on you another evening."

His hat was beneath his arm; he picked up his clouded cane.

"I thank your Grace."   Mrs Gunning's voice was stately.   It changed as she turned to Elizabeth. "And now, my flower, my dove, repose yourself on the couch, and Mrs Abigail will bring you the lavender drops, and let me find my treasure well and smiling on my return."

"What?   Does not Miss Elizabeth accompany her mama?"   The tone was alert.

"By no means, your Grace.   She has ailed all day with her head, and is not fit for a sick chamber. Farewell, child.   I wait your Grace."

He took Mrs Gunning's hand to conduct her to the coach; 't was as pretty a comedy as ever George Anne Bellamy played.   He laughed inwardly leading her to the door, and on the stairs discoursed charmingly on the last masquerade at Vauxhall.   Without the hall door he paused.

"Is Miss Elizabeth Gunning too ailing, Madam, to receive a friend for a few moments?   Permit me to assist you."

And before the lady could reply, he bundled the two into the coach, and was halfway up the steps ere Mrs Gunning could cry: "I know not, your Grace. A moment perhaps —"

He bowed from the door.

"Be easy, Madam. I will myself administer the lavender drops if needful."

It was impossible for the Duke to hasten himself, for this he had never done within the memory of man; but 't was scarce a minute since he had left the room when he reëntered, half fearing to find his pretty bird flown. Not so, however. She leaned against the shutter, her eyes fixed on the evening sky. It seemed she had forgot his Grace, for her expression was sorrowful and quiet, unlike the female trifling he expected, and he heard a faint sigh. She turned, startled.

"Forgive me, my Lord Duke. I think I can't stay. My head —"

She would have glided to the door. 'T was provocative, however meant, and he put himself in her way. She tried the other side of the table. He blocked that also, and was before her again. Finally she ceased the attempt and stood with eyes cast down.

"Child, don't hasten. Give me a few minutes. I see you alone for the first time and never so lovely as now. Is it your long hair, or what is it? Sure the angels have locks like this."

He lifted a heavy tress as if marvelling. She snatched it from him like an aggrieved queen; then, seeming to recollect herself, stood silent again. 'T was but a schoolgirl, with trembling lips and veiling hair. He took her hand like a man accustomed to be obeyed, as indeed he was.

"Child, your mama hath left you in my care, and

you can't desire I should relinquish the pleasure.
Such an opportunity no gentleman could resist. Be
seated, Madam, and let us discourse."

'T was all on one side, for she had not opened her
lips. But she obeyed him, and sat in the chair he
handed her to, as passive as a marble lady. He
seemed at a loss to continue, and stood looking at her
where she drooped, then took a chair beside her.

"You are pleased to be less cordial than I have
known you, Madam. Is it whim or anger? I like a
woman's pretty coquetries as well as any man, but
this silence —"

It still continued. She was snow and marble. Not
a word. Only the dark lashes like fans on her cheek.
Not a gleam rewarded him.

"A sullen beauty!" says his Grace languidly, "but
yet a beauty beyond all others. So here we sit!"
He drew out his jewelled timepiece.

"I give you a minute, Madam — nay, two. And
if by then you have not spoke, I will try if the
warmth of a kiss on those sweet lips won't thaw the
ice. I swear it!"

He laid the sparkling toy at her elbow on the table,
and stared in her face. 'T is certain his Grace had
dined. He was not wont to treat any woman thus
unless where it was asked for. A minute went by —
the tick was audible, but she moved not. And now
a slow hot tear scorched its way down her cheek.
If this followed mama's instruction, it bettered it.
The time was scarce out when he springs up and cries
with triumph : —

"I was not mistook. Your silence asks a kiss, child, and James Hamilton was never the man to refuse a woman's challenge. Give me your lips, and more."

His swashbuckling Border ancestors were stirring in his veins, and for a moment his face coarsened and his eyes were gross. He caught her by the two arms and bent his mouth upon hers.

In a flash the fair statue was living and dangerous. He was a strong man, she a wisp of a girl; but she flung him off and stood glaring at him.

"How dare you?" she panted, and could no more. The eyes were unveiled at last and rained fire on him. Never had any person seen her look thus; she faced him gallantly. He applauded as if it had been the Woffington or any other fair game.

"'T is prettily done — but I see your drift, Madam. If a young lady is left by her friends and her own desire to sit alone with one of the best-known men in town, she takes the consequences. Yet I would not have missed Lucretia — she lacked only the dagger in her hand. But the comedy may end. Give me your lips, child, and coquet no more."

"Sir — if you are a gentleman —"

"Madam, I am a lover."

"Oh, 't is too much — too much!" she cries. "I have undertook what was beyond me, and I can't — I can't carry it through. I would if I could — I cannot!"

The strange words, the despair in her face was no stage-play. The Duke knew sincerity when it cried aloud.   Still grasping her hands, he stood at arm's length, staring in her face.

"You cannot, Madam?   What mean you?   Are you in earnest?"

Not withdrawing her hands, fast held and quivering, she kept silence.   He could feel the pulses flutter in her wrists, and the fumes of wine cleared slowly out of his brain and carried the brutality with them.

"Have the condescension to explain yourself.   You are safe in my company now.   Possibly I was mistook, but I supposed you not unwilling for our tête-a-tête.   Accept my apologies if this is not the case. I thrust no attentions on women who dislike them."

"Sir, I will explain, and go, and never see your face again.   I die of shame."

He could still feel the pitiful flutter in her wrists. He relaxed his grip and handed her to her chair, — a gentleman again, — James, Duke of Hamilton and Brandon.   "I see myself gravely in error, Madam. I await your words."

She would not sit, nor he.   They stood apart now, and he could scarce hear the silver tremble of her voice.

"Sir, we are poor.   You know this.   And last night my mother did ask me whether I supposed your Grace had any feeling for me beyond careless goodwill.   I knew not.   What could I say?   And she then revealed to me — oh, how reveal it now! — that our little means is all but spent, and that gone, we must retire into poverty and misery again.   Also that there are debts, and prison for debtors.   Also that

any match for my sister is impossible to hope for —
No — how can I tell it! And she did say that if we
could hope — could but know that —"

Her voice died on her lips. She hung her head in
agony. He took her up.

"The task is too hard for you. Let me continue.
Your mama said that, if she and your sister withdrew and left you with me, if you put forth your
charms (and God knows there were never such!),
't was possible you might set the sweetest trap for the
rich man, and with his aid clamber out of the mud and
sit secure beside him. Confirm me if I don't err.
Confess!"

"I confess." The words scarce broke the silence.

"And love was not in the bargain," the cruel voice
persisted. "Mama did not enquire whether James
Hamilton was distasteful to you or the reverse. He
was a moneybag — no man. Confess again."

"I confess. Sir, we have used you very ill. I ask
your pardon. I was a fair mark for insult." Her
head dropped lower. She could not otherwise hide
her face, but shame overflowed it in waves of crimson.

"To be frank, Madam, I have never found your
mother congenial company. 'T was not for her I
sought this house. Tell me, was this her plot only?
Was it acceptable to you?"

"At least, I followed it. She is my mother. I am
one flesh and blood with her. If she is a plotter, so
too am I. I bid your Grace farewell, and pray for so
much pity as that you will never come this way again,
nor see me, lest I die at your feet."

"Madam, do I owe you no apology?"

"I think none, your Grace. You acted as the woman you took me for might, I suppose, expect. Let me go."

A singular thing happened here. The Duke, the haughtiest and coldest of men, bent his knee and carried her hand to his lips. So on Birthnights he kissed the late Queen's hand, she standing before the Throne. Then stood very grave. "Madam, I entreat your pardon. I have shown you a side of a man's character very unfitting for your eyes and you but the child you are. Forgive me, and ere we part for ever, answer me one question, in token of your pardon. Had I been but James Hamilton, the lowest of my clan — could you have honoured me with any regard?"

She stammered, trembling before this melancholy gentleness.

"I know not."

He persisted, gentle but firm:

"We have perhaps something to pardon each other. I ask again — would this have been possible?"

Constrained, she sought for breath. Because a cold handsome face softens, because distrust is melted, shall a woman let her heart fly like a bird to a man's bosom?

"Sir, you ask more than I can answer."

Still the eyes insisted, and now the strong hand held hers.

"Sir — I think — I believe — it had not been impossible."

"What — not James Hamilton — no more? — with a shieling on the moors, and the heather-cock for food, and a Hamilton plaid to wrap his heart's darling, and a fire of peats to sit by, and this hand empty but for love and his claymore? — Would the beauty of the world have come to his breast?"

His voice was a strong music — a river in spate. His eyes caught hers and held them.

"'T is not impossible. But oh, how should I prove it — prove it? There's not a word I say but rings false now. Leave me — leave me. I have said too much."

"You can't prove it? But you can, and if you prove it, I will distrust God's mercy before I will distrust my girl. All you have told me was known to me — known to all the town. It rings through the streets that the fair Gunnings and their mother are schemers; that they love none and seek only the best price for their charms. Marry me now, this hour, Elizabeth, and face the world that will call you plotter and adventuress. For they will so! There's no club in town but will ring with the story of how the beauty was cunningly left to a half-drunk man's advances. That's how Horry Walpole and all the old women of both sexes will have it! All this will be known through your mother's folly and your Abigail's chatter, and they will tell how you trapped me, how I would have escaped and could not for the snares about my feet. Marry me and face this, if you will, and I will believe you love me, for you will stand a disgraced woman for all time. Marry me not, and I will make your way easy with gold, and your mother shall tell her own tale, and not a smirch on your name, and fear not but another rich man will give you all I could, and not a spot on it.   Choose now once and for all.   I have seen and I know how my coronet will sting you with shame — with shame set in it."

He did not embrace her.   'T was the strangest wooing.   The clock pointed to eleven.   The house was dead silent.   Her eyes widened with pain and fear.   She looked piteously at him.

"They will say you caught me drunk, whom you could not catch sober.   They will say you forced the marriage, lest I escape.   There is nothing they will not say but the truth — that my sweetheart is the sweetest, the purest, the proudest woman alive.   Your delicacy will be trod in the mud, Madam.   Will you take your man at that?   Will you crawl through the dirt to his heart?"

His fire kindled hers.   Her eyes glittered.

"And if they believed me worthless — that is not what I ask.   What would your Grace think?"

He smiled with peculiar sweetness.

"Child, you know.   Look at me."

And still she trembled.

"Beloved, adored!" he cried.   "Think you I knew not 't was death to you to tell the truth?   Shall a man find a pearl in the dirt and not set it over his heart.   I have loved you since first I saw your fair face, and now I honour you.   Come to me and bless me; and when these fools cackle and gibber, I shall know how to protect my wife."

His arms went round her.

"I will do it," she said.

The minutes passed in an exquisite joy, plucked out of shame like a rose from a torrent. He left her and went to the door, and leaning over the balustrade, called down the stair : —

"Armitage !"

A young man, handsomely dressed and something of a fop after his valet-fashion, sprang up the stair — his Grace's gentleman. His master, very tranquil and haughty, was by the door — the fair Miss Gunning erect in her chair.

"Armitage, proceed at once to my house, and acquaint my chaplain, Mr MacDonald, that this lady and I are to be married immediately. Desire him to come hither with all that is necessary, and lose not a moment."

And seeing Armitage hesitate like a man wonderstruck, the Duke stamped his foot and set him flying down the way he came, calling after him : —

"Desire Mrs Abigail to come up this moment."

They heard the door shut violently, and Mrs Abigail came up, very demure and curtseying to the ground.

"Be seated, good woman. Your lady will excuse you. We wait the Reverend Mr MacDonald, with ring and licence, and you and Armitage shall serve for witnesses to the marriage. Now I think of it, call also the woman of the house."

He carried it masterfully, and Elizabeth, no more than any other woman, could be insensible to that

charming tyranny.   He stood behind her chair while
the woman called for Mrs Mann — who came, mor-
tally afraid of her company.

"Shall Mrs Abigail braid my hair? — it tumbles
all about me," says Elizabeth, questioning her master
timidly.

"'T is so great a beauty I will not have it hid," he
cries, standing behind her chair where the long locks
lay on the ground.

Silence again, and the time passing.

At last, a sound as if Armitage propelled somewhat
before him up the stair, and into the room walks his
Grace's gentleman, and before him a stout personage
in bands and cassock, so breathless from haste as to
be incapable of any speech.

"Hath he the licence?"

"He hath, your Grace, but he declares that the
occasion being so great, and the incumbent of Mayfair Chapel, Dr Keith, being at home and the chapel
open, for the greater solemnity 't were well to have
the marriage solemnised there.   'T is but ten minutes, and I have brought the chariot, if it please your
Grace."

And now, puffing sore, the clergyman put in his
plea, — not for delay, the Duke's face forbade that, —
but that all be done with ceremony.

"If a word more be said, I send for the Arch-
bishop!" swears his Grace, flushed and handsome.
"My chariot's at the door.   Bundle in all who can.
Madam, allow me."

He drew the bride's hand to his, and preceded them

down the stair, holding it high as in a minuet. The women followed without a word. Elizabeth went in a dream, half-enchantment, half-nightmare.

The chapel was dark and musty — no time to light the lamps; but Mr Armitage, the facile, the adroit, a perfect Mercury and old in experience, called in four linkmen waiting by their ladies' empty chairs in the street outside.

These grimy fellows stood upon the altar steps, two at a side, lighting the book the parson opened, his voice resounding through the silent place with startling loudness. Behind the bridal pair huddled the women.

"Dearly Beloved, we are met together —" and so to the close. But his voice was muffled beside the clear ring of James Hamilton's. His "I will" fell like a sword on the air. He was never a man to show his heart but to the one in whose hand it lay, and his tone disdained all but the woman who stood by him. He put his signet ring on her finger, and they turned from the altar man and wife.

"Give each of these men five guineas, and bid them light her Grace to her chariot, Armitage. Take you the women back to Mrs Gunning's lodging, where we follow. I thank you, Mr Keith, for the best service any man ever did me. It shall not go unrewarded."

He handed her into the chariot with the utmost ceremony; and when the door was closed, flung himself on his knees before her, clasping her waist.

"My dear — my girl, how shall I thank you? Think you I don't know what it hath cost you —

and the proof you have given me that your heart is mine. My wife — my sweetheart!"

'T was half after twelve when Mrs Gunning returned with Maria, being a prudent woman, and resolved that, if the criminal did not hang himself, it should not be for want of rope.

"The chariot's at the door and the light still in the parlour!" she whispered; "sure, he can't be there still? Heaven send he be not drunk and asleep. 'T was mere folly to leave the wine!"

Not a sound. They approached as it were on tiptoe up the stair, and softly opened the door.

My Lord Duke, attended by Armitage, stood before them, splendid in his dark red velvet laced with silver, the blue ribbon crossing his breast. He held Elizabeth by the hand, she pale as ashes but perfectly composed.

Mrs Gunning gave a fine dramatic start, Maria advancing behind her, devoured with curiosity.

"What — what can this mean? Little did I expect to find your Grace here at this hour. Elizabeth, I fear you have been vastly imprudent. Your good name — " She might have said more but the Duke came forward, very magnificent.

"Madam, permit me to introduce a *stranger*," says he, with emphasis on the word, "Her Grace the Duchess of Hamilton."

"Lord! Then 't is to be!" cries Mrs Gunning, all radiant, and mistaking his meaning. "O my sweet child, my Elizabeth — how have you took me by surprise! When shall it be, your Grace?"

"Madam, it is done. Miss Gunning became my bride in the Mayfair Chapel — was it twenty minutes since, Armitage?"

"Fifteen, your Grace."

"'T was all in order — a clergyman? — 't was legal?" pants Mrs Gunning, her hand to her heart.

"Assuage your maternal fears, Madam." His lip was disdainful — he set her a world away. "All was as you could have wished. Permit the Duchess and myself to wish you farewell and good night — or rather good morning."

He led Elizabeth to the door, which Armitage held open. It closed behind them, and their steps were heard descending. The Duchess had not said a word.

There was silence until the chariot had rumbled away, when Mrs Gunning found her voice.

"I did not credit her with such skill. She hath played her cards well indeed. I would give the world to know what passed."

"That we shall never know," says Maria. "He 's not the man to tell his secrets, nor she neither. Sure, they 're a pair."

"Well, Heaven send you show the like skill with my Lord Coventry. You can't do better. Lord, how my heart beats for joy!"

"I shall not need, Madam," says Miss Maria coolly. "She has ensured my match with her own. The Duchess of Hamilton's sister won't go begging for a husband. 'T is now but to choose my wedding silk. Come, let us to bed. These late hours hurt my bloom. Let us however drink a toast in this wine

to old Mother Corrigan and the Golden Vanity. 'T is
the least we can do.   Blow out the candles."

(*Elizabeth, later Duchess of Argyll, bore her honours
with dignity and became a very great lady.   Maria,
Countess of Coventry, died aged twenty-seven, not un-
touched by scandal, and a victim to her own frivolity.
Mrs Gunning received a valuable appointment as Housekeeper at one of the royal palaces.   "The Luck of the
Gunnings" became a proverb.*

*It has been disputed which of the two famous actresses,
Peg Woffington or George Anne Bellamy had the honour
of setting the beauties forth in life.   Mrs. Bellamy's claim
has the better evidence, especially in view of the Countess
of Coventry's distinguished impertinence to her a few
years later.*)

THE WALPOLE BEAUTY

MARIA WALPOLE

Countess of Waldegrave
Duchess of Gloucester
17(?)–1807

HORACE WALPOLE was convinced that even the Gunnings envied the beauty of Maria Walpole, his niece. "Yesterday," he writes, "t' other famous Gunning dined there. She has made a friendship with my charming niece, to disguise her jealousy."

To the surprise of all London, Maria, daughter of Sir Edward Walpole and Maria Clements, married the Earl of Waldegrave, "for character and credit the first match in England." At her husband's death, she refused the Duke of Portland, but secretly married the Duke of Gloucester, brother to the King. Her admirers point out the romance of her fortunes — how she was daughter of a milliner, granddaughter of a great Prime Minister, widow of an Earl, wife of a Duke, sister-in-law to the King, mother of the three ladies Waldegrave, and, in her second marriage, mother of Prince William and the Princess Sophia.

Sir Joshua Reynolds made seven portraits of the lovely "Walpole Beauty." Years afterward, when he was at work on his famous painting of her three daughters, Walpole begged him to pose them "as the three Graces, adorning a bust of the Duchess as the Magna Mater." "But," adds the veteran of Strawberry Hill, with what resignation he can muster, "my ideas were not adopted."

Reynolds, pinx.

Maria Walpole, Countess of Waldegrave,
and her daughter, Elizabeth Laura,
afterwards Countess of Waldegrave

V

THE WALPOLE BEAUTY

[From a packet of letters, written in the middle of the eighteenth century by Lady Fanny Armine to her cousin, Lady Desmond, in Ireland, I have strung together one of the strangest of true stories — the history of Maria Walpole, niece of the famous Horace Walpole and illegitimate daughter of his brother, Sir Edward Walpole. The letters are a potpourri of town and family gossip, and in gathering the references to Maria Walpole into coherence, I am compelled to omit much that is characteristic and interesting.]

May, 1754.

WHY, Kitty, my dear, what signifies your reproaches? I wish I may never be more guilty than I am this day. I laid out a part of your money in a made-up mantua and a petticoat of Rat de St. Maur, and for the hat, 't was the exact copy of the lovely Gunning's — Maria Coventry. And though I won't flatter you, child, by saying your bloom equals hers (for I can't tell what hers may be under the white lead she lays on so thick), yet I will say that your Irish eyes may ambuscade to the full as well beneath it, though they won't shoot an earl flying, like hers, because you have captured your baronet already!

But 't is news you would have — news, says you, of all the gay doings of the town.

And how is her Gunning Grace of Hamilton, you

ask, and do the folk still climb on chairs at Court to
stare at her? Vastly in beauty, child. She was
in a suit of fine blue satin at the last Birthnight,
sprigged all over with white, and the petticoat robings
broidered in the manner of a trimming wove in the
satin. A hoop of the richest damask, trimmed with
gold and silver. These cost fourteen guineas a hoop,
my dear. Who shall say the ladies of the present
age don't understand refinements? Her Grace had
diamonds plastered on wherever they would stick,
and all the people of quality run mad to have a stare
at so much beauty, set off with as much glare as
Vauxhall on a fête night, and she as demure as a cat
after chickens.

But 't is always the way with these sudden-come-
ups, they never have the easy carriage that comes
from breeding, and 't is too much to expect she should
be a topping courtier.

You must know Horry Walpole was there, in gray
and silver brocade, as fine and finical a gentleman as
ever, and most genteelly lean; and says I to him: —

"What think you, Mr Walpole, of our two coquet
Irish beauties? Do they put out all the fire of our
English charmers?"

So he drew himself up and took a pinch of rappee
(can't you see him, Kitty, my girl?), and says he: —

"Madam, to a lady that is herself all beauty and
need envy none, I may say we have a beauty to be
produced shortly to the town that will flutter all the
world, excepting only the lady I have the honour to
address."

And, Lord! the bow he made me, with his hat to his heart!

"La. man," says I, "who is she? But sure I know. 'T is the Duchess of Queensberry reduced a good half in size and with a new complexion."

But Horry shook his ambrosial curls.

"No, Madam, 'pon honour! A little girl with the vivacity of sixteen and brown eyes, brown hair — in fact, a brown beauty."

And then it flashed on me and I says : —

"Good God! — Maria! But sure she can't be presented. 'T is impossible!" And could have bit my silly tongue out when 't was said.

He shrugged his shoulders like a Frenchman, — 't is the last grace he picked up in Paris, — and turned from me to the new lady errant, Miss Chester, who models herself on the famous Miss Chudleigh.

But nothing could equal the horrid indecency of Miss Chudleigh's habit at the Ranelagh Masquerade some five years back, when Mrs Montagu, observing her, said : "Here is Iphigenia for the sacrifice, but so naked the high priest may inspect the entrails of the victim without more ado." And says Horry : "Surely, 't is Andromeda she means herself, and not Iphigenia!" I thought we should have died laughing. The Maids of Honour were then so offended not one of 'em would speak to her. They are not such prudes today, and Miss Chester has as much countenance as she looks for. Alas, it takes a wise woman, if not a good one, to know just where certainty should stop and imagination take its place!

But, Kitty child, who do you guess is the new beauty? I give you one, I give you two, I give you three! And if 't was three hundred, you 'd be never the wiser. Why, Maria Walpole, you little block-head! Maria, the daughter of Sir Edward Walpole, Horry's brother. What think you of that? But Sir Edward never was married, says you. True for you, Kitty, but don't you know the story? No, to be sure. There 's no scandal in Ireland, for St. Patrick banished it along with the snakes and their poison, because the island that has so many mis-fortunes would have died of another.

Well, take your sampler like a good little girl and hearken to the history of the lovely Maria that 's to blow out the Gunning candles. Let me present to your la'ship Sir Edward Walpole, brother to the Baron of Strawberry Hill. A flourish and a sliding bow, and you know one another! Sir Edward, who resembles not Horry in his love for the twittle-twattle of the town, is a passable performer on the bass viol, and a hermit — the Hermit of Pall Mall. But the rules of that Hermitage are not too severe, child. 'T is known there were relaxations. And notably one.

The Hermit some years since was lodged in Pall Mall; and in the lower floors was lodged a dealer in clothes, with prentices to fetch and carry.

Lord! says Kitty, what 's this to the purpose? Attend, Madam. The curtain rises!

'T is an old story: the virtuous prentice — and the unvirtuous. There was one of them — Dorothy

Clement, a rustic beauty, straw hat tied under the roguish chin, little tucked-up gown of flowered stuff, handkerchief crossed over the bosom, ruffled elbows. 'T is so pretty a dress, that I protest I marvel women of quality don't use it! However, this demure damsel looked up at Sir Edward under the hat, and he peeped under the brim, and when he left the house and returned to his own, what should happen but the trembling beauty runs to him, one fine day, for protection, swearing her family and master have all cast her off because 't was noted the gentleman had an eye for a charming face.

Well, child, 't is known hermits do not marry. 'T is too much to ask of their Holinesses. But he set a chair at the foot of his table for the damsel, and bid her share his pulse and crusts; and so 't was done, and whether in town or country, the Hermitess kept him company till she died. Sure the Walpoles are not too fastidious in their women, excepting only Horry of Strawberry Hill, who has all the finicals of the others rolled up in his lean body.

Well, Kitty, there were four children: a boy, — nothing to the purpose, — and Laura, Maria, and Charlotte. And the poor lasses, not having a rag of legitimacy to cover 'em, must needs fall back on good behaviour and good looks. I saw Laura, a pretty girl, in the garden at Englefield some years since, when I was airing in Lady Pomfret's coach; and as we looked, the little hoyden Maria comes running up in muslin and blue ribbons, all health and youth and blooming cheeks and brown curls and eyes

— a perfect Hebe. And 't is she — the milliner's brat — that 's to borrow the Car of Love and set the world afire. But she can't be presented, Kitty; for our high and mighty Royals frown on vice, and not a single creature with the bar sinister can creep into Court, however many may creep out. And that's that!

And now I end with compliments and curtseys to your la'ship, and the glad tidings that one of the virgin choir of Twickenham, those Muses to which Mr Horace Walpole is Apollo, has writ an Ode so full of purling streams and warbling birds, that Apollo says he will provide a sidesaddle for Pegasus, and no male shall ever bestride him again.

September, 1758.

O la, la, la! Was you ever at the Bath, child? Here am I just returned, where was great company, and all the wits and belles, and Miss Biddy Green, the great city fortune, run off with Harry Howe, and her father flourishing his gouty stick in the Pump Room and swearing a wicked aristocracy should have none of his honest guineas. But he 'll soften when he sees her presented at Court, with feathers stuck in her poll and all the city dames green with spite. 'T is the way of the world.

But to business. The town is talking with hundred-woman noise on the marriage that Laura, — by courtesy called Walpole, — the Hermit's eldest daughter, makes tomorrow. 'T will astound you, Lady Desmond your Honour, as much as it did your

humble servant. For Miss Laura honours the
Church, no less, with her illegitimate hand, and no
less a dignitary than a Canon of Windsor! Is not
this to be a receiver of stolen goods? Does not his
Reverence compound a felony in taking such a
bride? What say you? 'T is Canon Keppel,
brother to Lord Albemarle; and mark you, Kitty —
the Honourable Mrs Keppel has the right to be presented where Miss Laura might knock at the door
in vain! We come up in the world, child; but the
Walpoles had always that secret.

'T will set the other charming daughters dreaming
of bride-cake. All the world talks of Maria, a
shining beauty indeed. Horry Walpole is enchanted
at Miss Laura's match — sure, an illegitimate Walpole, if niece to the Baron of Strawberry, is worth
a dozen of your Cavendishes and Somersets! I
laughed like a rogue in my sleeve when says Horry
to me at my drum : —

"Colonel Yorke is to be married to one or both of
the Miss Crasteyns, great city fortunes — nieces
to the rich grocer. They have two hundred and
sixty thousand pounds apiece. Nothing comes amiss
to the digestion of that family — a marchioness or a
grocer."

Says I, flirting my fan : —

"'T is gross feeding, sure, Mr Walpole. Now,
had it been a royal illegitimate."

He looked daggers, and took a pinch of snuff with
an air. Never was a man with more family pride,
though he affects to scorn it.

What think you of this latest news of Lady Coventry? The people are not yet weary of gazing upon the Gunnings, and stared somewhat upon her last Sunday was se'night in the Park. Would you believe it, Kitty, that she complained to the King, and His Majesty, not to be outdone in wisdom, offers a guard for her ladyship's beauty. On this she ventures into the Park, and, pretending fright, desires the assistance of the officer, who orders twelve sergeants to march abreast before her and a sergeant and twelve men behind her; and in this pomp did the silly little fool walk all the evening, with more mob about her than ever, her blockhead husband on one side and my Lord Pembroke on the other! I 'm sure I can't tell you anything to better this, so good night, dear cousin, with all affectionate esteem.

April, 1769.

Great news, your la'ship. I am but just returned from a royal progress to visit the Baron of Strawberry Hill. Strawberry was in prodigious beauty — spring flowers, cascades, grottoes, all displayed to advantage in a sunshine that equalled June. The company, her Gunning Grace of Hamilton, the Duchess of Richmond, Lady Aylesbury, and your humble servant.

Says Mr Horace, leaning on his amber-top cane and surveying us, as the three sat in the shell on the terrace and I stood by: —

"Strawberry Hill is grown a perfect Paphos. 'T is the land of beauties, and if Paris himself stood where

I do, he could never adjudge the golden apple."

He writ the same to George Montagu after, who showed the letter about town : —

"There never was so pretty a sight as to see the three sitting. A thousand years hence, when I begin to grow old, if that can ever be, I shall talk of that event and tell the young people how much handsomer the women of my time were than they are now."

There's a compliment like a fresh-plucked rose from the Lord of Strawberry. It reads pretty, don't it, child? Horry was in vast wit — 't was like the Northern Lights hurtling about us — made us blink! The Duchess of Richmond pretending she could not recall her marriage-day, says Horry : —

"Record it thus, Madam. This day thousand years I was married!"

'T was not till a week later I discovered this to be a *bon mot* of Madame de Sévigné. His jewels are polished very fine, but 't is not always in the Strawberry mine they are dug. But to our news — What will your Honour pay me for a penn'orth?

'T is of our beauty, Maria — ahem! — Walpole. The pretty angler has caught her fish — a big fish, a gold fish, even a golden-hearted fish, for 't is Lord Waldegrave! A belted earl, a Knight of the Garter, no less, for the pretty milliner's daughter. You don't believe it, Kitty? Yet you must, for 't is true, and sure. If beauty can shed a lustre over puddled blood, she has it. Lord Villiers, chief of the macaronis, said, yesterday was a week : —

"Of all the beauties Miss Walpole reigns supreme

— if one could forget the little accident of birth! Her face, bloom, eyes, teeth, hair, and person are all perfection's self, and Nature broke the mould when she made this paragon, for I know none like her."

'T is true, but 't is so awkward with these folk that can't be presented nor can't meet this one nor that. Still, I have had her much to my routs and drums, where 't is such an olla podrida that it matters not who comes. But Lady Waldegrave may go where she will; and certainly the bridegroom has nothing to object on the score of birth, for he comes from James the Second by the left hand, and for aught I know a left-hand milliner is as good these Republican days. Anyhow, 't is so, and Horry, who would have all think him above such thoughts, is most demurely conceited that a Walpole — ahem! — should grace the British peerage. Remains now only Charlotte, and I dare swear she will carry her charms to no worse market than Maria, though not so great a Venus.

I went yesterday evening to the Bluestocking Circle at Mrs Montagu's fine house in Hill Street. I am not become learned, Kitty, but 't was to hear the lionesses roar, and because I knew the Lord of Strawberry would be there and was wishful to hear his exultations. Lord preserve us, child, what a frightening place! We were ushered into the Chinese Room, lined with painted Pekin paper, and noble Chinese vases, and there were all the lions, male and female, in a circle — the Circle of the Universe. All the great ladies of the Bluestocking Court were there: the vastly learned Mrs Carter, Mrs Delany over

from Ireland, the Swan of Lichfield Miss Anna
Seward, Mrs Chapone, and other lionesses and *cub-
esses*. My dear, they sat in a half-moon, and behind
them another half-moon of grave ecclesiastics and
savants, and Horry at the head of them, in brown and
gold brocade. 'T was not sprightly, Kitty. 'T is
true these women are good and learned, and some of
them well enough in looks; but 't is so pretentious,
so serious, — I lack a word! — so censorious of all
that does not pull a long face, that, when Mrs
Montagu rose to meet us with the shade of Shake-
speare in attendance (for no lower footman would
serve so majestic a lady), I had a desire to seize her
two hands and gallop round the room with her, that
I could scarce restrain. But sure she and the company had died of it!

I expected great information from such an assemblage, but 't was but a snip-snap of talk — remarks passed from one to another, but served as it
were on massy plate — long words, and too many of
'em. Dull, my dear, dull! And so 't will always
be when people aim to be clever. They do these
things better in France, where they have no fear of
laughter and the women sparkle without a visible
machinery. 'T was all standing on the mind's tiptoe here. And when the refreshments were served
I made for Horry —

> On silver vases loaded rise
> The biscuits' ample sacrifice,
> And incense pure of fragrant tea.

But Bluestockingism is nourished on tea as wit on wine.

"So, Mr Walpole," says I, "what is this news I hear of Miss Maria? My felicitations to the bridegroom on the possession of so many charms."

And Horry with his bow : —

"I thank your ladyship's partiality and good heart. For character and credit, Lord Waldegrave is the first match in England, and for beauty, Maria — excepting only the lady I address. The family is well pleased, though 't is no more than her deserts, and 't was to be expected my father's grandchild would ally herself with credit."

'T is when Horry Walpole gives himself these demure airs that I am tempted to be wicked, Kitty. For what signifies talking? The girl is a beauty, but Nancy Parsons and Kitty Fisher are beauties, too, and if the court and peerage are opened to women of no birth, why what 's left for women of quality? 'T is certain the next generation of the peerage bids fair to be extreme ill-born, and the result may be surprising. But I held my tongue, for I have a kindness for Horry and his niece, though I laugh at 'em.

I thought Mr Walpole looked ill, and doubted whether I might hope to see him at my Tuesday rout. Says he : —

"'T is the gout, Madam, that ungallant disorder, and had I a mind to brag, I could boast of a little rheumatism too ; but I scorn to set value on such trifles, and since your ladyship does me the honour to bespeak my company, I will come if 't were in my coffin and pair. May I hope your ladyship will favour us at Maria's nuptials. Sure the Graces were ever attended by Venus on occasions of ceremony."

He would have said more, but the Queen of the Blues swam up, protesting and vowing she had never seen such a goddess as Miss Maria Walpole; that were she to marry the Emperor of the world, 't would be vastly below the merit of such glowing charms. And so forth.

'T is a lady that paints all her roses red and plasters her lilies white, and whether 't is malice, I can't tell, but believe 't is possible to blast by praise as well as censure, by setting the good sense of one half the world and the envy of the other against the victim. So she shrugged and simpered and worked every muscle of her face, in hopes to be bid to the wedding; but Mr. Walpole only bowed very grave and precise, and turned away, and I with him. And no more circles for me, my dear; and here I conclude, and my next shall be the epithalamium.

18th May, 1759.

Kitty, child, when you was married, did you look about you from under your hat? — did you take a sly peep at the World, the Flesh, and the Devil, and wonder which was the bridegroom? I did, but I 'll never tell which he proved to be! Well, Maria was married two days since, and Horry Walpole favoured me today with a glimpse of the letter he writ to his friend Montagu on the occasion. 'T was very obliging; but you know all he writes is writ with one eye on the paper and one on posterity, so 't is no wonder if he squints a little by times. However, here 's to our letter.

"The original day was not once put off — lawyers and milliners all canonically ready. They were married in Pall Mall just before dinner, and we all dined there, and the Earl and the new Countess got into their post-chaise at eight and went to Nave-stock alone. On Sunday she is to be presented and to make my Lady Coventry distracted. Maria was in a white and silver night gown, with a hat very much pulled over her face. What one could see of it was handsomer than ever. A cold maiden blush gave her the sweetest delicacy in the world."

So far our doting uncle, Kitty; but 't is indeed a fair creature. I saw the long soft brown eyes lifted once and flash such a look at the bridegroom — I dare to swear Lord Waldegrave wished away then the twenty years between them. Poor Lady Coven-try, indeed! Her race is run, her thread is spun, her goose is cooked, and any other trope you please; for what signifies all the white lead at the 'pothecary's compared to the warm brown of Maria's complexion and her long eyelashes!

Lady Elizabeth Keppel had a gown worthy of the Roman Empress she looks, with that beak nose and nutcracker chin. 'T was a black velvet petticoat, embroidered in chenille, the pattern a great gold wicker basket filled to spilling over with ramping flowers that climbed and grew all about her person. A design for a banqueting hall rather than a woman; or indeed a committee of Bluestockings might have wore it to advantage. She had winkers of lace to her head, and her hoop covered so many acres that one could but approach at an awful distance and confidences were impossible — a sure reason why the modish ladies will soon drop the hoop.

I saluted the bride after the ceremony and says I : —

"Maria, my love, I attend your presentation on Sunday, and I bring my smelling-bottle for Lady Coventry. 'T is already said her guards will now be transferred to your ladyship, together with a detachment from each ship of the Fleet, to secure so much beauty."

She has the sweetest little dimple in either cheek, and twenty Cupids hide under her lashes.

"I have no wish, Madam, to dethrone my Lady Coventry, if even 't were possible," says she. "That lady has occupied the throne so long, that 't is hers by right, and the English people never weary of an old favourite."

'T was two-edged, Kitty, as you see, and I will report it to the other lovely Maria, and 't will be pretty to see the rapiers flash between the two. 'T is not only the men carry dress swords, child. But I thought Miss Maria a downy nestling, with never a thought of repartee, till now. 'T is born in us, child. It begins with our first word and is our last earthly sigh.

May, 1759.

Well, was you at the presentation, Lady Desmond, for I did not see your la'ship.

Says you: "How was that possible with the Irish Sea between us? So out with the news!"

The company was numerous and magnificent, and Horry Walpole in his wedding garment of a white brocade with purple and green flowers. 'T was a trifle juvenile for his looks, but I blame him not; for my Lady Townshend would choose for him, though he protested that, however young he might be in spirits, his bloom was a little past. I could see he was quaking for his nuptialities — lest Maria should not be in full beauty.

T' other Maria, — Coventry, — in golden flowers on a silver ground, looked like the Queen of Sheba; and were not our Monarch anything but a Solomon, I would not say but — A full stop to all naughtiness! But I must tell you her last *faux pas,* for you know, child, she's as stupid as she's pretty. She told the King lately that she was surfeited with sights. There was but one left she could long to see. What, think you, it was? — why, a coronation!

The old man took it with good humour; but Queen Bess had made a divorce between her lovely head and shoulders for less.

Well, into the midst of this prodigious assemblage, with Uncle Horry quaking inwardly and making as though Walpole nieces were presented every day, comes the fair Waldegrave, gliding like a swan, perfectly easy and genteel, in a silver gauze with knots

of silver ribbon and diamonds not so bright as her
eyes. I dare swear not a man there but envied my
Lord Waldegrave, and many might envy the beauty
her husband — a good plain man, grave and handsome. But the bride! She swam up to His Majesty,
like Venus floating on clouds, and her curtsey and
hand-kissing perfect. Who shall talk of blood in
future, when a milliner's daughter can thus distinguish herself in the finest company in Europe? 'T is
true 't is mixed with the Walpole vintage; but when
all's said and done, who were the Walpoles? If you
get behind the coarse, drinking Squire Western of a
father, you stumble up against Lord Mayors and
what not! So 't is a world's wonder, and there I
leave it.

As for Maria Coventry — do but figure her! I
saw her pale under her rouge when the bride entered,
and her eyes shot sparks of fire, like an angry goddess.
Could they have destroyed, we had seen her rival a
heap of ashes like the princess of the Arabian Nights.
I tendered her my smelling-bottle, but she dashed it
from her, and then, smiling in the prettiest manner
in the world, says to my Lord Hardwicke: —

"'T is said women are jealous of each other's good
looks, my Lord, but 't is not so with me. I am vastly
pleased with my Lady Waldegrave's appearance.
'T is far beyond what was to be expected of her
parentage. She looks vastly agreeable, and I hope
she will favour me with her company."

'T was cleverer than I supposed her, and sure
enough she did nothing but court the bride, and now

the two beauties go about to the sights and routs together and are the top figures in town, and all the world feasts its eyes upon two such works of nature — and Art it must be added, so far as Maria Coventry is concerned; she is two inches deep in white lead, and the doctors have warned her 't will be the death of her.

Kitty, I found my first gray hair yesterday. 'T is my swan song. I am done with the beaux and the toasts and the fripperies. When I spoke to Harry Conway at the Court, his eyes were so fixed on Lady Waldegrave that he heard me not till I had spoke three times. Get thee to a nunnery, Fanny! I shall now insensibly drop into a spectatress. What care I! To ninety-nine women life ends with their looks, but I will be the hundredth, and laugh till I die!

Why, Kitty, your appetite for news grows by what it feeds on. Sure you are the horseleech's true daughter, crying, "Give, give!" You say I told you not of Charlotte Walpole's marriage. Sure, I did. Maria married her sister well — to young Lord Huntingtower, my Lord Dysart's son. 'T is a girl of good sense. She loved him not, nor yet pretended to, but says she to Maria: —

"If I was nineteen, I would not marry him. I would refuse point-blank. But I am two-and-twenty, and though 't is true some people say I am handsome, 't is not all who think so. I believe the truth is, I am like to be large and heavy and go off soon. 'T is dangerous to refuse so good a match. Therefore tell him, sister, I accept."

And 't was done. I had this from Maria herself, who took it for an instance of commendable good sense; but I know not — somehow I would have a girl less of a Jew with her charms. Anyhow, stout or no, she will be my Lady Countess Dysart when his father dies; and now sure, there are no more worlds left for the Walpole girls to conquer. Their doting Uncle Horry could never predict such success. The eldest girl's husband is now Bishop of Exeter.

Poor Maria Coventry is dead — the most lovely woman in England, setting aside only t' other Maria. 'T was from usage of white lead, Kitty, and tell that to all the little fools you know! It devoured her skin, and she grew so hideous, that at the last she would not permit the doctors to see her ruined face, but would put out her hand between the curtains to have her pulse took. She was but twenty-seven years of age.

There was not a woman in the Three Kingdoms but envied the Gunnings, and was 't not yourself told me, "the Luck of the Gunnings" was become a proverb in Ireland, and the highest wish for a girl? What will the sermonizers say now? That 't is best to be homely and live to eighty? I know not; but 't is as well the choice is not given, for I believe there is not ten women living but would choose as did Maria Coventry. Her beauty was her god, and if she sacrificed herself on the altar, 't is but what the gods look for.

Sure, I am Death's herald, for I must tell you my Lord Waldegrave is dead of the smallpox, and the beauty a widow after but four years' marriage. I saw her but yesterday, full of sensibility and lovely as Sigismonda in Hogarth's picture. She had her young daughter, Lady Elizabeth, in her lap, the curly head against her bosom, the chubby cheek resting on a little hand against the mother's breast. Sure never was anything so moving as the two — exact to the picture Mr Reynolds painted.

She has a great tenderness for his memory, and well she may, when the position he raised her to is considered. 'T is like a discrowned queen, for her jointure is small, and she is now no more consequence to his party, so his death has struck away her worldly glory at a blow. Indeed, I pitied her, and wiped away her floods of tears with tenderness that was unaffected. But for such a young woman, I won't believe the scene is closed. What — are there no marquises, no dukes, for such perfection?

But 't is brutal to talk so when she is crying her fine eyes out. I wipe my naughty pen and bid you adieu.

Two days later.

I attended Mrs Minerva Montagu's reception, and there encountered the Great Cham of Literature, Dr Johnson, rolling into the saloon like Behemoth. Lady Waldegrave's bereavement was spoke of and says he : —

"I know not, Madam, why these afflictions should startle us. Such beauty invokes ill fortune, lest a human being suppose herself superior to the dictates of Providence."

"Certainly she is the first woman in England for beauty," says I, very nettled; "but 't is to be thought she had chose a little less beauty and rather more good fortune, had she been consulted. 'T is hard she should be punished for what she could not help!"

"Let her solace herself with her needleworks, Madam. A man cannot hem a pocket handkerchief and so he runs mad. To be occupied on small occasions is one of the great felicities of the female train and makes bereavement more bearable."

'T is a bear roaring his ignorance of the world, my dear. But he has a kind of horse sense (if the female train would but let him be) that makes him endurable and even palatable at times.

Mrs Montagu informed us 't is rumoured that my Lady Mary Wortley Montagu (who you know is her cousin's cousin) thinks to return to England after being absent half a lifetime. I have a prodigious curiosity to see such a rarity. As for her beauty, that must be vanished, but her biting wit may outlive it, and Heaven send her here safe, I pray, to give a lash to the follies of more than one I could name, had I the malice. Were she to write a book of her life, 't would be the best reading in the world, could one wash their eyes and mind after reading it.

1764.

Kitty, my dear, have you forgot that, when my Lord Waldegrave died, I writ, "Are there no dukes to pursue the lovely widow?" Give honour to the prophet! She refused the Duke of Portland, that all the fair were hunting with stratagems worthy of the Mohawks. She refused this, that, and t' other. And the town said: "Pray who is the milliner's daughter, to turn up her nose at the first matches in England? Has she designs on the King of Prussia, — for our own young monarch is wed to his Charlotte, — or is it the Sultan, or His Holiness the Pope that will content her ladyship?"

No answer. But, Kitty, 't is me to smell a rat at a considerable distance, and I kept my nostrils open! Our handsome young King has a handsome young brother, — His Royal Highness the Duke of Gloucester, — and this gentleman has cast the sheep's eye, the eye of passion, upon our lovely widow! What think you of this? That it cannot be? Then what of the King Cophetua and other historic examples? I would have you know that in the tender passion there's nothing that cannot be. It laughs at obstacles and rides triumphant on the crest of the impossible. I knew it long since, but 't is over the town like wildfire now.

Meeting my Lady Sarah Bunbury yesterday, says she : —

"Lady Fanny, sure you know the Duke of Gloucester is desperately in love with my Lady Waldegrave. Now don't mask your little cunning face with ignorance, but tell me what's known. What have you heard from Horry Walpole?"

"Nothing, your la'ship," says I, very demure.

"Well," says she, "'t is reported the King has forbid him to speak to his fair widow, and she is gone

out of town. He has given her two pearl bracelets
worth five hundred pound. That's not for nothing
surely. But for what?"

"Indeed, 't is an ambiguous gift, Madam," says I,
whimsically; "and may mean much or little. Give
me leave to ask whether 't is Pursuit or Attainment
as your la'ship reads it?"

But she tossed her head, the little gossip, and off
she went.

I can tell you thus much, Kitty: the Walpoles are
main frightened. It may be a cast-back to the principles of the milliner mother. And there was never
the difference between her and Sir Edward Walpole
that there is between Maria and a Prince of the
Blood. Her birth is impossible. My Lady Mary
Coke asking me if the mother were not a washer-
woman, says I, "I really cannot determine the lady's
profession."

Poor Lady Mary is run clean mad with jealousy
and spite, for 't is not so long since she believed herself on the way to be a Royal Duchess, imagining
the late Duke of York to be her lover — a gentleman
so passionately in love with himself as to leave no
room for another. She wore her blacks when he
died, like a widow. But, spitfire as Lady Mary is,
't is too true Maria is playing with fire, and there
should be nothing between him and her mother's
daughter. She is indeed more indiscreet than becomes her. His chaise is eternally at her door;
and, as my Lady Mary says, she is lucky that anyone
else countenances her at all. If they do, 't is as

much from curiosity as any nobler emotion. Indeed, I fear her reputation's cracked past repair. Meeting Horry Walpole last night at the French Embassador's, he was plagued with staring crowds, and he made off after braving it a while. I hear the King is highly offended and the Queen yet more. She has a great notion of birth; and though poor, the Mecklenburg family has as good quarterings as any Royals in Europe. For my part, Kitty, I know not. Yet, if we seek for pedigree in horse and dog, 't is to be supposed worth something in Adam's breed also. And this ill-behaviour in Maria confirms me.

Yet I have visited the fair sinner, for I love her well. She can't help neither her birth nor her beauty, but sure her kind heart is all her own. She wept and would reveal nothing, but asked me to be so much her friend as to think the best of her. 'T is pity her tears were wasted on a mere woman. The drops beaded on her lashes like rain on a rose. Well, God mend all! say I. Sure none of us have a clear conscience and if anyone was to come up behind us and whisper, "I know when, how, and who!" 't is certain there are few women but would die of terror. Yet I did not think Maria a rake — though a Prince's.

'T is pity Lady Mary, the Great Wortley Montagu, is dead, that would have relished all this talk to the full. Can I forget when I visited her two years since just before she died — her vivacity and the tales she told of the junketings of Queen Anne's Court and George the First's! Gracious powers, Kitty, to think of our grandmothers' conduct and our own

excellence in comparison! I have not heard a
scandal since, but I have vied it with theirs and found
it a mere caprice. 'T was almost affrighting to see
that old lady, propped up in her chair, and croaking
out tales of the grandparents of every person known
to me, not forgetting my own, and laughing with a
horrid glee and a fire in her ancient eye, till I expected
to see her fly off like a witch on a broomstick. Sure,
thinks I, no respectable young woman will be seen
conversing with her grandmother after this! Mrs
Montagu carried me to see her, and I could scarce
thank her for it. Lord help us! does the world grow
better or worse? I must take Mr Walpole's opinion.

1772.

Kitty, Kitty, 't is all come out! But I may say
the town knew it after the masquerade in Soho, when
His Royal Highness appeared as Edward the Fourth
and Maria as Elizabeth Woodville, the pretty widow
he made his Queen. You 'll allow 't was a delicate
way to let the cat out of the bag. It could not
longer be kept within it, for the lady's sake and more.
For there 's to be a little new claimant one day to the
Crown, if all the elder stem should fail.

They were married, Kitty, in *1766!* Sure never
was an amazing secret better kept! And I will say
she hath borne much for the Prince's sake, and with
good sense — let my Lady Mary Coke and all the
Furies say what they will. But think of it — think
of it! for indeed 't is scarce credible. Here 's Maria
No-name — the milliner's base-born daughter — to

be Her Royal Highness the Duchess of Gloucester,
Princess of Great Britain! Was ever human fate so
surprising? 'T was a secret even from her father
and uncle, by the Duke's command; but she has now
writ her father so pretty a letter that 't is the town's
talk, Horry Walpole having shewed it about. But
Horry — have you forgot his pride, hid always under
a nonchalance as if 't was nothing? I was at
Gloucester House, where she received *en princesse*,
two nights ago; and to see Horry kiss her hand and
hear him address her with, "Madam, your Royal
Highness," at every word — sure no wit of Congreve's
could ever equal the comedy! But if looks were all,
she should be Queen of England — a shining beauty
indeed! She wore a robe in the French taste, of gold
tissue, her hair lightly powdered, with a bandeau of
diamonds and the Duke's miniature in diamonds on
her breast. He, looking very ill at ease, as I must
own, stood beside her.

The King and our little Mecklenburger Queen are
distracted; the royal ire withers all before it; but
it can't be undone, though they will pass a Marriage
Act to make such escapades impossible in the future.

But the Walpole triumph! 'T is now proved in
the face of all the world that a Walpole illegitimate
is better than a German Royalty; for he might have
married where he would. No doubt but Horry
Walpole always thought so, yet 't is not always we
see our family pride so bolstered.

Meagre as a skeleton, he looked the genteelest
phantom you can conceive, in puce velvet and steel

embroideries. For my part, I am well content, and wish Her Royal Highness joy without grimace. 'T is true I laugh at Horry Walpole, for in this town we laugh at everything, from the Almighty to Kitty Fisher; but I have a kindness for him and for Maria, and had sooner they triumphed than another. 'T is not so with the town. O Kitty, the jealousy and malice! 'T would take fifty letters to tell you the talk, from the Court down.

Well, Her Royal Highness gave me her hand to kiss, very gracious. She will not let her dignity draggle in the mud, like others I could name. But whether she would have been more easy with Portland or another, I will not determine. The Fates alone know, and sure they can't be women, they keep their secrets so well!

A BLUESTOCKING AT COURT

FANNY BURNEY
MADAME D'ARBLAY
1752–1840

"SEND me a minute Journal of everything," begs Mr. Crisp, "and never mind their being trifles — trifles well-dressed are excellent food, and your cookery is with me of established reputation."

Fanny Burney's letters, full of "trifles well-dressed" are as delightful as the novels, "Evelina," "Cecilia," and "Camilla," that made her famous. The skill of her writing and the charm of her character, "half-and-half sense and modesty," won her the friendship of Burke, Sheridan, Walpole, Warren Hastings, Hannah More, the Queen, and Dr. Johnson.

"She is a real wonder," said Johnson to Mrs. Thrale.

When Queen Charlotte made her second-keeper of the robes, her novel-reading friends protested that she had been "royally gagged and promoted to fold muslins." After four years of it, she returned to her home, her writing, and her marriage with General d'Arblay. With the proceeds of her most profitable novel, she built Camilla Cottage, where, with her good Alexandre and her gay little son, she could live and write, "Pleasure is seated in London, joy, mirth, society; but happiness, oh, it has taken its seat, its root, at West Humble!" She lived to be eighty-eight.

Yet the world still thinks of her on those youthful visits at Mrs. Thrale's in Streatham, when, if she seemed about to take her leave, Dr. Johnson would exclaim, "Don't you go, little Burney, don't you go!"

after E.F.Burney   Emery Walker, Ph.Sc.

Fanny Burney

VI

A BLUESTOCKING AT COURT

[The following is endorsed: "Miss P.'s Narrative of the causes leading to the celebrated Miss Burney's retirement from Court in the year 1791."]

THE intention of this narrative of Miss Burney's later residence at the Court of Their Majesties King George the Third and Queen Charlotte is simple. I am informed that reports spread among her friends have given birth to the notion that she was harshly treated, her genius slighted, and herself subjected to an odious tyranny from Mrs Schwellenberg, the Keeper of the Robes, and that she fled from the scene of such cruelties as the only means of preserving her health and life. As an eyewitness, I may be permitted to set forth another view which, though uncoloured by the rosy or lurid hues of the genius of the author of "Evelina," may be received as a plain account of what took place, especially with regard to the Honourable Colonel Digby and the causes of the lady's quitting the circle of the attendants on Royalty. These humble notes will not appear to the world until all concerned are reposing in the dust of the tomb.

I had the distinction to be early made privy to Miss Burney's intention to resign her appointment; but this less from any wish of her own, than as I concluded from my own observation. She did not suspect this, nor that the Queen's ready penetration had

prepared her also for the coming resignation before
it was respectfully laid at her feet.   Indeed, much of
what follows she was a total stranger to, and might
have found it difficult to credit had it been known to
her.

It was the custom that, while Her Majesty's head
was powdering and her powdering-gown had been
placed upon the Royal person, she should be left *sola*
with her *friseur*, when she usually read the news-
papers.   On a certain day, however, she despatched
Miss Burney for me, adding that she need not return;
and when I arrived, addressed me as follows — the
man not comprehending what was said : —

"There is a little matter which I have wished to
open with you.   I have some reason to believe Miss
Burney's spirits a little sunk.   Do you, Miss P., remark any failure in this respect?"

Her Majesty, all sweetness and benignity, fixed her
eyes on me as well as the operation she was under-
going would permit (the man casting clouds of powder
about her), and awaited my reply.   Much embar-
rassed, for it is the first rule of courts to make no comment on the affairs of others to the ear of Royalty, I
stammered a few words, to the effect that I thought
Miss Burney imagined her health a little declined,
but could offer no opinion of my own.

"She is a lady," continued the Queen, "no longer
in her first youth, who has been accustomed to much
adulation in her own circle, and may miss that in-
cense."

I murmured that it might be supposed the dignity

of a life in the Royal service — but was gently interrupted : —

"No. We have neither the time nor the inclination to make the Court a Bluestocking circle, and Miss Burney may prefer such surroundings. But, why I address you, my good Miss P., is to enquire whether Miss Burney has made any observation, of course not confidential, which would lead you to suppose her unsettled in her intentions?"

I believed that I realised Her Majesty's views. She would probably prefer that the severance should come from herself and not from the lower quarter. Alas, how little did I do justice to the benevolence of her character! I hurriedly replied that I knew nothing of Miss B.'s mind further than all the world might know, and within myself earnestly wished Her Majesty might turn the subject of her remarks. She, however, thought proper to continue with a mingled dignity and sweetness which distinguishes all she utters.

"All this is spoke in a confidence which must not be broke. But if there were any little agitation of the affections which —"

Here the Royal speaker was herself interrupted by a cloud of powder which the unconscious *friseur* flung over the edifice then erecting. It gave me a moment for hasty reflection. Impossible ! — who could suppose that Her Majesty, in whose presence every look was restrained, every word calculated, could have remarked the preference by which I had long known Miss Burney distinguished Colonel Digby? He, in the first anguish of bereavement of a lovely and beloved partner, did undoubtedly seek Miss Burney's sympathy. So much was visible to all. There was even a certain luxury of grief, — a heightening of the loss, — which gave his very handsome and attractive person an interest few could resist. Many indeed might have been ready for the tender office of consolatrix, but it was Miss Burney who was specially chosen, and the conviction formed in my own mind that the sympathy she so feelingly tendered was not untinged by a rosy flush of expectation. The caution incident to life at Court hindered my breathing so delicate a suspicion to any, and that Her Majesty's calm but piercing eye should have discerned any preference did indeed animate my soul with astonishment.

"Ma'am, your Majesty's observation so far exceeds my own poor powers," said I fluttering, "that, while it is impossible for me to deny, it is equally impossible for me to confirm it. Miss Burney's superior talents, her reserve, constitute a barrier which — "

"I know — I knew," interrupted the Queen, "that I could not expect any confirmation from you. You are discretion itself. I am surrounded by discretion. We will not now pursue the subject further. Will you oblige me, my good Miss P., by preparing the pocket-case which I give Lady Harcourt today."

The hint was an order. I respectfully retired at once, leaving Her Majesty almost concealed in the cloud of powder which was casting about her headdress.

Any little unusual occurrence at Court causes comment, and I was obliged to meet the questioning gaze
of the ladies in attendance with composure. I mentioned that Her Majesty had given me directions
about Lady Harcourt's pocket-case, and said no more.
Miss Burney followed me to the room where it was
laid out in readiness for wrapping — a trifle of extreme elegance, pink satin spangled with silver and
fitted with all the little furniture of gold scissors,
bodkins, thimble, and so forth, which the venerated
friend might accept as a compliment both royal and
affectionate. Miss Burney admired it with me.

"It resembles that formerly given to sweet Mrs
Delany," said she. "Dear excellence — sweet heavenly angel departed to her kindred sphere! What
wonder that Their Majesties' discernment should
single her out for the veneration due to age and piety
so unaffected. She is gone, but how will this gift
presented to the equally worthy Lady Harcourt bring
the tear to her eye and the almost pang of gratitude
to her bosom!"

I made an appropriate reply, but reflected. These
gushes of feeling on the part of Miss Burney sometimes appeared to me a little overwrought and de-
signed to conceal a sharpness of wit and observation
which she feared to exercise in courtly circles. In
this resolve she was doubtless discreet, but it gave
her conversation a turn of unreality which impressed
as might the use of some perfume of Araby to conceal
a less romantic odour. It affected my own candour
disagreeably. Possibly the praise received by the

author of "Evelina" might cause her to abandon the
common modes of conversation and talk literary, if
I may so express it; but it was, to my knowledge, a
great disappointment to the Queen, who loved good
talk and in her position could expect but little of it.
She had formed great hopes of the wit and originality
of Miss Burney, and was always met only by a sentimental silence, coupled with an affected modesty
which promised nothing fresh. Her reading-aloud
was also not of a high order, and her slender knowledge of books, apart from her own, astonished the
hopeful Queen, who had looked forward to much
pleasing entertainment in her company.

There were also other difficulties. Miss Burney's
extreme sensitiveness to her own dignity operated as
a hindrance to herself as well as her friends. Never
can I forget her expression on hearing that a bell
was to be the means of her summons to attend her
Royal Mistress. She was ever ready to anticipate a
slight; and that I may not be supposed malicious
in this statement, I will cite what was said by her old
friend, the brilliant Mrs Thrale-Piozzi on this circumstance : —

"I live with her in a degree of pain which pre-
cludes friendship — dare not ask her to buy me a
ribbon — dare not desire her to touch the bell, lest
she should think herself slighted."

It can readily be imagined that slights would in
such a case be imagined where none were intended.

It was a habit Miss Burney encouraged in herself
to use the longest words to express the simplest opin-

ions. Colonel Manners, who laughed at all and everyone, declared she had made the illustrious Dr Johnson her model, and would slyly note down some of her most flowing periods to deliver them, enhanced by humour, when she had left the room. I mean only to imply that she chose the *corporeal* style of the famous Doctor without acquiring the zest and gusto of that great man.

But this is to digress.

"The equerries will attend us at tea today, Miss P.," she observed. "Colonel Manners and Colonel Digby will be present and Mr de la Giffardière. Colonel Digby's spirits depend much upon female support and sustentation. He loves to contemplate the melancholy aspects in a way which cannot but be harmful to a character so feeling."

I replied collectedly : —

"Colonel Digby owes much to Miss Burney for all the consolations of literature and religion so charitably offered. But indeed who would not sympathise with his bereavement of a partner so lovely that, should he ever think of replacing her, beauty of the first order must be his object."

This was perhaps a little pointed, but I could never agree in Dr Johnson's estimate of her as "Pretty Burney," and she was not reckoned a pretty woman by others. She had not the graces of height nor elegance in movement, and might in complexion be called a brown woman. The eyes, while expressive, were decidedly green. If I add that she slightly stooped, though by no means sufficiently to be a deformity, and that her features were, on the whole, pleasing, I have been honest in my description.

While we were speaking, the Princess Royal entered, fresh and bright as the day, to inspect the case and add to it her own little tribute, a posy of beautiful satin flowers made by her own fair hands. This she attached to the case.

"I really think it very pretty," she said, adding in the most winning manner, "I hope Miss Burney and Miss P. approve it. Princess Elizabeth's gift is a fairing from Cheltenham — a most elegant little box, containing a bottle of rose perfume which came to mama from India, in the great box from the Bengal Nabob."

This would add interest to the gift, these bottles consisting of a minute tube of the precious oil of roses, enclosed, as it were, in a thick tube of embossed glass, ornamented with gold and sealed. Each of the lovely Princesses now brought her gift, and each spoke with us with the most conciliatory softness. Princess Elizabeth said laughing : —

"How go the equerries' teas, Miss Burney? Do they still insist on their right to wait on you, even when Mrs Schwellenberg is present?"

Miss Burney curtseyed, a little out of countenance. I put in my word : —

"Why, Ma'am, they are very constant. We have much entertainment from Colonel Manners and Mr de la Giffardière — especially the latter."

"I can believe that," said she, laughing again. "His spirits grow more boisterous daily. Mama

says an hour of his company is like a walk in a high
wind. But you know how we all value and respect
him. What a contrast to poor Colonel Digby!"

"I imagine, Ma'am, that Colonel Digby too is re-
covering his spirits a little under our united kind
treatment. He was even observed in a melancholy
smile yesterday," said I.

Her Royal Highness smiled with a soft meaning
kindness on Miss Burney, whose eyes were fixed on
the floor. This convinced me, if I had needed conviction, that the Queen intended the allusion she had
made to Colonel Digby, and there had been a something in her tone, indescribable but audible, which
indicated disapproval. I considered myself that the
man had quite as much encouragement as he needed
if his intentions were serious. I could not make him
out. There were times when I saw a growing interest in Miss Burney, and he indeed haunted her
parlour; yet was I assured that in London he was as-
siduous in waiting on Miss Gunning — a young lady
with every advantage of fortune, beauty, and connection. I own the thought sometimes occurred to me
that he might be that most despicable of characters —
a male flirt. I had thoughts sometimes also of a
word of warning to Miss Burney, but was restrained
by fear of her displeasure.

Two days later Colonel Manners and Colonel
Digby waited on us to tea, Mr de la Giffardière following. Colonel Digby wore his Vice-Chamberlain's
uniform, being to wait on the Queen, and a very
handsome sight he made, adding all the advantages

of birth and breeding to extreme good looks. Miss Burney, with a pleasure she could not conceal, found the conversation turn to "Evelina."   Colonel Manners praised it in his gay light-hearted way, and declared its special glory in his eyes to be the character of Captain Mirvan. He asserted it was that which gave rise to the suspicion that the author was a man, since a lady could scarcely be supposed capable of drawing a portrait of such vulgarity in such bold strokes. I now saw Miss Burney wavering whether to receive this as compliment or insult, when immediately Colonel Manners, whom no awe can check, broke out into Dibdin's song, applying it, as it were, to Captain Mirvan : —

> I 've a spanking wife at Portsmouth Gates,
>   A pigmy at Goree.
> An orange-tawny up the Straits,
>   A black at St. Lucie.
> Thus whatsomedever course I bend
>   I lead a jovial life —

Miss Burney rose indignantly, and the more so as Mr de la Giffardière, who could never resist the absurd, was applauding vehemently, and even Colonel Digby smiling. She cast one awful glance upon the offender, and was quitting the room, when Colonel Digby threw himself in front of the door.

"Miss Burney shall not deprive us of the happiness of her company without a word of entreaty," said he, fixing his eyes upon hers, "My friend Manners would be the first to deplore having offended the delicacy of any lady, and especially that lady whose genius created Captain Mirvan. But Miss Burney will condescend upon forgiveness when she hears he has been sharing His Majesty's barley water after a day's hunting. It always goes to his head with most boisterous results."

It was drolly said, indeed, though with his usual languor, and no other intervention would have stopped the exit. She graciously consented to return to her seat, and Colonel Manners immediately and absurdly fell on his knees before her, offering to kiss her shoe like the Pope's, if she would but pardon him.

"Alas, I was compelled to drink the barley water, Ma'am. I think it right to be civil to the King, though Heaven knows a violent drink like that is not what one should prefer after a hard day's hunting. I had chose something milder, had it been in my power."

She smiled faintly, and Colonel Digby, visibly to please her, uttered a very handsome praise of "Cecilia," specially dwelling on the chapter of the Opera Rehearsal. Her eyes followed his every movement. I perceived but too well the growing interest, and pitied the poor lady were her feelings to be deeply engaged; for I believed he turned his melancholy to as good account with others as with herself. I could not but note how his visits to her were made at times when he could almost count upon finding her alone. If his intentions were serious, all was well. Otherwise I could not approve it.

"Miss Burney is so evidently the Muse of Comedy," cried Mr de la Giffardière, "that I wonder you,

Manners, and you, Digby, do not fear her ironic pen. What if she record this scene in the third volume, for which all the world attends! There are only two persons who will emerge with grace — Miss P. and myself. We tread on awful ground with a lady so gifted."

Mrs Schwellenberg now made her appearance, and the talk changed, with Colonel Manners gravely enquiring after the health of her pet frogs, and the gentlemen shortly after left, a circumstance not very pleasing to her.

"What for they always — what you call — run away when I come?" she cried. "I like it not. Or if he stay, — that Colonel Manner, — he sleep! Sleeps he with you, Miss Burney? He sleep always with me. It is not to bear!"

We could not forbear laughing, and it was good-humouredly taken.

The cloud of fearful blackness which was to overshadow the nation soon broke upon us in His Majesty's illness. I had for some time suspicion that all was not well. It was his habit to talk with most condescending frankness to all whom he trusted, and I, as an old servant, had the happiness to be thus honoured. It could, therefore, be no secret to me that his mind was often agitated in the highest degree about public matters, and to my thinking had never recovered its tone since the disasters with regard to his American colonies. His outward fortitude was astonishing at the time of the rebellion; but it preyed inwardly and undoubtedly was the first and most galling link in the chain of misfortune which surrounded him from private and public sources. I have been told on high authority that the falling of the largest diamond from the Crown on the Coronation Day was a prognostic which His Majesty supposed awfully fulfilled when those rebellious colonies broke away from his sceptre.

It is not in my power, as it would not be my duty, to give an account of circumstances which involved the whole nation in mourning when it beheld the reason of its Monarch eclipsed. Be mine rather the female task to describe how it affected the celebrated lady who is the subject of these notes.

All then was confusion, and the habits of the Royal family so intermitted, whether at Windsor or Kew, that those attached to the household came and went as they pleased, although the strictest inquisition followed all that was allowed to pass outside the walls, lest reports adverse to His Majesty's health should reach the party of the Princes, his sons, who caught eagerly at any facts they might distort in a way to gain the Regency for the dissolute Prince of Wales, and cast the Queen completely into his power. It so happened that one day I was seated to my knotting behind the Japan screen in the parlour apportioned by the Prince to Her Majesty at Kew. My knotting had fallen on my knee as I gazed pensively at the prospect of oaks and beeches in all their verdure, when I heard voices, and Her Majesty and the Princess Royal entered, talking earnestly as if continuing a conversation.

"Mama, I do indeed think the news is true, and if so you will desire that we should soon give Colonel Digby joy. It is not absolutely certain —"

Here I stepped forth from behind the screen, curt-seying deeply. The notion in my mind was that Colonel D. had announced his coming engagement with Miss Burney. He had visited her sedulously during the King's illness, and, I might add, some-what in defiance of Her Majesty's hints to that lady, and had brought his little son more than once to visit her — a step which could not but appear very partic-ular.

The Queen saw me advance with her usual gracious composure, and the Princess greeted me charmingly. She wore a morning *négligée* embroidered all over with roses, and looked what she was — the Rose of England.

"You have appeared at an opportune moment, Miss P.," said Her Majesty. "The matter in hand is one where I rely on your discretion. Princess Royal, inform Miss P. of what you have heard."

She took her seat, and the sweet Princess, stand-ing behind her mother's chair, related to me with her own artless candour that she had heard, from a source which she did not give, though unimpeacha-ble, that an engagement subsisted or shortly might subsist between Colonel Digby and Miss Gunning, and she thought — she feared —

Here she hesitated in the most pleasing manner. I now fully understood, but it became me to remain silent and hear the Queen's pleasure. My beloved

Queen spoke presently and even — marvellous to
relate — with a touch of the gentle archness which so
adorned her before His Majesty's all-overshadowing
malady.   Her fortitude was astonishing.

"My good Miss P., you have heard the Princess
Royal, and I am full sure the announcement you expected was of a kind far nearer home.   Am I wrong?"

I hurriedly said I had indeed expected and hoped —
Her Majesty would pardon my confusion.   I scarce
knew what I was saying, for it rushed on my mind
that, if this were true, the effect on Miss Burney's
health and spirits might be serious — his attentions
having been so public.

"I have noticed and heard how frequent Colonel
Digby's visits to her have been," continued Her
Majesty; "and if this has reached me, it is certain
that others must have felt his attentions to be particular.   I cannot acquit him."

"Nor I, Ma'am," I cried eagerly, and interrupted
myself in such a breach of etiquette.   She proceeded
composedly : —

"I believe Colonel Digby is frequently with Miss
Burney.   You have the same impression, Princess
Royal?"

The fair Princess softly murmured that she had.
I could not but suspect Mrs Schwellenberg the in-
formant, nor yet blame her.   All must depend upon
the colouring given.

"Colonel Digby's confidential favour with us all
disappoints me the more in the course he has taken,"
continued the Queen.   "There has been a touch of

something insincere. And I have heard also that the poor Schwellenberg is left entirely to herself while these visits take place. I thought this hard and so dropped a hint to Miss Burney, which I failed not to see was resented. Have you, my good Miss P., observed anything of this?"

Catching the encouraging eye of the Princess, I ventured to say I was not wholly a stranger to the fact that Mrs Schwellenberg felt herself somewhat dropped out in these visits, so agreeable to the gentleman. Miss Burney I alluded not to.

"Another hint I offered," proceeded the Queen, "when my hair was dressing one night, and I was informed the Schwellenberg was very unwell and needed company, but found Miss Burney was engaged as usual with Colonel Digby. I asked Miss Burney, without leading up to the subject, whether he had been here. She coloured very high and admitted it and, on further questioning, displayed a knowledge of all his movements which I own surprised me, especially on her complaining of the want of variety here — a fact that made any visitor welcome, as she told me."

"Can it be possible, Ma'am," I cried, "that at this time of universal sorrow, Miss Burney should so far forget the cruel facts as to reproach —"

I was softly interrupted in my turn.

"I am far from blaming Miss Burney," said the amiable Queen. "It has been a time of gloom for all. I am only considering, from these circumstances and others I could name, how sharp and severe may be her disappointment when she hears the news which has reached the Princess Royal."

Such goodness did, I confess, moisten my eyes, for had I been the commentator, I might have been tempted to say that any little coquetries were misplaced at a time of national grief, and especially so in Miss Burney, whose extreme sensibility, somewhat paraded in words, was in its highest flight as regarded the King's health. Only that morning she had cried out: —

"What must be the guilt of that implacable country which, in breaking away from his mild majestic sway, sowed the seeds of the malady which reduced the best of kings and men to a condition where this fell disease could prey upon his overcharged heart and brain! Surely the blessing which disowns its present cannot attend its future!"

But this is a digression.

"What we are to consider, Miss P.," said the benignant Queen, "is how best to hint this news to Miss Burney so that her mind may be gradually accustomed. It is to be remembered that, in her confined home circle, she can have met but few so distinguished and eligible as Colonel Digby. I am perhaps not wholly free of blame from having introduced her to so new a sphere. I never contemplated that she would so soon liberate herself from the control of the Schwellenberg."

Gracious Powers! I, who had once accidentally heard Miss Burney term Mrs S. "Cerbera," could have told Her Majesty that Miss Burney was the last person in the world to permit Mrs S., or any other person in the world, to control her, as might appear by her rejoinders to Her Majesty herself.

"If," said the Princess, interposing with a gentle civility, "such a hint could be dropped to Miss Burney, it might spare her much pain. She is so gifted — so high-strung —"

"We leave it to your good heart," said the Queen. "We wish all that is good to Miss Burney. You will see I cannot commit it to the Schwellenberg. These literary ladies have high flights, I believe, and are a more fragile porcelain than ordinary folks. Do your best, my good Miss P., and I shall be well satisfied."

The Princess sweetly requested permission to retire with me and we were about to withdraw, when the Duchess of Ancaster entered, and the Queen informed her of Colonel Digby's supposed engagement. The Duchess laughed with all her own humour.

"What, Ma'am? Miss Gunning? No, surely Miss Burney! I am Miss Burney's advocate as regards her just rights and claims. Miss Gunning is but an interloper.

"I will wager that Miss Burney at last secures Colonel Digby, whatever his struggles. He is but a bird hovering a few inches above the charming serpent's jaws, which are open to receive him. I know not how our sex has ever acquired the reputation of flight, for it has ever appeared to me that apparent flight was but a feint to encourage pursuit not otherwise forthcoming. Believe me, Ma'am, that your Majesty will yet see Colonel Digby overtaken

and captured by the united arts of 'Evelina' and
'Cecilia.'"

"Come, Duchess," said Her Majesty, with the little
arch smile she sometimes wears; "you would not
have us believe the Duke made a very desperate race
of it, would you?"

"Indeed, Ma'am, I did my part as well as others,"
the kind Duchess said, laughing, "and but for my
efforts, who knows what indiscretion he might have
committed? Do but consider the late marriages
made by noble lords who shall be nameless! Miss
Burney probably is Colonel Digby's destined saviour,
or so believes herself."

So the lively lady rattled on, until I withdrew,
following the Princess.

"Pray do your best, Miss P.," she whispered softly
at the door. "I feel for poor Miss Burney — I do
indeed. Colonel Digby has been so particular in his
attentions. And her health is never strong."

She sighed as she glided off to join the Princess
Elizabeth for their sketching-lesson. Sure never was
such a bouquet of beauty and warm hearts as these
Royal sisters! I know not which I can distinguish
more than another, though perhaps the Princess
Royal is my pattern for all that is excellent and
sweet.

I took my doubting way to Miss Burney's parlour.
She was writing, as was her wont. If it were not
another novel, it must have been a daily mass of
information to her friends. In all she did seemed a
little mystery that promoted not the unreserve so

essential to friendship. Perhaps it might be a part of the profession of a writer of fiction; but it made itself felt.

She looked up smilingly.

"Pray take a seat, Miss P. I hope your gratifying entry is with good news of that precious health on which Britain hangs. I hear this black cloud begins to turn its silver edges."

I agreed, and she then spoke of cheerful details she had had from Lady Charlotte Finch. It appeared that there were now much longer intervals of rational quiet. He had alluded to public matters with a piety and reason the most exalted, which moved all who heard almost to tears. Oh, that those rebellious subjects beyond the ocean could have heard their Monarch! Yet why should this be my aspiration when there were rebels, and *filial ones*, close at hand, to rejoice in his misfortune!

I was about to reply when the door opened without knocking, and Colonel Digby glided in, with the words : —

"How does Miss Burney? May a friend, a friend of the faithfulest, enter to make his enquiries?"

He did not perceive me behind the opened door. Miss Burney blushed visibly, and instantly seeing me, he bowed with his own finished good-breeding and no sign of discomposure. I sat, as it were on thorns, until, Mr Smelt entering later, the talk became general and I retreated, more and more confused at the part expected of me, especially as Colonel Digby's manner appeared as softly ingratiating as ever. I felt I should be compelled to sink the truth a while longer and could only hope the Princess Royal misinformed.

The coolness between Miss Burney and Mrs Schwellenberg about this time began to be much warmed by many little kindnesses on the part of the latter as she observed Miss Burney's somewhat careworn brow. It has since been confided to me that the account given of her by Miss Burney to her friends was one of uncontrolled malignity; but though my testimony is humble, it is sincere, and I can describe Mrs Schwellenberg, apart from her acknowledged devotion to her Royal Mistress, as possessing a much more kindly heart than Miss Burney would consent to allow her. Her imperfect knowledge of English often did her an injustice and made it easy to be witty at her expense. While she thought she saw Miss Burney inflated with the pride of a caressed and flattered author, and rebelling at the necessary restrictions of court life, she certainly was watchful and sometimes disapproving; but in the time of trouble she opened out into an attention which Miss Burney's candour should have gratefully owned.

Time went on. Our beloved King recovered the use of his invaluable senses, thus escaping the snares set for him and the Queen by enemies the most difficult to subdue. This enabled us to return in triumph to Windsor — in triumph, do I say? No, but ecstasy — a kind of rapture which pervaded the whole nation, excepting the party of the Opposition.

The inhabitants of every place we passed flooded out to greet their King. The people, stirred as by an earthquake, broke upon him in a wave of loyalty; and we, who almost adored him for his private benignity and public virtues, seemed swept away in the torrent. As for the Queen, what joy sat upon her sweet but wearied countenance, as she turned her eyes, swimming in tears, upon him who was the centre of all rejoicing!

I never came so near loving Miss Burney as when one day, in walking with Her Majesty's little dogs, Badine and Phillis, in the Park, she broke out into feelings warmly expressed of her sense of what the Queen's conduct had been during the scenes of agony we had witnessed. For once she forgot herself nobly, and I shall never forget her countenance as she paused and said : —

"Indeed, Miss P., when I consider Her Majesty's complicated suffering, — increased as it was to misery by attacks from quarters whence only love and duty might have been expected, harassed by politics and cabals, torn by national and foreign dissension, herself deprived of all protection, and yet protecting with almost masculine fortitude a beloved husband and King, — I say with all my heart that to have attained such heights of courage, resignation, and ability, is much, much more than to be Queen of England, or possessed of the most shining genius the world has known. I bow the knee in spirit as in body before a Mistress so truly Royal."

The generous fire in her voice was quenched by the

tears in her eyes.   I grasped her hand, but could not reply.   Here was indeed the cry of sincerity.   We walked pensively for some time in the shrubberies, and ended our airing on the great terrace.

How exquisitely pastoral, yet soul-stirring, is the view from that majestic height!   The towers of Windsor Castle behind us breathing of the historic past; the Thames unrolling its silver windings below; the meadows;   the roofs of Eton College lifting through the veil of foliage — can aught on earth surpass it?   A distant sound of cheering from the Eton playing-fields reached us, to announce that some young votary of athletic games had reached his goal.   Over all floated the sunshine.   Why seek foreign shores for recreation which these sylvan bowers, so richly charged with memories of departed greatness, afford to all?

A quick step on the gravel roused me from these thoughts and, turning, I saw Colonel Digby proceeding quickly to the Queen's Lodge.   To my astonishment he only bowed hurriedly and went on his way without a word.   Miss Burney looked the amazement she naturally felt; and it flashed across my mind that here might be the long-sought opportunity.   I seized it with a beating heart.

"We have seen but little of Colonel Digby since the King's recovery," said I.

"Oh," she replied nervously, "you know the King's attachment to him, and also the Queen's; they impose on him many important errands to London. We cannot expect — I should be the last — "

She paused.

"He has many friends in London," I ventured.

"Certainly. A disposition so generous, affectionate, and kind must be entitled to all the blessings of friendship."

"And even warmer sentiments —" I hesitated.

She turned her face from me, but I could see the perturbation. I would not for the world that she should misconceive me then. Though feeling to the full the difficulty of my position, I tried to turn it lightly.

"There is one fair lady in London who is said to have a warmer interest in His Majesty's recovery, since it enables Colonel Digby to be more constant in his attendance."

There was a moment's silence.

"You allude to Miss Gunning," she replied coldly. "On the few occasions I have seen her I have thought her so cool in her likings and sentiments, so self-sufficient, that I could not think her attractive to a nature so warm as Colonel Digby's. Nor do I think her mental attainments such as to render a real friendship possible between them."

"It is difficult," I breathed, "to name the qualities which attract the other sex. But I have heard certain rumours to the effect that Colonel Digby finds Miss Gunning attractive."

She flashed her eyes on me with a kind of indignant scorn, as if suspecting some meaner motive in what I said, and coolly consulted her watch.

"I too have heard those rumours and their denial.

We must return, though I am loath to quit this enchanting scene.   Shall I leave you, or shall we return together?"

We walked in silence, I feeling I had miserably failed in my commission, and she discoursing of the national fêtes in prospect, in a way which bespoke her hurry of spirits.

A few days later, Colonel Gwynn came into waiting, and told us Colonel Digby was taken ill in London and could not hope to resume his duties for some time. I saw the concern on Miss Burney's face.   We all shared it in a measure but, alas, her pallor showed but too well how deep the shaft had pierced.

I was present that evening when she was in attendance on the Queen.   Her Majesty, rousing herself from thought, said somewhat abruptly: —

"I am much displeased with Colonel Digby" (instancing her reasons and adding): "He will not come here.   He has set his mind against coming. For some reason he cannot bear it.   He has been in London in perfect health, and I have it on good authority that he desired it might not be told here."

I dared scarcely glance at Miss Burney.   She was perfectly white and stood with her eyes fixed on the ground.   The Queen, seeing she had alarmed us, glided with her benignant grace into another subject. I, who knew her mind, could perceive what was intended; but to Miss Burney it must have been a thunderbolt.

Next morning the Princess Royal, coming to my room, lovely in her flowered sacque, and without her hoop, her curls twisted with rose-hued ribbons, seemed to cast a radiance before her. She paused at the door, and said condescendingly: "May I come in?"

I hastened to set her a chair, and after a little indifferent discourse she said with a touch of melancholy: —

"I think Miss Burney has not been fairly treated. It is the Queen's opinion that Colonel Digby's conscience prevents his coming hither. We are to offer our formal congratulations to him and Miss Gunning at the Drawing-Room. I own I shall present mine with very little heart. Do you not think, Miss P., that the poor lady should be told the truth? It might come as a shock, but would be best from a friend like yourself. If all else failed, I would gladly do it. But indeed, I dare not."

I implored Her Royal Highness not to put herself out. I would be the messenger.

"That Miss Burney should have been given any pain under our roof, and by one connected with our service, is very painful to mama, who fully values Miss Burney's gifts of the mind," added the beloved Princess. "If it is to be done, however, there is no time like the present, for the news is now very generally known."

She left me, and with a trembling step I rose to seek Miss Burney's room. She was seated by the window, a large black hat with ostrich plumes shading her face, and a muslin handkerchief folded across the bosom. I had never seen her look so becoming.

She was then thirty-seven or-eight years of age, as I
have since learned (for that was then a carefully
guarded secret), but did not look near so much;
and her expression, intensely absorbed, had the
pensive sweetness of a day in autumn ere the golden
leaf yet flutters to its fall.

"Miss Burney," I said timidly, "I believe I intrude, but may I ask you to favour me with the copy
of verses you made for Her Majesty on 'The Great
Coat.'"

This was graciously granted, and a seat offered.
A light conversation ensued, and at last, summoning
my resolution, I said : —

"We are soon to congratulate an old friend on his
approaching nuptials.   Colonel Digby —"

She turned angrily, but restrained herself with a
distressing effort.   I continued : "I hear his engagement with Miss Gunning is confirmed."

"I too have heard it," she said haughtily; "I am
therefore no stranger to your news."

She half rose, and taking the hint I hurried away,
confident that she believed me not at all.   I met the
Princess Royal with Princess Augusta on my way,
and they stopped me eagerly.

"Did you succeed, Miss P.?" asked each fair
sister, with such sympathising faces as made me love
them the better, if that were possible.   The elder
Princess shook her head sadly.

"Poor, poor lady!   I fear he is a very heartless
man.   I cannot easily forgive this treatment of one
we esteem."

She linked her arm in her sister's, and the two hurried away to attend the Queen, who was to consider their Drawing-Room robes just then inspecting.

Willingly would I have softened the blow, but fall at length it must! After the Drawing-Room, it became known to Miss Burney that Miss Gunning had attended and had been given joy by all the Princesses. The Princess Royal herself breathed this, with a voice like a dove and her eyes considerately averted, adding: —

"Miss Gunning was most elegant in a dress of purple gauze and silver; but I cannot think her beautiful, though some find her manners pleasing. Colonel Digby was not present."

There was a pause and then Miss Burney, deplorably pale, replied: —

"I had already heard this, Ma'am. I believe she is thought handsome. The Drawing-Room must have been particularly elegant from the rejoicing crowds who would wish to pay their duty."

No more was said on the subject. Later, she complained of headache to me, and I, breathing it into the sympathising ear of Her Royal Highness, Miss Burney was recommended, nay, commanded to return to her room, and the truly amiable Queen dispensed with her attendance.

The marriage took place in due course, and in a private house, a circumstance which met with Her Majesty's warm disapproval, as considering that a contract so solemn needs all the blessing and ratification imposed at such times by the church's ordinance.

During all this time, Colonel Digby did not appear at Court, though whether by his own choice or the kind concern of Her Majesty, I cannot tell. Miss Burney visibly drooped — I could see suffering written on her face, and it awoke a sympathy which I dared not offer. The Queen's consideration for her increased, and the lovely Princesses avoided with true delicacy every subject which could recall the image of the past, making what soft amends lay in their power.

Yet but a very short while after, will it be believed that Colonel Digby sent his bride to call upon Miss Burney, having himself resumed attendance upon the Court immediately after his marriage! I sincerely felt for Miss Burney when a bustle was heard and before us there appeared the bride, glowing in health and happiness, and dressed in the last perfection of the milliner's art. Triumph, visible and exultant, sat on her brow; and as she took her place on the sofa by Miss Burney, who looked wan and aged beside so much splendour, I felt it would have declared a better heart had she deferred her visit. Miss Burney, with an effort of courage, parried all the speeches which could hardly fail to have the appearance of thrusts, and undertook to deliver the bride's duty to the Queen with a calmness which did her honour.

I have more than once in my life seen reason to congratulate myself on passing through life untroubled by the attentions of that sex which, while the blessing, is also the curse of our own, and felt this with peculiar energy during that scene, when I saw one so justly celebrated, triumphed over almost publicly by a young lady whose face was her chief recommendation.

I concluded that we should soon now lose Miss Burney and could not harshly censure (though disapproving) the course she took in attributing her waning health to the tyranny of Mrs Schwellenberg and even to the hardships of her attendance on the Queen. Nevertheless, Her Majesty more than once favoured me with the remark : —

"Large allowance must be made for Miss Burney. I foresee she will before long wish to be among the healing influences of her own home circle; and as I would not for the world dismiss her, all must be done on the foot she herself chooses, and with reluctance on my part. I know her good sense will dictate a commendable course."

Of this I was by no means certain, but could, of course, make no rejoinder; and Her Majesty's face, beneath her becoming fly-cap, beamed with a true benevolence as she pronounced these words. I have certain knowledge that she favoured Mrs Schwellenberg also with this injunction, and that she also exerted herself to show many little pleasing attentions on our return to Windsor. It was that day Miss Burney came in, with an animation to which she had long been a stranger, to say she had met Mr Boswell — friend and survivor of the Great Lexicographer — near St. George's Chapel, on his way to view the alterations, and he had arrested her steps.

"It was like a breath of fresh air in a shut room!"
she cried; "and indeed almost too much for my
weak health. 'O Ma'am,' he said with energy,
'when do you return to us? You must resign —
you must indeed. It won't do, Ma'am. We can
put up with it no longer!' I laughed and stared,
but he continued: 'We shall address Dr Burney
in a body. It was so resolved at the Club last week
— Charles Fox in the chair. I need your aid in my
book on the Great Man, soon to appear. You are to
lighten the picture. In my hands he is grave Sam,
great Sam, learned Sam. With your aid we will
deck him with all the graces. He shall be gay Sam,
agreeable Sam, and, to that end, I claim all the little
pleasing billets he has written to your fair self.' So
he rattled on, and I could with difficulty extricate
myself. But, O Miss P., though your goodness will
not repeat the scene, it was such a view of home and
its surroundings as may greet the returning sailor
when his country rises on his view."

I sympathised and venturesomely said : —

"I would not presume to counsel, Miss Burney,
but if you so crave for your family and friends, were
it not well to seek their healing company? None
can doubt that your health suffers under the restraints
of court life, and Miss Burney's is a health valuable
to the world at large."

I ever found that a little well-turned compliment
softened her sense of injury. She smiled gratefully
upon me and was silent; then softly pressed my
hand.

I related this little scene to the tender-hearted Princess Royal who took the pains to make an opportunity with Miss Burney, when we were in attendance for that walk on the Windsor Terrace which so often presented the Royal Family to the view of a delighted people. The procession was not yet formed, Their Majesties not having appeared. She detached herself from her group of sweet sisters, holding the little darling Princess Amelia by the hand, and said: —

"Are you fit for the walk, Miss Burney? You appear tired and unwell. Permit me to make your excuses to the Queen."

She paused, and Miss Burney warmly thanked her and said tremblingly that she believed she could support herself through the walk.

"But why?" exclaimed Her Royal Highness. "Indeed, we are not such tyrants, and allow me to say, my dear Miss Burney, that if you should feel — should think you need a long rest — *a releasing* rest, there need be no hesitation in mentioning it to the Queen."

She repeated this with emphasis and glided away. I saw Miss Burney's eyes moisten as she turned and retreated.

Events now succeeded each other slowly but surely. The Queen had with reluctance accepted her resignation, the successor had been found, and the time drew near for departure when, most unexpectedly, my whole view was changed with regard to Miss Burney's feelings.

We were walking in the Park on a fine sunny day, having chosen the Long Walk which leads to the eminence and its noble prospect of the Castle, though scarcely with hope of reaching it so slow were our footsteps. I had led the talk to her writings and she gave me some interesting particulars of the praise "Evelina" had received from such judges as Mrs Delany and the Duchess of Portland, who agreed in thinking it a book likely to do more good than any other ever published, from its high principles wrapped in a glitter of entertainment. This was a subject on which she never wearied, and I was pressing for its continuance, when we beheld a lady approaching, leaning on a gentleman's arm — a handsome woman in a rich pelerine and jewellery — and with a start my companion caught my arm, crying softly: "Mrs Thrale — Mrs Piozzi. Good heavens! For years we have not met. Oh, could we escape."

I was no stranger to the fact that they had been the closest friends and that Mrs Thrale's most injudicious marriage with a Roman Catholic and a foreigner had ruptured the friendship on Miss Burney's very proper objection to such an alliance. It is known how society, how even the papers, rung with the scandal of a lady of birth and fortune thus forgetting what was due to herself and others. And a fresh blaze had lately been kindled by the publication of Dr Johnson's Letters and many anecdotes relative to the life at Streatham, all of which Miss Burney had entirely disapproved. I could not sympathise with Mrs Thrale-Piozzi — impossible that any right-minded person should, but I own to the deepest curiosity to see her, and above all to witness her meeting with this discarded friend, having understood from my own friends that feeling run very high between them. Consequently I did not hurry my steps.

"For Heaven's sake, hasten!" cried Miss Burney. "'T is Mr Piozzi himself. Was ever anything so mortifying!"

Unfortunately Mrs Piozzi heard these words and recognised the speaker.

"Mortify not yourself, Miss Burney, I entreat. Mr Piozzi is obliged to hasten into Windsor to bespeak apartments at the White Hart. Delay not, Piozzi. I will follow. Do I see my Burney in good health?"

I was never so affrighted in my life. The lady, though short, had such an air of resolution and her eyes shot such lively sparks of anger hid under a show of good humour that I looked to see Miss Burney sink at my feet. She also was in a horrid fright if panting breath and fading cheeks may be trusted. I would now have fled but she detained me by the hand and presented me to a sweeping curtsey from Mrs Piozzi. Doubtless she thought my presence would confine the meeting to the forms of politeness.

Accustomed to courts, I could not consider the lady high-bred, but her energy and intelligence were overpowering.

"I have not seen you since my return, dear Burney," says she, "but am glad of this favourable

opportunity to ask if what I have been told is true —
that Baretti was inspired and abetted in his attack
on my marriage by friends I could the least suspect.
Pray emulate my candour.   An open enemy is preferable to a stabbing friend."

"Surely, Madam, before a third person —" began
Miss Burney, but was interrupted : —

"I have learnt to know a witness is very valuable
on occasion.   All I require is a plain 'Yes' or 'No.'"

"Then 'No' — a thousand times 'No,'" cried Miss
Burney with immense spirit.   "I know nothing of
Baretti — would know nothing — a violent unprin-
cipled man, that frightened myself.   That I disapproved your marriage is known —"

"And on what impertinent grounds !"   Mrs Piozzi
was now trembling with rage — and as pale as Miss
Burney.   "Let me tell you, Madam, that a gentleman of good birth is not to be despised, and his means
of £1200 per annum, though not splendour in comparison with my own revenue, set him above all
mercenary imputation !"

'T was with the greatest effort my companion now
clung to her cautious decorum, for she was palpitating
violently as she held to my arm.

"Madam, money was not in question.   A woman
who will marry a foreigner and a Roman Catholic, in
both respects her country's foe, must expect —"

I looked for an explosion but, as happens when
women quarrel, Mrs Piozzi's humour took the most
unexpected turn.   She laughed : —

"Ah, Fanny, Fanny, that was the world's voice.

Time was you loved me kindly; but the world you always did and will love reverentially. Well — continue! — 't is worth it. The world has its prizes to give and I have none now. I did not even provide a husband for my friend, and your Royals have not been more successful — I know not why. The day may come when you yourself may fall back on a foreigner and Roman Catholic, and, if so, may he be as good as mine and may you live as happy with him!"

She curtseyed and made to move on. I thought of this later when Miss Burney married M. D'Arblay, a Frenchman and Roman Catholic. I wondered then if she recalled this scene and her own strictures. She bridled with dignity.

"I can scarce imagine Dr Burney's daughter doing the like, Madam. My tastes are all English. But is it well to prolong this talk? Our ways of life are now so different —"

"Truly all is changed — and you with it. But I was ever a prophet, Fanny, and I venture to tell you that you have so overloaded your heart and your wits with caution and fear of the world's opinion that when you take pen in hand once more you 'll find it clogged and heavy. 'T will move on stilts instead of the light heels that danced 'Evelina,' and the ungrateful world will say, 'There goes a woman that if she had shut her eyes on forms and opened them on nature had been the glory of her age.' You are too fearful of the world, Fanny. I flew in its face and found its bark worse than its bite, and that if you kicked it, it crawled to kiss your feet. And so now good-bye."

They both curtseyed angrily, and Mrs Piozzi proceeded quickly down the drive, then suddenly turned and ran back, both hands outstretched : —

"Fanny, Fanny, I can't —" she panted. "It all so rose on me with the sight of you. My master at the table, and Johnson in his chair booming out his wisdoms, and Burke, and poor Goldie — Oh, the poor dead days — the sad dead days — and you a part of them all; and could I say a word to wound you, no matter what you did to me! You that were a part of it all — I felt as if I would kill it outright if I left you in anger. Can one kill ghosts? — they are but ghosts, and yet — Oh, Fanny !"

She held out her shaking hands. I knew this shockingly disordered Miss Burney's notions of propriety and that a lady out of favour with the great world should be seen by me thus familiar with her, and she at Court. She barely touched the hand.

"It was to the memory of those days your friends looked to keep you in a becoming path," said she. "Indeed I share your affection for them, but to remember them thus —"

"Do you so?" says the other a little wildly, and drawing back to dash the tears from her eyes. "Then remember them your way and I 'll remember them mine, and so our paths go east and west : (then turning to me,) I 'm sure I ask your pardon, Ma'am, for what must appear so declamatory and high-flown. We Welsh folk, like all the other poor Celts, are

allowed romantic flights sometimes to make sport
for the sober English. Farewell, Miss Burney. My
best compliments and respects attend your father."

She ran off again very quick and tripping. We
stood looking after her till Miss Burney spoke: —

"The tenderness I had and have for her is not to be
expressed nor compared save with the love of David
for Jonathan. How have I been wounded! Yourself, my dear Miss P., is a witness to her ungoverned
passions. Your delicacy will not prefer to entail the
misery of explanation on me."

I hurriedly disclaimed any wish to pursue the subject, and she was silent as if revolving the scene.
But why should I now hesitate to own that though
all the propriety of speech and silence had been on
Miss Burney's side, my own sympathies were engaged with the poor lady. I thought a heart that
less weighed opinion must have melted at her appeal
to fond memories, gushing warm from a sensibility
that she could not control. Since that interview,
when I have heard Mrs. Piozzi censured I could comprehend the high romantic notion with which she
had entered on her marriage, and the more so, since
I had been credibly informed that Mr Piozzi was
in all respects admirable could he but have had the
blessing to be born an Englishman and Protestant.

"Dear Miss P., I trust to you to keep this painful
meeting a secret," said my companion. "I know
your serious and respectable character too well to
doubt you will draw the veil over the wild ungoverned temper of one once so honoured."

I promised and reserved my thoughts and we turned back to the Castle. But the events of this astonishing walk were not yet at an end. We were nearing the gates of the gardens, when we saw Colonel and Mrs Digby beneath the trees on the further side. They were not conversing and the whole width of the path was between them. It gave rightly or wrongly an air of dissatisfaction, of weariness in each other's company, that struck me as instantly as it did my companion, though of course it could be no surprise to see them where all the Household took their airings when they would. She drew me sharply behind a tree.

"Miss P.," she said in breathless agitation, "it is not the least of my sufferings here that I know it is supposed they are caused by this marriage. I beg you would not deny it (for I would have spoken) — it is too palpable that this is believed. Yet you are wrong — completely wrong. Those who have ceased to give us pleasure very soon lose the power to give us pain; and I view his marriage with an indifference that wishes him neither well nor ill. My heart was never engaged. I will not deny that he risked it and all my peace with it, but he succeeded not. I do not form one wish to be in her place whom we have just seen. They will have what happiness they deserve and, if I am not mistaken, I think it will be little indeed."

She turned and gazed after them with an expression of bitterness the most concentrated. Never again did I doubt that it was not wounded love but

wounded pride which was driving her from Court
into the retirement of her home.   Let others more
capable than myself judge which is the severer pang !
She had never regarded him further than as he had
flattered her vanity as woman and genius, and a
burning resentment at the public slight was all that
needed commiseration.

She added composedly : —

"Your kindness deserved this explanation and will
accept it.   There is no man on earth so indifferent to
me as Colonel Digby, and later events will prove to
you that I speak the truth."

I said I could but rejoice to hear it, and we returned from these agitations to her room.

All this confirmed the opinion I held that she
was naturally a person of agreeable disposition but
spoiled by her literary success.   I never doubted that
her acceptance of Court office was with a view to a
brilliant establishment such as she had given her own
"Evelina."   She was as much her own heroine and
hoped for as romantic advancement, very sensibly
preferring a social triumph, could it be secured, to a
mere literary one, which she always took a little
doubtfully as somewhat that might be disparaged.
Disappointed, and openly disappointed, in this hope
by the heartless behaviour of Colonel Digby, she felt
retreat to be inevitable and also the only hope for a
future settlement.   Yet had she been wiser to remain !   I have ever been convinced that her taste
for the pen was gone by and that only the narrowness
of her means drove her to it again.   At Court she

would have been valuable from a natural caution
which received a fresh lesson in this foiled love-affair.
When I add that Mrs Schwellenberg offered her the
reversion of her own place when ill health should
cause her retirement and that I know this would have
been confirmed, it will be seen what she most im-
prudently sacrificed to sentiment.

It will be objected that marriage was her object.
If so, there were opportunities at Court she could not
have elsewhere, and among the grave clergy who attended, a suitable settlement might have been found.
Miss Burney, as the lady of a Bishop, dispensing a
serious hospitality and amending his Charges to his
clergy, would have been in her right place.   I am
told that her later manner of writing was far more
suited to Episcopality than to fiction, and can answer
that when reading her "Memoirs" of her father I
was unable to trace the sense through the verbiage,
which appears to confirm this view.   But it was not
to be, though I believe from the eagerness with which
she ever visited the Royals and took every opportunity to keep her name in sight, that she regretted
her folly and would have repaired it.   But how was it
possible for Their Majesties to assist a needy Frenchman and Roman Catholic?

In her final parting with her Mistress she received
much kind notice, including permission to retain half
her emolument as a pension — and this after but five
years' service!

The sweet Princesses successively pressed her hand
at the parting scene and she quitted the room with

her handkerchief at her eyes and a profound final curtsey. The Princess Royal whispered aside to me : —

"Poor soul, she might have made others happier but for the cruel wound her heart has received. I cannot — cannot forgive Colonel Digby!"

The gay and pretty Princess Elizabeth, much livelier in disposition, leaned on her sister's shoulder, whispering also : —

"I think, sister, that Miss Burney will not always be inconsolable, for at the trial of Mr Warren Hastings the Duchess of Ancaster observed that Mr Wyndham was very particular in his attentions to Miss Burney and that she did by no means *froisser* them. And have you not thought that she will certainly meet him much oftener in town than here?"

I could but smile at the young discerner whose thoughts agreed so fully with my own. For some time after she would ask me merrily what news of Mr Wyndham, and I certainly expected it. However that was not to be, and my expectations were verified next year by Miss Burney's marriage — a truly amazing one — even to M. D'Arblay, a refugee Frenchman and Roman Catholic!

Would that I could have heard Mrs Thrale-Piozzi's views on this circumstance!

Here I end. I design these notes as a strong corrective of what might place the Queen and others of less moment in an unamiable light. Let it be remembered that Miss Burney was the spoiled child of genius, who would still be first and who throbbingly aspired to a social eminence denied her. She received all attentions from the Royal Family as her due, and knew not how to draw the distinction between what was due to her own merit and what was given by these personages as due to their *own* high standard of courtesy and compassion. This is a distinction seldom drawn by those unused to high circles and a mere literary society cannot teach it.

I have often desired that I could have had the honour to be admitted to Her Majesty's private thoughts on Miss Burney, and should not be wholly surprised if they favoured my own.

No doubt allowance may be made for the vagaries of genius, but none the less do I rejoice that this, my first meeting with uncommon talent, was also the last. It is entirely out of place in courts, and certainly a happy mediocrity is the soil in which flourish the domestic virtues.

Though I defend not Colonel Digby it is possible he showed his judgment if not his delicacy in his retreat, it being very difficult for him or any man to preserve in Miss Burney's company that sense of superiority which is so essential to matrimonial peace. There was that in her eye which, if suddenly surprised, indicated satire; there was that in her demeanour which hinted depths which might or might not be soothing. To be candid, what we do not understand is feared rather than loved. And it is to the author of "Evelina" I owe this conviction.

Peace be with her manes when what I have so doubtfully written shall be read!

THE DARCYS OF ROSINGS

ELIZABETH BENNET

Mrs. DARCY

"I MUST confess," observed Jane Austen, when Elizabeth Bennet, who had been created in 1796, was at last introduced to the world of readers in 1812, "I must confess that I think her as delightful a creature as ever appeared in print, and how I shall be able to tolerate those who do not like *her* at least, I do not know."

Miss Austen had the whimsical habit of diverting herself, when visiting portrait galleries, by looking for faces that resembled those of her heroines. She was continually on the watch for Elizabeth, but never came upon her. She found Mrs. Bingley, "in a white gown with green ornaments," but not Mrs. Darcy herself. "I daresay Mrs. D. will be in yellow."

The exhibition in Spring Gardens promised well, but no Elizabeth appeared. "We have been both to the exhibition and to Sir Joshua Reynolds's, and I am disappointed, for there was nothing like Mrs. D. at either. I can only imagine that Mr. D. prizes any picture of her too much to like it should be exposed to the public eye. I can imagine he would have that sort of feeling — that mixture of love, pride, and delicacy."

We could wish that Miss Austen had found the portrait; but since she never did, there is none of Mrs. Darcy in this book.

VII

THE DARCYS OF ROSINGS

[A reintroduction to some of the characters of Miss Austen's novels.]

Whitethorn Manor, HUNSDON, KENT.
4th *May,* 1814.

YOU will be interested to learn, my dear Sophia, that we are arrived at our new home a se'nnight since, having posted from London with every comfort. Already I feel sure we shall not regret fixing here. Now that the Admiral has retired from the naval service, a rural retreat was his object, and we had a strong recommendation to Hunsdon from Mrs Colonel Brandon, the Marianne Dashwood of your early days and mine. She spoke of the little domain named as above, and investigation soon convinced my dear Admiral that this was what he had hoped to secure. My approbation followed as a matter of course, and I hope an early visit will convince me of Sophia's. If a fair dawn promises a cloudless day, we may look forward with the highest degree of confidence permissible in human affairs.

The journey from London to the village of Hunsdon is agreeable, and through an affluence of English scenery which must surely compare favourably with any in the world : swelling hills embowered in green; placid rivers enlivened by a delightful concert of feathered songsters; villages clustered about the

churchyards, where sleep their rude forefathers;
though it were to be desired that a judicious restora-
tion could obliterate the savage Norman and Gothic
architecture too often found in the churches, and that
they could be restored in harmony with the more
elegant taste of the present day.   I could never agree
with Mr Walpole's love of the Gothic!   Still, I am
not to deny that the perspective is sometimes pleasing, and the intention of a ruder age merits respect.

The Admiral, who is not an amateur of scenery,
slumbered most of the way.   We alighted from the
post-chaise at Sundale for a night's rest, and ordered
a light repast, with tea for me, and that heady ale
which I could wish my Admiral would renounce, both
on account of his increasing weight and his tendency
to inflammatory gout.   But you are not now to learn
that it is vain to remonstrate with gentlemen where
the pleasures of the table are concerned.   Our rooms
being unprepared, we sat downstairs, though the inn
was full in anticipation of some horse races tomorrow,
and some of the gentlemen decidedly in liquor.   My
attention was early engaged by a lady of prettyish
appearance at a table near by, whose bonnet and
spencer bespoke a florid taste hardly in keeping with
her uncurled ringlets and — dare I add it — un-
washed hands.   She was accompanied by a good-
looking man in regimentals, of handsome but, as I
thought, somewhat dissolute presence (so different
from the solid worth of my Admiral!), who was evidently an officer from Chatham, not far distant.   I
judged them to be husband and wife from their

yawning inattention to each other's remarks. Finally, the gentleman, rousing himself, said in a low clear tone: —

"It signifies not, Mrs Wickham, what your opinion may be, for the thing must be done. Money we must have, and your sister's influence with Mr Darcy is our only prospect of relief. Your father will do no more. Mr Darcy's prejudice against me is fixed, and therefore your journey to Hunsdon, now they are staying at Rosings, will be necessary. Argue no more. My mind is made up."

She pouted angrily.

"I am quite as sensible as you are, Wickham, of our need of money; but you know how I hate travelling alone, with all the men ogling me and the servants looking for vails that I have it not to give. Come with me, and all will be well." Her tone was cajoling.

"Oblige me with the letter you received from Mrs Darcy a week since," was his only reply.

She pulled out a dog's-eared letter from her reticule, and he read aloud: —

"'I regret, my dear Lydia, to be obliged to speak plainly and say that the less Mr Darcy meets Mr Wickham the more likely is his benevolence to continue.' Now, Mrs Wickham, in view of that statement, where is the sense in urging me to accompany you to Rosings?"

He threw it back to her, and leaned in his chair, staring at his boots with a very discontented expression. I am no eavesdropper, Sophia, but the Admiral was still engaged with his plate, and I could not withdraw; and though I looked pointedly at the lady, she took no notice.

"It would show more consideration for me, Wickham, if you was to come. You know how poor my nerves are, and the flutterations I suffer from at the thought of seeing Darcy. Such a stiff, starched man — I don't know how Elizabeth endures him. And the last time I stayed at Pemberley, the airs of her maid sunk my spirits altogether. I have not a gown equal to her black silk. The miseries our marriage has brought upon me — Good God! what a fool I was!"

"It was certainly not forced upon *you*, Madam, whatever it might be on me."

"A pleasant allusion, I must say," said Mrs Wickham, tossing her ringlets; then, beginning to giggle: "But you was always a quiz, Wickham, and don't mean the half you say. You know how I hate travelling alone, whereas you and me could pick up some friends on the way, and have a hand at cards. Don't drink no more now. You will want your head clear for the races. Did you ever see such a scare as that bonnet yonder?"

There was no mistaking who she meant, my dear Sophia; and though it is true I had on my beaver bonnet and blue veil, a little disordered by the wind, still there was no excuse for her unladylike freedom. I felt my complexion heighten indignantly. Mr Wickham took no notice.

"I wish to heaven," he said gloomily, "that I could perform if it were the most trifling service to Darcy,

to lessen this load of obligation. There are times —"
But his lady was giggling, and waving her hand to a
lady at some distance, and, rising, he strode away.

But what was I to think? For I had been informed by Marianne Brandon that Mr and Mrs
Darcy are the chief residents at Hunsdon, where he
inherited the noble estate of Rosings from his aunt,
the Lady Catherine de Bourgh, whose daughter and
heiress died. Mrs Darcy was formerly a Miss Elizabeth Bennet, and this sister, Mrs Wickham, had been
of by no means irreproachable conduct. And this
was she! Such impropriety of demeanour! Such
a vulgar insipidity! If Mrs Darcy in any way resembled her, I feared our hope of pleasant society
was destined to disappointment. Such connections!

I broke the matter with my dear Sir Charles; but
he pooh-poohed my anxieties in his sailorly fashion,
saying : —

"There's many a bad egg from a good nest, my
Lady, and Mrs Darcy may be a valuable woman, for
all her sister looks such a slut. And I would have
you by no means be cackling about this meeting all
over the neighbourhood."

Cackling! But you, my dear Sophia, know the
energy with which the Admiral expresses himself.
It was his mode of recommending discretion.

Next morning we started, and saw them no more;
but I understood from the remark of one waiter to
another that Mr Wickham was a well-known figure
in the betting ring, and the races would engage their
stay.

As our chaise and four rolled into Hunsdon, my spirits were elevated by the beauty of the prospect, where a flourishing peasantry dwells in prosperity under the protection of the worthy Darcy. The cottages, with their rose-decked gardens and beehives, the rich pastures, with grazing cattle and dotted with sheep, all expressed the idea of pastoral plenty; and the handsome carriages and curricles passing gave us a high opinion of the consequence of the neighbourhood. I roused the Admiral to partake my pleasure, as we passed a beautiful little church with a handsome portico in the Italian taste. We next drove by the Parsonage, standing in a green lane and faced by the park palings of Rosings; and as we passed I observed a sensible-looking lady at the window, whom I judged to be Mrs Collins. The Rector, a tall heavy-featured man, tying up his carnations, hastened at once to the gate, and by low bows, repeated until we were out of sight, gave us our first welcome to Hunsdon. I would have prevailed on the Admiral to stop in response to so much civility; but he refused, and putting his head out of the window, desired John to drive on. I could only hope Mr Collins did not hear him.

How shall I describe, my dear Sophia, the gratification with which I beheld our new home! It is a long, low, white house, covered with roses and clematis, with pleasant windows opening to smooth green lawns, and an air of purity and order within which is peculiar to English homes. Having travelled to Boulogne, I may be allowed to be a judge. The rows of curtseying servants, headed by good Mrs Williams, the housekeeper, and the Admiral's faithful butler, Sampson, gave us a rude but honest welcome, and were ordered a couple of bottles of port to drink our healths.

Next day Mr and Mrs Collins waited upon us. She strikes me as a woman of judgment, much inclined to reserve, and with a demure and settled manner; but this, in her position, may be very necessary. The Rector — what shall I say? This was his greeting: —

"It is with profound pleasure I have the honour to welcome Sir Charles Sefton and your Ladyship to your magnificent abode in our humble village of Hunsdon. We are indeed honoured by the choice of newcomers so distinguished, to whom the highest circles of London or the amenities of the world are alike open. But the refined and elegant society of this neighbourhood will be found worthy of even such a mark of approbation. Mrs Collins shares my sense of the distinction thus conferred upon us, and I speak for her as well as myself."

She looked somewhat uncomfortable at this exuberance, accompanied with a formal bow for every comma, but is probably used to it, for she quietly made me a sensible little speech of welcome, to which I responded in kind.

"I thank you, Sir," replied my Admiral bluntly; "and you will find us regular attendants at Divine Service, where we hope to benefit by your discourses, which I hope excel in quality rather than quantity. Ha, ha!"

"My discourses, Sir Charles, never exceed half an hour, that being the length preferred by the Right Honorable Lady Catherine de Bourgh, who presented me to this parish; and though she is now elevated to a sphere higher even than that which she adorned on earth, I still observe her wishes, and the rather that I have not had any intimation to the contrary from Mr Fitzwilliam Darcy, her nephew, or his amiable lady, to whom I have the honour to be related."

"Indeed?" I said; "I was not aware. Do Mr and Mrs Darcy always reside here?"

"They divide the year between Rosings and Pemberley in Derbyshire, your Ladyship. But their daughters, the Misses Darcy, prefer Rosings, so they are oftener here. And I am frequently in the habit of saying to Mrs Darcy that when these fair flowers are transplanted to Pemberley, the gardens of Rosings droop and wither. Elegant females are very susceptible to these little attentions, as you are aware, and I never hesitate to offer them."

"Flummery and females!" interjected the Admiral. "I hope, Sir, it is not your intention to spoil my Lady Sefton's digestion with this sort of whipped cream!"

Mr Collins bowed and sidled, and Mrs C. observed: —

"The Misses Darcy are two extremely handsome young women — sixteen and fifteen respectively. Miss Darcy is most prepossessing. I feel sure your Ladyship will agree with me."

"Don't omit the Admiral, Mrs Collins!" said Sir Charles. "I like a pretty face as well as anyone, as you may judge by my Lady."

The dear man! He expresses himself with bluntness occasionally, but the heart is gold!

"Are you as good a judge of pigs as of ladies, Mr Collins?" he added; "for if so, pray accompany me on my first visit to my pigsties, and we will leave the ladies to their gossip."

Mr Collins went, with a rueful glance at his boots, but bowing and smiling all the way. I learnt much of the neighbourhood from Mrs Collins, but with the warm colouring she judged amiable. I must except, however, the poor of the parish. There she spoke, with a censure no doubt deserved, of thriftlessness and ingratitude. These indeed are tokens of a spirit of discontent which we cannot view with composure, especially in the light of late events in the unhappy country of France — the prey of impiety and revolution.

The visit was, on the whole, pleasant, though Mr Collins's courtesy is overstrained, and the Admiral, throwing himself into his chair when they departed, made use of language which, however suitable for gentlemen, the female pen declines to record, adding : —

"When Mr Collins's foot slipped, and he fell prone in the muck, he got up and apologised until I fairly ran for it."

Next day Mr and Mrs Darcy waited upon us, having thoughtfully sent a mounted messenger to

enquire if we felt equal to receiving company after
our journey.   On our agreeing, they presented themselves in the most unostentatious way, having walked
through their park and down the lane, though the
weather was showery.   All forebodings were instantly
banished.

Mr Darcy is a tall well-formed man, in early
middle life, distinguished in bearing and manners, a
little haughty, but not more so than is becoming in
his position.   Mrs Darcy, some years younger, is
veritably charming.   You know, my dear Sophia,
that I am not rash and do not use such words unguardedly.   She smiled, disclosing beautiful teeth,
and, as I observed, has the peculiar grace of one whose
eyes smile in harmony with her lips.   Nothing could
be more obliging than her manners, and I could
scarce think it possible that the tawdry, noisy Mrs
Wickham could be her sister.   Her eyes are dark
and animated, with long eyelashes which soften their
somewhat alarming brilliance.   She is extremely
conversible.

"I am glad you were pleased with the village, Lady
Sefton.   What did you think of the church?   The
old one was a venerable structure, dating from the
Plantagenet kings, and I personally should have preferred that; but Sir Lewis de Bourgh, who had made
the grand tour with Mr Horace Walpole and other
notable amateurs, had acquired a passion for Italy,
and when restoring the church, Italianised it.   Had
he also presented us with Naples, where the original
stands, the gift would have been complete; but to my

mind it stands as ill in little Hunsdon as would the dress of an Italian Signora on good Mrs Collins."

She smiled so archly that I laughed, and the Admiral joined in.

"Quite right, my dear Madam," he exclaimed. "There can be no greater folly than sticking the buildings of one country in the surroundings of another. What the English builders built is good enough for English men and women, and more suitable than any Greek and Roman temples and such idle gazebos. They will be having Divine Worship in a Belvedere next!"

I blushed for my dear Admiral's taste, but was unable to check his loud voice. Mrs Darcy applauded with her gloved hands, and sparkling eyes.

"I make a point of applauding any judgment which agrees with my own," she said playfully; "and I congratulate you, my dear Sir, on an excellent taste, and vigour in expressing it. I foresee we shall be always applauding one another. Am I not fortunate in our new neighbours, my dear Darcy?"

He agreed, with the utmost kindliness and a graceful touch of formality, and requested permission to examine the exquisite set of ivory chessmen presented to the Admiral at Bombay. They are a superb work of art, all the pieces being mounted on elephants, camels, and horses, elegantly carved. Having bestowed his meed of admiration, he added:—

"Since you are acquainted with India, Sir Charles, it will give me the utmost pleasure if you and her Ladyship will do me the honour to inspect those

which Mr Lorenzo Darcy, my uncle, brought from
that wonderful country. The Ivory Shrine is considered a masterpiece, and some have recommended
that it should be in some public collection. But
family associations —"

"Public collections!" interrupted the Admiral (I
could wish, Sophia, that the dear man would not interrupt when persons of consideration are speaking).
"They are an encroachment by the lower orders,
on all accounts to be resisted. What? Are private
treasures to be exhibited to their pawings and ignorance? No, Mr Darcy! Preserve the Ivory Shrine
as an heirloom, and let those who would engage the
votes of the vulgar be —"

I will not record the end of the sentence. Mrs
Darcy apologised for her daughters not waiting upon
me by mentioning that they had a prior engagement
with Mrs Collins, relative to a treat for the village
school in honour of Mr Darcy's natal day.

"I bespeak your kindness for them, my dear
Madam," she was pleased to say. "My elder, Charlotte, has a strong taste for sketching and music, in
both of which I am aware you excel. Rumour, as
you see, has preceded you with her trumpet! Caroline is more studious. We hope, when your son is
here on leave, that many little pleasure parties and
balls may be made up. My young people and all
those of the neighbourhood are excessively fond of
dancing."

I protested this was a taste my Henry shared, and
was very sensible of her attention. Indeed, Sophia,

I trust you will not set me down as a Mrs Busybody (a character I detest) if I say that certain possibilities flashed across my mind at the moment. No young man can be more attractive nor stronger in moral principle than Henry, and if these young women — But I need say no more! Miss Darcy is so great an heiress as to be an object to many.

"You have met Mr Collins as well as his wife, I conclude?" she added smiling.

"We have had that distinction!" I said, and could not forbear smiling also.

"A worthy man! But there are peculiarities of manner. His discourses are always adapted to the occasion, and his allusions — He will, no doubt, tomorrow refer to your arrival in his sermon."

"My dear Mrs Darcy," said I, much alarmed, "have you any real reason to suppose this? I have never been the object of public comment. And the Admiral! I trust you are mistaken."

"I may be," she replied archly; "but can only say that the Sunday after we settled at Rosings, Mr Collins preached from the text, 'Who is this that cometh from Edom, with dyed garments from Bozrah,' and made it very clear that Mr Darcy was that individual."

I could only gaze at her in dismay, but was obliged to check my impulse of consulting the Admiral, lest he should take some compromising step as regards Mr Collins, who might be entirely innocent of such an intention.

When our visitors rose to take leave, and Sir

Charles and I attended them to the gate, I felt a friendship was commenced which might have the happiest results for both families. At the gate we were joined by the young ladies, who had walked up the lane from the Parsonage, and the introductions were made. They curtseyed with the prettiest air of good breeding. Charlotte, the elder, is a glowing brunette. Her purity of expression and correct features positively charmed me. The younger, not so unusual in beauty, is still extremely attractive, and has her mother's penetrating and sparkling eyes.

The next day brought us a visit from my old friend, Marianne Brandon, who settled here with her Colonel Brandon after Delaford was sold to Mr Edward Ferrars on his second marriage. Her chief inducement at Delaford being thus removed by the death of her sister, Mrs Edward Ferrars, they decided to fix nearer London.

I need not describe to you, who know her, the warmth of her greeting. Her feelings are always strong and strongly expressed.

"It adds delight to delight itself," she cried, embracing me, "that you should be settled here, my dear Anne. What happy days are in store for us! With our pencils we will seek the beech woods of White-thorn, and transcribe the various moods of nature."

"Beechmast," said the Admiral, "is one of the most fattening things I know for swine, and if you will not object to their presence, Mrs Brandon, I doubt not they will allow of yours. What say you, Colonel Brandon?"

Their old friendship makes this permissible, however unromantic, and he has always rallied her thus. She continued with ardour: —

"I look forward to the most delightful *al fresco* meals in the green shades. We will make up little parties to recline on the moss —"

"In that case, my dear, I fear I must ask you to leave me out!" said dear Colonel Brandon, smiling mischievously. "You forget my rheumatism and flannel waistcoats!"

She bit her lip. It is a point on which she is sensitive, for she would not have him thought much older than she, though there is twenty years' disparity.

"Let us leave them to their own dullness, my dear Marianne, and tell me all your news," said I.

She drew her chair to mine and talked with all her old animation. Pity they have no children! Her excellent qualities and his deserve repetition. One of her items, I own, surprised me. They are expecting a visit in August from — whom do you think? You cannot guess, nor could I. Young Willoughby, now twenty-one years old, son of her ancient flame, John Willoughby! She speaks of him now without any consciousness, and there is evidently no painful feeling. Spending his wife's large fortune, Mr Willoughby, senior, on her death accepted an appointment at Calcutta, where he has since resided. This is his only son, landed in England after the Cape voyage, and he has written them with a very proper letter of introduction, begging that the young man may present himself and bespeaking the patronage and civility for him of Colonel and Mrs Brandon. Her kindly heart gives her a peculiar pleasure in this opportunity, for you will remember Mr Willoughby, senior, made explanations which removed much of the seeming heartlessness of his treatment of her. I might be mistaken in supposing that Colonel Brandon was less eager for the visit; but such was my impression. He is not impulsive as she. Their visit was in all respects a delightful one.

We attended Divine Service next day, and naturally there was a little curiosity, especially among the white-headed village children, as we approached our pew, a handsome enclosure with armchairs, which I feared but too truly would soon invite Sir Charles to the arms of Morpheus. I think, Sophia, it were to be desired that there should be a certain rigour in the design of church furniture. I myself sometimes — but today my senses were on the alert, especially when Mr Collins ascended the pulpit, and pompously announced his text: "A mighty man of valour."

The beginning was harmless, and my thoughts became a little indistinct, when suddenly I was aware that the allusion was to the Admiral, and to his services in our actions with the French. Special allusion was made to his victory in the Arrogant off Ushant! I sat in such apprehension as cannot be expressed in words. You are as well aware as I that the modesty of a hero will admit of no encomiums, and the prayer formed itself on my lips (I hope without impiety) that his sleep might continue, as I could not be answerable for the consequences. I sat on tenterhooks, and meanwhile the Admiral slumbered placidly, his gentle snores punctuating Mr Collins's discourse, his mouth open, nor dared I push him with my foot as is my custom. Fortunate indeed was I that the height of the pew prevented my catching Mrs Darcy's eye. I cannot but think all this was in deplorable taste. What think you? As we left the sacred building, the Admiral said: —

"An excellent discourse! I know not when I have heard a better. Pointed and instructive. I shall offer a word of commendation to his Reverence."

I could but look at him with an imploring eye as Mr Collins bowed.

"I am happy, Sir Charles," he rejoined, after the encomium, "to have met with your approbation. Ensamples of heroism may surely as justly be drawn from modern instances as from Alexander and Cæsar, and I am not now to be informed that such ensamples are of more interest to the infant mind when the illustrious model is seated among them in all the majesty of success and honour."

The Admiral stared, but Mrs Darcy, joining us, staved off the disclosure.

"I told you so!" she whispered in my ear, her eyes dancing with humour.

I pressed her hand for silence and it blew over, the Admiral later demanding jealously: "What was it all about, my Lady?" when I replied with a show of countenance: "A droll allusion of Mrs Darcy's, my dear." So it ended.

So also must this letter, my dear Sophia; but I do not apologise for its length, knowing your interest in all that touches us.   Your truly aff^e sister,

ANNE SEFTON.

4th *September*, 1814.

I resume my pen, my dear Sophia, to narrate the most extraordinary series of incidents which can have ever taken place in such surroundings.   You may have seen some reports in the public journals, but cannot have heard the details.   Let me strive to impart my news in as collected a manner as they merit.

I should premise that my Henry arrived on his leave, and the very day after received cordial invitations from Mr and Mrs Darcy to wait on them and join in all the parties of pleasure consequent on young Willoughby's arrival.   A number of friendly gatherings took place, and Captains Gilbert and Ord from the Chatham garrison were visitors at Rosings.   Still, I ventured to hope that though thus besieged, the lovely Charlotte did sometimes cast an eye on Henry, though Willoughby was ever at her side.   An invitation to inspect the Indian rarities followed later, and we drove in my pony carriage to Rosings, and were received with all Mrs Darcy's obligingness.   She was attended by her two daughters, and I observed Charlotte's complexion heighten in the most interesting manner as Henry made his compliments, though young Willoughby was by her side, and very much at his ease.   The young man is extremely handsome — very brown-complexioned and with piercing eyes, of a good height and person. His manners I thought a little disposed to be familiar; but from the beginning of the acquaintance, I had set this down to the account of an Indian life and its freedoms. He remained fixed to Miss Darcy's chair, a manœuvre I could not see with comfort. Elegant refreshments — cold meat, fruit, etc. — were immediately served, the Collinses being present and the Brandons arriving later.

When all had been refreshed, Mr Darcy led the way to the library, and the curiosities were produced. The Admiral was in his element, and young Willoughby was called on for explanations which he gave well enough. At last the famous Ivory Shrine was removed from its glass case, and set upon a round table where all could view it.

I must now be particular in my description. It was a cabinet of the richest ivory, carved with images of idols whose histories I know not.

"The thinking mind," said Mr Collins, "must lament to see such skill lavished on such a worthless subject, were it not the happy destiny of this cabinet to become an appanage of the great. In the magnificent mansions of our nobles (titled and untitled) such objects afford the instructive contrast of an inferior civilisation with all that is Christian and elegant."

Mr Darcy slightly bowed. He then threw open the doors of the cabinet, disclosing a surprising object indeed — a seated figure of clumsy proportions with the head of an elephant, supposed by these poor heathen to be a god, of whom the name escapes me. This also was ivory, with a necklace and girdle of small jewels inset. Mr Darcy applied to young Willoughby, by his side, for information of the attributes of this strange being, which he gave with an elegance as much out of the common as his figure, Mr Darcy following with the story of its acquisition by his uncle, Mr Lorenzo Darcy. We all drew near to examine the carvings, the hideousness of the image precluding admiration; and Mrs Brandon was gratified, as she told me, to find her *protégé* distinguish himself by his address.

"We find his company very agreeable," she said aside, to me and Mrs Darcy. "He. is a young man of parts, and his travels have made him very conversible. Our servants find his Indian attendant, Tippoo, an endless source of surprise. He cannot speak a word of English, and to see him roll his black eyes and gesticulate causes laughter which penetrates even to our end of the house."

Mrs Darcy enquired if he were a troublesome inmate on account of caste prejudices; but Marianne assured her that such was not the case. He was perfectly obliging.

Still, Sophia, I felt one should be on one's guard where foreigners are concerned. A young man, though of English parentage, brought up in India and surrounded by wily Orientals, can scarcely be expected to have the solid principles of an English training. I am told that attendance on Divine Service is sadly lax among our wealthy nabobs; that it is even a practice to give entertainments on the Sabbath, when other than sacred music is performed. What must be the result on the young mind?

The afternoon ended, as I feared, in Mr Darcy giving Willoughby an invitation to spend a week at Rosings, that he might assist him to classify his Indian collection, a proposal to which the young man instantly agreed. That I thought it imprudent, I must not deny, unless indeed there were a settled intention as regards Miss Darcy, since it would throw them so much together, and already they were more easy than my judgment could approve. I observed Henry's spirits, like my own, a little sunk at such a distinction, though to him also the manners of both Miss Darcy's parents were conciliatory in the extreme. Both have a generosity of disposition which will suspect no evil. Yet, Sophia, we hear on the highest authority that the wisdom of the serpent is equally desirable with that of the dove.

Willoughby now became a guest at Rosings, and the parties of pleasure were fewer, the young officers from Chatham having left. The week passed, and the invitation was extended by a few days, the lists of Indian rarities still being unfinished.

I was seated in the late afternoon at my embroidery frame, when Mrs Collins was ushered in, so pale, so trembling and overcome, that I cried without any ceremony, "Good God! what is it?" and fell back in terror. She sunk into a chair and endeavoured to collect her spirits, the Admiral hurrying in from the lawn. At length she spoke, but with difficulty.

"Miss Darcy is fled with Willoughby!" and could utter no more.

The Admiral hastily fetched a glass of Constantia, and on partaking, she resumed with more composure. O Sophia, how express our feelings!

It now appeared that, when Willoughby was summoned to a cold collation, prepared in view of an afternoon excursion, he could nowhere be found. Tippoo was called, that he might seek his master, but to the consternation of all, his scanty possessions were removed and the room entirely empty; and the servants, hastening to his master's chamber, found a dressing-case known to stand on his table disappeared.

Theft was the first suspicion, and Willoughby's presence doubly desirable. Again they sought, and in vain. Miss Caroline was seated with her mother, and hearing all this, she rose with a countenance pale as ashes and trembling in every limb, and cried: —

"O Mama, where is Charlotte? I saw her last after breakfast in the shrubbery with Willoughby. The lake — O God, can it be possible!"

These fears at once communicated themselves to her parents and, hastily summoning help, Mr Darcy ran to the lake. The boat was loose and floating on the water, with an oar beside it, and a coat of Willoughby's on the bank; instantly the worst was feared and Tippoo forgotten. The lodge-keeper and his men were summoned with drags, poor Mrs Darcy on the bank wringing her hands in speechless affliction.

"Thus," pursued Mrs Collins, "were two valuable

hours lost in dragging the lake, and more might have been the case, owing to the success of this vile scheming, but that the gamekeeper — Ward, you know, Ma'am — came running up in hot haste. One of his underlings had seen, hours before, a post-chaise standing in the road before the north gate, as if awaiting a party, but took no particular notice at the time. Returning later to the east gate, he observed the same post-chaise dashing along at full speed, and will be positive he saw Miss Darcy's face at the window and Willoughby with her. Such was the speed, that he could say no more than that the driver was a dark handsome young man in a triple cape. Thinking it was merely one of the parties of pleasure which had been so common, he loitered along, resumed his work, and only by a chance mentioned it to the gamekeeper, who with more presence of mind ran at once to his master.

"O my dear Lady Sefton," continued Mrs Collins, "What a scene of horror was here! An elopement! And with a man virtually unknown, and of whose parent Marianne Dashwood's experience was dreadful! Pursuit was immediately ordered, and Mr Darcy mounted his horse, though none can be sure what way they will have taken at the crossroads. Who — who could have supposed this of a young lady so virtuously brought up as Miss Darcy?"

"A sly little jade!" said the Admiral; and actually smiled! Such are even the best of men!

Scarcely able to articulate for horror, I was able to say : —

"True, dear Ma'am. Yet must we not own there was imprudence in permitting a young girl of Miss Darcy's beauty and expectations to be so unguardedly in the company of Willoughby? Forcibly indeed has that thought struck me more than once. Poor unfortunate parents! Let us hasten to condole with them."

Mrs Collins was too overcome to attend us, and the Admiral giving me his arm, we set off through the Park, he speaking his mind with the bluffness of a sailor on Miss Darcy's behaviour. Well did she know, he said, that her parents would never consent to a match so far below her pretensions, and therefore — But I dare not emulate his frankness.

We found Mrs Darcy pale but composed, a mounted messenger having returned from Mr Darcy with the news that he had heard of a post-chaise going at full galloping speed on the road to Merton, and was following it up. He begged Mrs Darcy to sustain her spirits, and call on the Admiral for aid if occasion should arise in his absence.

O Sophia, how describe the looks of fear and horror which surrounded us on all sides in that hitherto so happy household! Caroline fainted in her mother's arms and was instantly conveyed to her room, where we attended her until consciousness was restored and misery with it. The Admiral employed himself in the library, in questioning the men and women, with a view to discover some more certain clew to pursuit, or possibly some accomplice, his experience as president of courts-martial standing him in such good stead that he terrified them all, and I feel certain, had any been a party to the flight, it must have been known. So valuable is manly presence of mind in such emergencies! Nothing, however, transpired.

Time advanced, and Mrs Darcy requested we would remain. The shades of night darkened, and still no news. It was impossible not to admire Mrs Darcy's fortitude, for indeed this must have forcibly recalled the time when her sister Mrs Wickham (as I have learnt from Marianne Dashwood) made the fatal elopement with Wickham which has secured her a lifetime of wretched poverty and uneasiness. I readily understood her deplorable appearance at the Sundale inn on hearing her story. Fatal indeed, Sophia, are the steps of female error, and how impossible to be retrieved!

We are not to judge Providence, yet it certainly appears that masculine imprudences are viewed more leniently from on high. Rectitude, no doubt, is demanded from all; but it must be owned the consequences are less severe when a man forsakes the narrow path of virtue. As the Admiral frequently observes — woman is the weaker vessel and therefore much more is rightly expected from her, and the punishment justly more severe, as we observe in the case of Eve and other examples for our learning. This, however, is a bewildering subject, and more suited to my dear Admiral's understanding, so I pursue it no further.

We were all unable to eat, and were sitting listless in the parlour as midnight approached, when my ear caught the gallop of a horse. "Mr Darcy!" I cried, starting to my feet and trembling with agitation.

Mrs Darcy, exercising an almost superhuman composure, sat rigidly in her chair. The door was flung open and in rushed *Mr Wickham* — disordered with speed and riding, but recognisable to me as the handsome, dissipated-looking man we had seen at the inn at Sundale. He seized Mrs Darcy's almost lifeless hand and cried : "Courage, Ma'am! She is safe. She is with Mrs Wickham at Sundale, and the miscreant fled."

How is it possible, Sophia, that I should describe the scene that ensued?

Hearing the commotion, Caroline tottered downstairs and swooned again at our feet, yet was scarcely heeded — all crowding round Wickham, who obligingly soothed our anxiety.

"When," he said, "the officers of our regiment returned to Chatham from the enjoyment of Mr Darcy's hospitality, the incidents of their stay were naturally broached, and Willoughby spoken of. Nothing, however, transpired until Colonel Vaughan returned from leave, when the subject happened to come up again. 'But, good God, who is this?' cried Colonel Vaughan. 'Young Willoughby died eight months ago at Calcutta, and was an only child. My own brother attended his obsequies. Who can this person be?' All was astonishment. His brother, Mr James Vaughan, was hastily summoned from his residence in the Dockyard, and fully confirmed this, he having lately returned from India. He looked

very gravely upon the matter, and mentioned that
Mr Willoughby, senior, had formed years ago an
illicit connection with a Portuguese female, of which
there were two sons of most disreputable character.
I waited not to hear more, but called for my horse,
and in regimentals, as you see me, rode at full speed
for Sundale, where Mrs Wickham was awaiting me
for the Sundale Steeplechase, that being the nearest
way here."

Mrs Darcy pressed his hand, but was still unable
to speak. He proceeded : —

"It was now almost dusk and she pressed a little
necessary refreshment on me in the inn parlour. I
was swallowing it hastily, when a post-chaise drew
up at the door and a man alighted, supporting in his
arms an almost senseless female, a large veil concealing her bonnet and face. He called for a private
room and refreshment in a haughty impatient tone,
and was turning to the stair with his burden, when,
struggling from his arms, she tottered toward Mrs.
Wickham exclaiming, 'O Aunt Lydia, save me —
save me!' and dropped at her feet."

A sob broke from Mrs Darcy's pale lips, but still
she spoke not.

"Mrs Wickham removed her veil, and there was
Miss Darcy, in a truly pitiable condition. The
baffled villain, little thinking how he had run into a
trap of his own making, stood one second a mask of
terror. I made for him instantly, sword in hand,
but he ran with the speed of lightning through the
ostler's yard and was lost in the beech woods behind.

I gave directions for search to be made and returned to the ladies."

Mrs Darcy lifted his hand in both hers and pressed it to her lips. "The hand that saved my Charlotte!" was all she could murmur; and indeed we were all in tears of thankfulness and joy. Mr Wickham's own manly tones trembled as he resumed: —

"Between the agitations that ensued, the dear girl told us how he had forced her into the post-chaise and driven off at full speed, determined so to compromise her that a marriage would be insisted on, or even besought by her parents. He had sent a decoy chaise on the Merton road, and driven furiously to Sundale, counting on the coast being clear. I waited not, however, to hear more, but left her in Mrs Wickham's arms, and rode on hither."

"Brother, you are weary — famished!" cried Mrs Darcy, ever considerate. "Are we to have no thought for you, who have had so much for us? I knew — I knew my Charlotte could not so fearfully be lost to all sense of propriety, and knowing this, can now recover. Oh, could my Darcy but know his girl is safe!"

O Sophia, what a scene was here — all pressing refreshments on our deliverer — all joyful excitement. The only element lacking, dear Mr Darcy's presence! And two hours later, — for none could go to rest, — that also was supplied; for finding his pursuit of the Merton chaise mistaken, he returned home, drooping and almost despairing, in the faint hope of tidings. Words sink beneath the effort to describe his manly gratitude to Wickham, and the relief of hearing he had not been deceived in his belief in Miss Darcy's principles. Never have I seen his majesty of demeanour so softened. He also addressed Mr Wickham as "Brother," and the latter was profoundly touched. If I mistake not, this will be an epoch in his career and that of his unhappy wife. Mr Darcy's is a spirit that will never leave an obligation unacknowledged. They rode together next day to escort Mrs Wickham and the interesting victim to Rosings — Miss Darcy in a pitiable condition, but yet fully sensible of her safety.

"On such occasions," observed Mr Collins to the Admiral, "it cannot be denied that a special Providence appears to attend the great. Had Miss Darcy been a humbler female, had she not been possessed of relatives willing and able to defend her, what might not have been dreaded! This leads us to devout admiration of the discriminating bounties of heaven, so well bestowed where most needed and deserved. For what, Sir Charles, is the downfall of a female of low birth, however worthy, compared with that of a young lady who has adorned elevated circles and is the cynosure of all eyes and hearts!"

The dear Admiral owned to me later that this exordium so bewildered him that he knew not "at which end to take hold of it," to use his own expression. I feel the difficulty myself.

The public prints will have informed my Sophia that the miscreant escaped, and that it is now known the pair were brothers, a dark stain for the complexion having converted the younger into the attendant, for the visit to Hunsdon. Reassuming his own appearance, he acted as the driver and was of course wholly in his brother's interest in securing a wealthy prize in Miss Darcy. What machinations, and what a deliverance!

Mrs Darcy, who is all candour, said later to me that she had suspected the beginning of an attachment in my Henry's mind, and that, if it were so — Here she hesitated in the most interesting manner.

I took her hand in mine. "Hesitate not to open the subject, my dear Ma'am," said I, "for I can confirm your view. Henry is deeply, deeply interested in your sweet girl — poor lovely innocent! And if there is any hope —"

It was my turn to hesitate. She resumed more calmly : —

"Then, if it be so, Lady Sefton, I may speak plainly. Candour is a necessity of Mr Darcy's character and mine. I cannot deny that Charlotte's imagination was touched, however slightly, by Willoughby's romantic tales and appearance. Young minds are susceptible —"

Indeed, Sophia, there was a false glitter about him which I, for one, instantly distrusted; but the inexperience of the young will ever be a danger. I said as much and she continued : —

"Calm recollection and these frightful events have, however, wrought a complete cure and a revulsion of feeling which has turned her mind to Mr Sefton's worth with full appreciation. If later — *much* later

— he should make an application, I believe he might hope for a success which I venture not to promise. Her parents are also to blame for incaution. But the future may yet be all brightness."

As for Henry, his affection is unaltered, and perhaps deepened, by these occurrences. And it has impressed me, Sophia, that possibly Mr and Mrs Darcy might have had more exalted aspirations for their lovely heiress than a mere baronet's son had not this shade fallen on her opening flower. I think it is the Swan of Avon who observes that there is a soul of goodness in things evil, and so it may have proved in this instance.

As to Marianne Brandon, the whole affair has cost her a severe illness, in which she incessantly deplored her own impulsive nature, though all did their utmost to mitigate the blow. "Shall I never acquire the calm judgment and sober reason which alone can preserve from such errors?" was her cry. "Surely I, who have so much reason to distrust the name of Willoughby, should have hesitated to introduce one of that fatal race to the notice of friends."

I fear she will never forgive herself; but it may prove a warning to a being whose only fault is incaution, and a too warm belief in human nature. The Colonel is, and will be, her unfailing support.

Although nothing definite has yet been said, the Admiral is now inspecting Hoddesden House, with a view to our young couple's occupation, and I hope ere long to send you the joyful news of the addition of a daughter to my comforts.

I should not conclude without dwelling on the danger of insufficient introductions; and something might also be said of the impiety of admitting false gods to adorn a Christian library, even as objects of art. But my Sophia is well able to draw her own conclusions and her affectionate sister will now, with all good wishes and endearing thoughts, conclude.

ANNE SEFTON.

Postscriptum. — Mr and Mrs Wickham are now visiting at Rosings.

McGrath - Sherrill Press
GRAPHIC ARTS BLDG.
BOSTON